Savannah Martin has always been a good girl, doing what was expected and fully expecting life to fall into place in its turn. But when her perfect husband turns out to be a lying, cheating slimeball - and bad in bed to boot - Savannah kicks the jerk to the curb and embarks on life on her own terms. With a new apartment, a new career, and a brand new outlook on life, she's all set to take the world by storm.

If only the world would stop throwing her curveballs...

When Savannah's real estate company, Lamont, Briggs, and Associates, finds itself embroiled in a closing scam, broker Timothy Briggs asks Savannah's help in figuring out what happened and who's behind it.

The task is a welcome distraction for Savannah, whose private life is rocky. Carmen Arroyo is in prison in Nashville, nine months pregnant, and no one knows whether the baby is Rafe's or not. And while Rafe doesn't seem too worried about it, Savannah can't say the same.

Meanwhile, down in Sweetwater, Savannah's mother Margaret Anne is hitting the brandy while trying to come to terms with her late husband's love child and her best friend's thirty-four year silence on the subject.

Between one thing and another, it's all Savannah can do to keep everything moving along smoothly. The very last thing she needs is someone rocking the boat...

OTHER BOOKS IN THIS SERIES

SCARED MONEY

Savannah Martin Mystery #13

Jenna Bennett

SCARED MONEY

Savannah Martin Mystery #13

Interior design and formatting: B. Gallagher
Cover Design: Dar Albert, Wicked Smart Designs

Magpie Ink

One

"Thank God you're here!" Tim said.

I had just walked through the door of LB&A—Lamont, Briggs, and Associates, real estate company to the stars—and into my office, a converted coat closet off the lobby. Just enough time to hang my purse on the hook by the door and pull out the office chair, but not time enough to sit in it—and for Brittany, the receptionist, to beep the boss to let him know I had arrived.

"I'm sorry," I said, since he was clearly distraught. I wasn't really sorry, though, since I hadn't done anything I needed to be sorry for. It's not like I had an obligation to show up at nine sharp every morning. I was self-employed, not working for Tim. "What's wrong?"

"Come into my office."

He grabbed my arm and pulled me after him: out of the coat closet, through the lobby, down the hallway to the back of the building, and into his own office, which is the biggest and best in the firm, and approximately ten times the size of mine. Tim has enough room for several filing cabinets, a fancy U-shaped desk, and a fancier leather chair he inherited from our previous broker, Walker Lamont.

He closed the door behind us and pushed me toward one of the large visitors' chairs. "Sit."

I arched my brows, but sat. I'm going on seven months pregnant, so it's always nice to get off my feet.

Tim, meanwhile, walked around the desk and got comfortable in Walker's leather chair. "I wasn't sure you'd come in today," he told me.

Honestly, it had been touch and go. I had spent the best part of the last week in my hometown of Sweetwater, an hour and a little more south of Nashville. First for my mother's birthday last week, and then because my husband, TBI agent Rafe Collier, had been involved in a gang war and had wanted me tucked away somewhere safe until it was over. But that issue had resolved itself yesterday afternoon, and since I'd had some things I needed to talk to Rafe about, I'd come home to Nashville.

"I'm sorry I missed the meeting," I told Tim, in reference to the weekly sales meeting that takes place every Monday morning. "I would have been here, but I was still in Sweetwater yesterday morning. Family stuff."

The last time Tim had asked for a one-on-one, it had ended with him firing me. He had taken me back a week or two later, after finding out that the person who wanted me fired had had ulterior motives for wanting me out of the way, but I admit I was a little leery of what might be going on. As a result, I was perhaps explaining a bit more than I should have been. My family stuff was none of Tim's business.

"Is everything all right?" Tim asked.

He sounded concerned. It was a masterful performance. Once upon a time, Tim had gone to New York to try to make it as an actor on Broadway—and failed. At the moment, it was hard to see why. I knew he wasn't concerned about me at all, but he sure sounded like he was.

And then the truth came out. "It isn't Rafael, is it?"

Tim has a crush on Rafe. It doesn't matter that Rafe is a hundred percent heterosexual and married, and that even if he weren't, he wouldn't swing Tim's way.

But since I'm also crazy about Rafe and understand the sentiment, I refrained from rolling my eyes. "Not at all. Rafe's fine."

"Yes, he is," Tim said, and smacked his lips.

This time I did roll my eyes. At myself. I fall for that one every single time. "What do you want, Tim?"

"Other than your husband?" Tim said. I opened my mouth, and he added, quickly, "A favor."

"What kind of favor?" And if it had anything to do with Rafe, he could forget it.

He glanced at the door before leaning forward and lowering his voice. "This doesn't leave this room."

I leaned forward, too. I had to, or I wouldn't be able to hear him. "What doesn't?"

"What I'm about to tell you," Tim said.

I sat back. "I'm not sure I can promise that. I mean, I have to leave the room. This is your office. I can't stay here indefinitely. And when I go, whatever you tell me will go with me."

"You can't talk to anyone about it," Tim said.

"Nobody? Not even Rafe?" Because I don't like to keep secrets from Rafe. We've only been married a few months, and besides, nothing good ever comes from not telling him things.

Tim considered, baby blues pensive. "I guess you could tell him," he conceded eventually. "He might be helpful."

That sounded interesting. And maybe a little ominous, since my husband has spent the past ten years undercover, rooting out organized criminals of various sorts. Now he was supposed to be training the new TBI recruits and staying out of trouble, but it rarely worked out that way.

"Helpful with what?"

"We have a problem," Tim said.

"We?" Because I knew *I* had problems, but Tim wasn't part of any of them.

"The firm."

Uh-oh. "What's happened? Is it Walker?"

A year ago, our former broker and founder of the company,

Walker Lamont, went to prison for murder. Several counts of murder. Then, about six months later, he escaped and came after me, since it was my fault he was caught in the first place. He was supposed to be back in prison now, under much stricter guard, but under the circumstances, I might have reason to worry.

"He didn't kill anyone else," I added, "did he? Who's dead?"

"No one's dead," Tim said. And added, "yet. But when I find out who did this..."

"Did what?"

He leaned forward again. "This is between us."

"And Rafe," I said.

Tim nodded. "It's about Magnolia Houston."

Oh, God. Magnolia—whom I suspected was born Margaret, or maybe even Margery—was one of Tim's clients. And when I called LB&A the real estate company to the stars, it was Magnolia I was thinking of.

Not that she's that big a deal. Or only in her own mind, I guess. She's a minor star. A very minor star. Maybe even a dwarf star. And I'm not referring to her stature.

She's a singer. Country music. This is Nashville, and we get a lot of that around here.

What Magnolia is, is a YouTube sensation. First she did one of those TV talent shows, which she didn't win, but she parlayed her fifteen minutes of fame into a career making and uploading YouTube videos. Those videos are popular enough to earn her a very healthy seven-figure income every year. Magnolia sings, she dances, she talks, and she comes quite close to taking her clothes off. Men love it. Women maybe not so much. She looks like a Barbie doll, with big boobs, a tiny waist, masses of bleached hair, and vacant, blue eyes. She can't be much over twenty-five, either, which only makes it worse.

Sometime in the early summer, she had retained Tim to find her a mansion, something befitting her stature, or what she thought she deserved.

Now, mansions don't come along every day, and Magnolia, for all her other failings, didn't want a modern mansion, a subdivision McMansion. She wanted the real deal: a true antebellum like the one I grew up in, in Sweetwater.

The Martin Mansion isn't for sale, but after a few months of digging, Tim came up with an alternative. He found an old lady rattling around in a decrepit antebellum farmhouse north of town, just off what used to be Buffalo Trail and is now Dickerson Pike. It had been in the family for generations, but Miss Harper was the last member standing, and the place was falling down around her ears. She had no one to help her fix it up, and no money to spend on it. But even so, she was a hard sell. All about how the place had been in her family since before the War Against Northern Aggression, and where would she go now? Tim had to sweet-talk and cajole for quite a while before she agreed to move, and Magnolia had to come up to the top of her budget for the run-down property. But the place had so much potential, and so much history she could wallow in, that it must have been worth it to her. She went under contract sometime in June, and seemed happy as a clam, even as she made plans to turn the mansion into some horrible hybrid of old and new.

Closing was supposed to have taken place last Friday, as I recalled. I had been out of town then, as well as through the weekend. Something must have gone wrong, and I only now heard of it.

"What happened? Did the place burn down? Did Miss Harper die, so the place is caught up in probate?"

"Nothing that simple," Tim said gloomily.

Probate is nothing but simple. However— "Why didn't you close?"

"Who said we didn't close?" He shook his head, bright blond curls bouncing. "We closed, all right. Because it was a Friday, and because it was a lot of money, funding didn't happen."

I nodded. That's not unusual. With the new settlement

regulations, things take a little longer than they used to. And it's not like one can just hand over a check anymore. One bank has to wire the funds to the closing company's account, and then the closing company's bank has to wire the money from there to the seller's account. It can take time. But— "Surely that wasn't a big deal. It wasn't like Magnolia planned to move in over the weekend."

She couldn't, of course, since—if funding hadn't taken place—the house hadn't actually become hers. The funds have to be received by the seller before the deal is done. But I doubted she had planned to camp out there anyway.

Tim shuddered. "Of course not. She has months of repairs and renovations ahead."

"And I can't imagine Miss Harper minded two more days in the ancestral home."

"She's already out," Tim said. "And into a facility somewhere."

Well, good. As long as it was a nice place, she'd probably be better off there. It can be hard for these older people to take care of themselves at home when they're all alone. And in a facility— as long as it was a nice one—she'd have medical professionals on hand if she needed them. She'd also be able to make friends and do things she wasn't able to do now.

"You found her a good place, didn't you?" When I first met Rafe's grandmother, Mrs. Jenkins, last August, she had been cheated out of her home by another unscrupulous realtor—not Tim—and dumped in the Milton House retirement home. It was a horrible place, and as soon as Rafe could prove that he was her grandson, he moved her back into the house. And then, when he had to go out of town, and the live-in nurse he hired was murdered, and it became clear that Mrs. Jenkins wasn't safe by herself, he moved her into a different home. This is a nice one, and they know how to deal with her increasing dementia, so we've left her there. She's happy. She has company and people taking care of her needs, and she's safe. In the old neighborhood, she'd wander off and get lost, and half the time she doesn't know who we are, anyway.

"Of course," Tim said, sounding insulted. "With the money she's making from this deal, she'll be set for life."

Good. "So what's the problem?"

Tim sighed. "Like I said, funding didn't take place on Friday. Nothing unusual there."

I shook my head.

"I didn't give it any thought over the weekend. Took a trip to Atlanta, and didn't worry about it."

I nodded.

"I went to work on Monday, and everything was normal. Magnolia started work on the house, since she'd paid her money on Friday and we assumed funding had taken place."

I nodded.

"On Monday around three o'clock, I got a phone call from Mr. Peretti."

"Who's Mr. Peretti?"

"Miss Harper's closing attorney," Tim said.

"She didn't use DeWitts?"

DeWitt Title and Escrow is Tim's favored closing company. They're located right around the corner, and he recommends them for all his transactions. Most of his clients end up using them. Unless they have someone else they prefer to use, which must have been the case for Miss Harper.

"She wanted to use an old friend in Goodlettsville," Tim said. "The same guy who made her will and looked over the sales docs for her. They go back a century or more."

Surely not that much, but she had obviously trusted this guy. "What did he want? When he called?"

"To ask why he hadn't gotten the wire transfer," Tim said, "and to tell me that he'd been over to the house and had seen Magnolia's crew working. He said they had to cease and desist until Miss Harper had her money."

"But surely the transaction should have funded by three on Monday, if closing was Friday?"

A small delay was to be expected, but not something like that.

"You'd think," Tim said. "So I contacted DeWitts to see if they'd wired the money."

"And?"

"They wired it Friday afternoon."

The seller's attorney should have had the money first thing Monday morning, then. Certainly by Monday afternoon, when he had contacted Tim. "Did you double check the wiring instructions? Make sure you'd written them down right?"

"He communicated directly with DeWitts," Tim said, "but I made him give me the numbers anyway, and then I called DeWitts back to double check."

"And?"

Tim's voice got tight. "They said I had emailed them a week ago to change the wiring instructions."

"You did?"

"Of course I didn't!" If it wasn't quite a shriek, his voice got rather shrill.

I made sure mine was soothing. "But that's what they said? That you'd contacted them to change the wiring instructions?"

Tim nodded.

"And you didn't?"

"Of course I didn't!"

I took a breath. And then one more. I had a feeling I knew where this was going, and it wasn't anywhere good. "Where did they send the money?"

Tim shrugged. His usually smooth and elegant movements were sharp, jerky. "No one knows."

"It's too late to stop it?"

"Much," Tim said bitterly. "That money was in Switzerland

by midnight on Friday."

"They sent it to Switzerland?"

"Probably not," Tim admitted. "But they might as well have. We'll never get it back."

I swallowed. The words threatened to stick in my throat. "How much?"

Tim closed his eyes, like he couldn't bear to look the facts in the face. "Half a million dollars."

"In cash?" Who buys a five hundred thousand dollar house with cash?

"It's Magnolia Houston!" Tim said indignantly. "Of course in cash!"

Of course. No mortgage loan for Magnolia. So it had been half a million in cash winging its way across the airwaves from one closing attorney to the other—and being intercepted midway and rerouted to Switzerland.

Or somewhere else. Someone else.

"Can you trace the account and get the money back?" Maybe whoever received it would be nice enough to return it. Or maybe it could just be quietly withdrawn from the account where it had ended up. The owner of the account might not even realize it was there.

"You're missing the point," Tim said. "This wasn't an accident. Half a million dollars didn't suddenly take a wrong turn somewhere and get lost. Someone sent DeWitts an email telling them to send the money somewhere else. And DeWitts did it, because they thought it was from me."

"And now DeWitts are out five hundred thousand dollars."

Tim nodded. "That they're trying to pass off onto me, because of the email."

Oops. "Do you have five hundred thousand dollars?"

"No," Tim said. "And even if I did, I wouldn't spend it on this. This isn't my fault."

"Whose fault is it?"

"DeWitts!" Tim said. "They should have checked with me before they changed the wiring instructions. Or checked with the seller's attorney."

"Why didn't they?"

He shrugged again, helplessly this time. "I guess, since the email was from me, they just did what it said."

"Because you bring them a lot of business."

Tim nodded, looking sick.

"What'll happen now?" I wanted to know.

Tim leaned forward. "That's what I wanted to talk to you about."

I had a feeling I knew where this was going, too. "What do you want me to do?"

"Figure out what happened," Tim said.

"How do you expect me to do that?"

"I don't know. Do... detective things."

"I'm not a detective." But that brought up a good question. "Have you called the police?"

"Of course not," Tim said.

"Why not? Someone's stolen five hundred thousand dollars. Why wouldn't you report it?"

"Because the email came from here," Tim said. "From inside LB&A. I can't prove that I didn't send it. I know I didn't, but I can't prove it. I can't prove that anyone else didn't send it, either. Someone did. Someone we work with."

That was an uncomfortable thought. That someone we worked with, someone we saw every day, was capable of stealing five hundred thousand dollars. Of taking Magnolia Houston's money and ripping off poor, old Miss Harper, who was now stuck in an assisted living facility somewhere with no money to pay for it.

And not only that, but was willing to implicate us—Tim and the company—in the scam.

"Who do you suspect?" I asked Tim.

He shook his head.

"Well, how do you know I didn't do it?" Since he was asking me for help, I had to assume I was off the suspect list.

"You married a TBI agent," Tim said, checking reasons off on his fingers. "Your best friend is a cop."

My best friend was actually a housewife and mother in North Carolina, married to a plastic surgeon with a couple of kids in tow. But she was my best friend from high school. High school was a long time ago. So for all intents and purposes, maybe Detective Tamara Grimaldi was my current best friend. She'd been my maid of honor at the wedding, not Charlotte.

Funny, I hadn't really thought of it that way before.

"And you come from a family of lawyers," Tim added. "Your brother's a lawyer. Your sister's a lawyer. Your brother-in-law is a lawyer. Your father was a lawyer. Your grandfather..."

"I get it. And you're right. I didn't do it. I wouldn't do it." And not just because I'm married to a TBI agent, and my best friend is a cop, and I come from a family of lawyers. Stealing is wrong. Taking advantage of people is wrong. I was brought up to be better than that.

"So you'll help me figure out who did?"

I guess I would. I didn't honestly care a whole lot about Magnolia Houston's half a million dollars—all she had to do was film herself in some risqué position and upload the video to YouTube and watch the dollars roll in to recoup it—but my heart went out to Miss Harper. After spending her life in the family home, taking care of it to the best of her ability, and then having Tim come along and convince her to sell it... well, the last thing she needed, was this kind of mess.

"Isn't DeWitts insured against something like this?"

"I'm sure they are," Tim said. "But they should have double-checked the email before paying out the money. Since they didn't, the insurance company may refuse to pay. They pay for losses when it's nobody's fault, but this was gross negligence on

DeWitts' part. And that's probably why they're trying to pass it off onto me. Because the insurance won't cover it and they don't want to have to pay out-of-pocket."

I nodded. "And if the insurance won't pay, and DeWitts won't pay, and you won't pay—"

"I shouldn't have to pay!"

"—and I'm sure Magnolia Houston won't want to pay again—"

Tim shook his head.

"—then Miss Harper is the one who's out of luck here."

Tim nodded, trying not to look relieved. "So you'll do it?"

"I have no idea what to do," I told him. "I'm not an investigator. I don't know where to start, or how to go on from there. But I'll see what I can dig up. We can't let that poor old lady lose her house *and* her money because some sleezebag thought he'd rip her off."

Tim shook his head, looking pious.

I leaned forward. "So tell me who you suspect."

Two

"Nobody!" Tim exclaimed, scooting back in his chair as if I had launched a personal attack on him.

"Are you sure? If it was someone from here, there has to be someone you think is a more likely suspect than someone else."

He didn't answer, and I added, "Who do you know who could use half a million dollars?"

"Everybody," Tim said.

I nodded. Too broad a question. "Who do you know who could use it and might steal to get it?"

Tim hesitated.

"You know everything that goes on here at the firm," I coaxed. Tim has an ego, and he likes for it to be stroked. "You sign every check that's paid out. You know exactly who is and isn't making money."

"You're not," Tim said, unable to resist getting a little dig in.

I nodded in acknowledgement. No, I wasn't. "But as you've already established, you don't suspect me. So there has to be someone else. Unless there's a chance the email didn't come from inside LB&A?"

"Lane DeWitt said it did," Tim said.

But Lane DeWitt was probably not an expert on cyber crime. And he had every incentive to make Tim believe the email could only have originated here, at LB&A. That didn't mean it was true.

"If you want me to do this," I told him, "I'm going to need access to everyone's email. And everyone's paperwork. Tax forms, sales, commissions paid and received. Do you do any kind of background check on people when they come to you and want to join LB&A?"

"No," Tim said, sounding bothered that I asked. "They're licensed real estate agents. The state makes sure they have clean records."

Yes and no. You can't get a real estate license if you have committed a crime in what they call a 'substantially related field.' To quote the Real Estate Licensing and Registration Act, § 501: "Licenses shall be granted only to persons who bear a good reputation for honesty, trustworthiness, integrity, and competence to transact the business of a broker or salesperson."

So anyone with a conviction for fraud, for instance, or embezzlement, or anything like that, shouldn't expect to get a real estate license.

Anyone with a conviction for drunk driving or fishing without a license, on the other hand, might not have anything to worry about. There's nothing 'substantially related' about driving under the influence, or catching illicit catfish, and selling real estate.

"So you don't know whether anyone here has a criminal record."

"I know the state of Tennessee gave them all real estate licenses," Tim said. "That's always been good enough for me."

Trust is a nice thing. However— "You should consider running criminal background checks on everyone before you take them on."

Tim looked mutinous.

"And we should definitely run them now. If someone who works here has a conviction for any kind of crime, that might be who's behind this. Someone who's been inclined to one kind of crime, might be inclined to another."

"Or not," Tim said.

Or not. Sometimes there are extenuating circumstances. And some people go to prison and serve their time and come out different. Just look at Rafe.

But... "Fine," I said. "We don't have to run background checks on anyone. Do I at least have your permission to look at everyone's email accounts and paperwork?"

Tim sighed. "I guess. If it will help you find who did this. Talk to Brittany about getting you what you need."

"Is Brittany off the suspect list?"

Tim opened his mouth. And didn't say anything.

"Because Brittany could probably use that half a million as much as anyone else. Maybe more." She was the receptionist, and salaried. Everyone else worked on commission. Something that can be a blessing as well as a curse. Brittany got a salary every couple of weeks, and could count on that amount, even if it—probably—didn't amount to a whole lot. The agents, meanwhile, only got paid when they had a closing. And while it's possible to make a nice chunk of change as a realtor—Tim was doing quite well, and so were several of the others—it's also possible to be like me, and make less than Brittany.

Really, sometimes I wonder why I bother. When the baby came, maybe I'd just quit real estate and stay home and write that bodice ripper I've been toying with in the back of my head.

"You can sit at Brittany's desk when she goes to lunch," Tim said. "I'll let Heidi know."

Gee, thanks.

Heidi Hoppenfeldt usually did the honors at the reception desk whenever Brittany wasn't around. She started out at LB&A (back in the days when it was Walker Lamont Realty) as Brenda Puckett's protégée, but after Brenda was killed, Tim made her his assistant instead. I'm pretty sure Brenda was grooming Heidi for real estate greatness, although Tim uses her more as general dogsbody and Jill of all trades. She's still here, so she must not mind.

On the other hand, that might make her a candidate for Tim's little problem. If she resented his treatment of her, and she needed money, she might have felt it was poetic justice to put him on the hot seat by using his email address and getting him in trouble with DeWitts.

"I'll do that," I said, since it would give me access to Brittany's computer and all the records on it. "And give Heidi a break."

Maybe she'd appreciate it. She and I haven't ever gotten along especially well, either.

Tim nodded. "Anything else?"

"Nothing I can think of at the moment. If you hear anything else from DeWitts or Miss Harper's attorney, let me know."

Tim assured me he would. I braced my hands on the arms of the chair and heaved myself upright. "I'll be in my office until lunch."

"I'll let Brittany know you'll be relieving her," Tim said.

"Maybe you should give Heidi a project, too, so she doesn't wonder about the change. Send her on an errand or something."

"Good idea." Tim smiled approvingly. "You know, Savannah, you're smarter than you look."

"Thank you," I said, since there was no point in saying anything else. And after all, he must think I was reasonably smart, since he'd asked my help with this. He wouldn't have if he'd thought me dumb as a box of rocks. Or so I assumed.

I retired to my office and started doing the stuff I'd come to LB&A to do in the first place.

A week or so ago, I had signed up for lead generation software, to help me find more buyers and sellers. Between you and me, real estate hadn't turned out to be the moneymaker I had hoped it would, when I got my license to practice last year. I haven't sold many houses, and it's not always easy to find new clients. In an effort to change that, I'd gone in with several other agents on this lead generation software that supposedly would fix the problem. Every morning now, I'd sign into my email and see if there was a *New Lead!* message. If there was, I'd have to contact the new lead and introduce myself and see how I might be able to help them. Nine times out of ten, they were looking for rentals. I don't help people find places to rent. The tenth time, the house they were interested in was under contract. At that point, I'd take their contact info and offer to send them information about other houses with the same criteria—price, size, location— and that would be it. I'd do a search for like houses, send it off, and sit back and wait. In the five days I had had said lead generation software, I'd gotten four leads. No one had called me back a second time.

I went through the motions again. Ten minutes later, with the list of properties dispatched to someone I'd probably never hear from again, I sat back on my chair, just as Heidi walked into the lobby and stopped at Brittany's desk.

"I have to go to the office store. We're out of manila envelopes."

I glanced through the gap in the door, as Brittany furrowed her brow and tucked the wad of bubblegum into her cheek so she could talk. "Are you sure? There were plenty yesterday."

"I checked," Heidi said. "Tim said that Savannah can take over while you go to lunch."

She glanced toward my door. I'm pretty sure the look was smug.

"Of course he did," I said, and tried to sound as if this was the first I'd heard of it.

They both waited. I sighed. "Fine. Let me know when you're ready to go, Brittany."

Brittany smirked. Heidi waddled off down the hall toward the parking lot. I tried not to think unkind thoughts about the way she moved, since I was getting to the waddling stage myself.

It can't have been more than fifteen minutes later that Brittany got up from her desk and pulled her purse out of a drawer. "I'm going."

"Seriously?" I glanced at my watch. "It's ten-fifteen." Who goes to lunch at ten-fifteen?

"Appointment," Brittany said.

"Convenient." I got to my feet and walked into the lobby. "I guess I'll be manning the desk for longer than an hour, then."

Brittany smirked. "You can always call Tim if you have to pee."

I'm pregnant. I always have to pee.

And then she was gone. The door slammed shut, and Brittany trucked past the window at a good clip, a big, self-congratulatory grin on her face.

I stuck my tongue out—just in case anyone was watching— before taking her place behind the desk. And just in case she realized she had forgotten something and decided to come back, I waited five minutes before I turned to the computer and started searching.

It was all there. Paystubs and salaries, gross sales and commissions. Home addresses and social security numbers. If I'd been inclined to larceny, I could have had a field day with all this information.

Maybe the guilty party hadn't been Brittany after all. She'd had all this at her fingertips for over a year, and hadn't done anything with it.

She took home an OK, but hardly generous salary. More than I made, for sure, since I was dependent on my non-existent commissions, and only got paid when I sold a house. But she didn't make a lot. A few of the other agents were in the same boat I was, and didn't make much, either. They were people I hardly ever saw, so they may have had other jobs and practiced real estate only on weekends. Or perhaps they had a business of renovating houses, and only sold the houses they renovated. One every three months or so. Either way, they were in the slim-to-none category along with me and Brittany.

Heidi Hoppenfeldt did better than I thought she would be. I had assumed, since she mostly worked as an assistant to Tim, that she was salaried, and that the salary was small, like Brittany's. But while that was true, Heidi got bonuses. Whenever Tim had a closing, Heidi got a percentage of Tim's proceeds. Not a big percentage, by any means. But since Tim is one of those agents who sells a lot of houses, many of them expensive, Heidi did all right.

That didn't take her out of contention for being the guilty party in this case, of course. It just meant that if she was the guilty party, she wasn't motivated solely by money, but perhaps equally by getting Tim in trouble.

And speaking of Tim... he made more money than most of us put together. He got paid for being the broker, and being in charge of us all—the place where the buck stopped. That was done with a percentage of what the rest of us pulled in. And then he made his own money in addition to that, and plenty of it. He certainly had no reason to want to steal Magnolia Houston's half a million dollars... not to mention how bad the whole thing made him look. And besides, if he'd been behind it, chances were he wouldn't have asked me to investigate. Tim might not think a whole lot of my abilities in the real estate realm, but he couldn't deny that I'd solved my share of mysteries. And that was in addition to my special agent husband and my friend the homicide detective. If he'd had a hand in this, I doubted he would have involved me. Too risky, just in case I did figure it out and pointed the finger at him.

Several of the others had healthy incomes, too. I looked at their 1099s for last year, and their income so far for the current year, and was envious. Those people went down to the bottom of my mental list, since they had no need to steal. They were making plenty of money honestly.

Although that thought made me sit back and think. What were the reasons why someone might have done this?

And speaking of mental lists: it was getting a little disorganized up there in my head, so I pulled a legal pad out of Brittany's desk drawer, grabbed a pen from the mug beside the computer monitor, and proceeded to take notes.

So what were the reasons—financial or otherwise—someone might have done this?

The need—or desire—for money was the obvious number one reason. Someone either needed or wanted Magnolia Houston's half a million dollars.

There was a difference between needing and wanting—and I don't mean the obvious one.

Someone who needed the money, didn't have enough money of their own. Either didn't make enough, or had some unexpected expense they didn't know how to cover. Accident, illness, or maybe just a new house.

Someone who wanted it... well, that was a different story.

Someone might just want more than they had, not because they needed more, but just because it was there and they could figure out a way to take it. Some people just don't have a very clear concept of 'enough.'

On the other hand, it might be someone who didn't want Magnolia to have it. Taking the money away from her was the goal, rather than appropriating it for themselves.

Someone who didn't think she deserved it? Someone who shared my opinion of her 'talents' and my incredulousness that she could make money—and such a lot of money—bouncing her boobs in front of a camera?

I guess I'd need to talk to Magnolia—or have Tim talk to Magnolia—about who might have had it in for her in a financial way. Or maybe not even in a financial way. Someone who just didn't like her, and wanted to hit her somewhere where it might hurt.

Or—with a slightly different angle—maybe someone who wanted to make sure she didn't get her hands on Miss Harper's antebellum home. Either because they didn't think she deserved it, or because they were afraid of what she might do to it.

That probably meant I'd have to take a closer look at both Miss Harper herself, and her attorney. The money hadn't been wired where it was supposed to go, no... but what if Miss Harper's attorney, or Miss Harper herself, were on the take? They arranged for the half a million to go to a secret account somewhere, and kept the house. Or kept the first half a million, and then got another half a million from the insurance company eventually. Or from Tim.

Maybe Miss Harper was resentful that he'd talked her into selling her family home. Maybe this was a way for her to keep both the house and the money, and get Tim in trouble at the same time.

It was a lot of calculation to attribute to a little eighty-year-old woman. But on paper, at least, it made sense.

And then there was Tim. Not Tim himself, but someone who didn't like Tim. Someone who didn't want Tim to benefit from his association with Magnolia, or just someone trying to get back at him for something he'd done. In that scenario, the money was a nice bonus, but getting Tim in trouble was the main goal.

So any enemies of Tim went on the list.

I sat back and contemplated it. It was getting lengthy. And I had no idea how to approach anyone on it. I mean, it was one thing for me to sit here and look at people's taxable income and say that so-and-so—Brittany, for example—had reason to steal Magnolia Houston's half a million dollars and implicate Tim, because she wasn't making a lot of money and Tim was bossing her around. Brittany might disagree. Hell—heck—if she wasn't involved, she'd certainly disagree.

After all, who was I to say what would constitute a motive for theft in someone else's mind? What might seem like a good reason to me, might not be anything resembling a reason—good or bad—to the person in question. They say that everyone has a price, but some people are just inherently honest and wouldn't steal, no matter how big or small the amount.

Whoever did it, had some computer knowledge. And enough understanding of real estate to know how closings worked, not to mention enough information about LB&A to know the parties involved in the Magnolia Houston closing.

I added the cleaning crew to the list. They had access to the office, to the computers, to information about our pending transactions. And they could use the system while they were here, cleaning. After hours, when the place was mostly empty. If that email had originated here, the cleaning crew was a good place to start looking for suspects.

Chances were, one or more of them would have a financial motive. Cleaning offices at night isn't something that'll make you rich.

Or they could all be honest as the day was long, and would never consider stealing.

I leaned back with a sigh. I was getting nowhere. And somewhere, someone I didn't know—or maybe someone I knew—was gloating over an unexpected windfall of half a million dollars.

Three

By the time Brittany came back, it was close to two o'clock, and I was starving. The baby lets me feel it if I don't feed it regularly, and I was past my usual lunch time by almost two hours.

"About time you came back," I told her when she sauntered in, hands laden with shopping bags. "I'm about to pass out. I haven't had anything to eat since breakfast. The baby's chewing on my stomach lining."

Brittany made a face. "Ewww. TMI."

She's in her early twenties, and hasn't quite moved past that teenage stage where pregnancies are gross and pregnant women are fat and ugly. And while she must be getting her job done somehow, since she still has one, pretty much all I ever see her do, is polishing her nails and leafing through fashion magazines.

I eyed the bags as I got up. "I thought you had an appointment."

"At the county clerk's office," Brittany said, dumping the bags in the area behind her chair. "Then I went to get something to eat, and since I was at the mall anyway, I figured I might as well look around."

She nudged me out of the way and folded her skinny frame into the desk chair, reaching out a pink-tipped hand to wiggle the mouse. "What did you do?"

"What do you mean, what did I do? I answered the phone when it rang. Other than that, I didn't do much of anything."

"You used my computer."

"Of course I used your computer. It wasn't like I could go back and forth to my own."

I waited a second, and when she didn't say anything else, I added, "And it isn't your computer. It's LB&A's computer. The reception computer. Everyone has access to it."

And if I'd known just a little more about how computers work, I might have been able to figure out whether the email to DeWitts had been sent from this particular computer. As it was, I had checked the email program, the sent emails and the deleted emails, and had found nothing. Which was exactly what I had expected to find. If whoever had sent the email to DeWitts had sent it from here, he or she had probably been smart enough to delete it—completely, from the entire email program—after they did it. A computer tech might be able to dig it out, but I wasn't one of those and didn't know where to find one.

"I'm back now," Brittany said, and waved those pink talons. "You can go back to your own office."

It was almost like she wanted to get rid of me. And because it was, I lingered. "What did you buy?"

"Nothing that would fit you," Brittany said, which was more than a little rude, if accurate. She's skinny as a snake, and I wouldn't have fit into her clothes even before I got pregnant.

"I probably wouldn't like anything you bought, anyway." She dressed like a tramp, not that I'd ever say so. My mother raised a lady. Obviously Brittany's mother didn't.

She sniffed. "Not that it's any of your business, but Devon and I are going to get married on Friday. That's what I did at the county clerk's office. Got a marriage license."

Devon's the boyfriend. They've been together more than a year. Brittany was dating him when I started working at Walker Lamont Realty, when Walker was still with us.

"How romantic," I said. "Don't you think maybe you should wait until you're a little older?"

"I'm twenty-two," Brittany informed me, with a toss of the

ponytail, "and Devon's twenty-three."

"I was twenty-three when I married Bradley. It didn't work out well." In fact, it had lasted less than two years before I discovered that he was sleeping with his paralegal. The fact that I'd been young and stupid had certainly had something to do with it. Not with his sleeping around—although he tried to tell me it did—but with my not realizing he would.

"I'm not you," Brittany said. The implication, of course, was that she wasn't stupid, and it couldn't happen to her.

I had only met Devon a couple of times. I didn't know him, certainly not well enough to be able to tell whether he'd cheat. He had struck me as just another long-haired musician type, who probably was a musician, since half of Nashville is involved in the music industry in one way or another.

Was it in any way significant that he and Brittany had suddenly decided to get married, and that Brittany had spent a bunch of money at some very expensive stores, just a couple of days after five hundred thousand dollars had gone missing from Magnolia Houston's account?

If Brittany had rerouted it, was she stupid enough to draw attention to the fact that she was suddenly flush by buying a bunch of stuff she wouldn't normally buy?

Getting married was a good excuse. A bride needs a trousseau, and nobody would think twice about a prospective bride going a little crazy at the mall.

Nobody but me, I guess.

I wanted to stay and chat longer, but by now my stomach was starting to cramp, and I swear the baby was kicking me in the ribs to get my attention. Brittany probably wasn't likely to tell me anything beyond what she already had, anyway. I went to my own office for my bag. "I'm going to get something to eat."

Brittany nodded. "Is Heidi back?"

"I haven't seen her." And that wasn't cool, either. A trip to the office store for manila envelopes shouldn't take the best part of four hours. Not when the nearest office store was fifteen minutes away, tops. "She might have come in the back." And avoided me.

"I'm going out that way," I added, since the parking lot was back there and it's where my car was parked. "If I see her, do you want me to send her up here?"

Brittany shook her head. "I'll page her if I want her."

"Suit yourself." I put the strap of my purse over my shoulder and walked away.

Heidi's office—a little anteroom across the hall from Tim's office, was empty, though. So she must still be out there getting manila envelopes, and God knew what else Tim had come up with for her to do. Since it doesn't take more than three hours to buy office supplies, she must have moved on from there and into another activity. Maybe she was getting married too, and was shopping for a trousseau.

I hesitated for a second before I slipped through the door and pulled it shut behind me. Not all the way shut; I wanted to hear if someone came down the hall. But shut enough that someone walking by wouldn't immediately notice me being in there.

It wasn't the first time I'd been snooping in Heidi's office. Just about a year ago, after my colleague Brenda Puckett had had her throat slit in Rafe's grandmother's house, I had taken it upon myself to search her office, and her assistant's office, and Heidi's office, for any clues as to why the crime had been committed (and whether it was likely that Rafe had any part in it).

Back then, it had been dark, after hours, not the middle of the day. The place had been empty. And Clarice, Brenda's assistant, had still come in and caught me in the act.

It occurred to me that it would probably be smarter to wait until after hours to search Heidi's office, too. Why take chances?

I was on my way back to the door when it opened and she walked in.

I stopped. So did she. And looked around suspiciously.

"What are you doing here?"

"Looking to see if you're back," I said. And—offense being the best defense—I added, "It took you long enough to go to the office store for manila envelopes."

"I stopped for lunch," Heidi said.

She didn't have to tell me that. Her ample bosom showed evidence of recent consumption. Sesame seeds, unless my eyes were playing tricks. Maybe a burger bun?

My own stomach rumbled audibly at the idea, and I moved a step closer to the door. "Well, I'm on my way to lunch now. Brittany came back and took over the front desk. She asked if you were back, so I stepped in to see."

Heidi moved aside so I could make my way to the door, but her eyes were still narrowed in suspicion.

"She said she'd page you if she needed you," I added as I moved past her, "but you might want to check in with her, just in case there's something specific she wants."

Heidi turned to watch me go through the door and into the hallway.

"She went shopping," I added. "Maybe she bought something she wants to show you."

I didn't wait for an answer, just hot-footed it down the hallway to the back door and out.

My pale blue Volvo—the only thing, along with my self-respect, that I had salvaged from my short-lived marriage to Bradley Ferguson—was parked in the lot. I didn't get into it, though; just gave the rear corner a little pat as I made my way past. There are a couple of eateries within a block of the LB&A office, at the Five Points intersection in East Nashville, and one of them, the FinBar, has a nice selection of burgers. I wanted one.

Three minutes later I was tucked into a booth by the window, waiting for a vanilla milkshake and a bacon cheeseburger with a side of fries. All the major food groups.

The waitress had taken pity on me and had brought me a little bowl of pretzels from the bar, just so I could put something in my stomach while I waited. Maybe the rumbling had gotten so loud she'd been able to hear it when I came in.

So I sat there with the pages I had torn off Brittany's yellow legal pad, covered with all my scribbles, and stuffed myself with pretzels while I looked them over.

I didn't know much about anything yet, so I had made a list of things I needed to find out. And things I needed to do.

I should probably drive up to Goodlettsville and take a look at the Harper house, just so I could say I had. I didn't know what I'd learn by doing it, but it seemed like I ought to. At the same time, I should perhaps stop by Miss Harper's attorney's office, just to get a look at him. Not that it's possible to tell by looking at someone whether they're crooked or not, but just in case he seemed shifty.

I had to go back to the office tonight, and look through Heidi's desk and computer. I didn't think I'd find anything of interest, but it had to be done, if for no other reason than to eliminate her.

If she was guilty, I'd probably have more luck going through her townhouse. I knew where she lived, but going there would entail breaking and entering, and I didn't like Tim enough to risk going to prison for him. If I found anything that pointed to Heidi being involved, I'd tackle that prospect then.

I also needed to find out about the ins and outs of email. I use email, but I don't know much about how it works. DeWitts had said that the email changing the wiring instructions for the money had to have come from within LB&A, but was that true? Could it have come from somewhere else instead?

I don't know enough about it to be able to say one way or the other, so I'd have to find someone who did.

And somehow I'd have to find a way to look into Magnolia Houston, just in case this was something she could have done herself, to keep her half a million smackers. A big hoax to get Miss Harper's house and the money too, by seeming to lose it, while actually siphoning it off into another account somewhere, and then having DeWitts' insurance company cover the loss.

Getting a half a million dollar house for free is nice work if you can get it. And since she'd have to put about the same amount into renovations once she got the house, getting it free would make the deal all the sweeter.

Not that Magnolia was any higher on my suspect list than anyone else. I just didn't know her—and didn't like what I did know—so it was easy to consider her a suspect. Easier than suspecting people I actually knew. And I didn't have much of a problem there.

The burger arrived, and I wolfed it down, along with all the fries and the milkshake. My mother would have been appalled. A Southern Belle is supposed to have a wasp waist and the appetite of a bird. I don't have either at the moment, and really never did.

However, the thought of Mother reminded me that I hadn't heard from my brother yet today.

Yesterday, I had started the morning in Sweetwater, in the Martin and McCall law office on the town square, with some shocking news. Shocking to me, Dix, and Catherine—my brother and sister—who had discovered that we had another sister we'd known nothing about.

And devastating for Mother, who had learned that her best friend had been in love with her husband—Mother's husband, my father—and had borne his child.

When I left Mother yesterday morning, after following her home to the mansion, she'd been looking at the bottom of a bottle of brandy. She'd been angry enough about the whole situation that when I registered disapproval of the brandy, she had told me it was her house and her brandy, and if I didn't like her drinking it, I could get out. So I had. Dix and Catherine had dried her out, and by evening she was reasonably sober but still angry. I didn't know what was going on today, since nobody had bothered to call me, and since—frankly—I had had some personal matters of my own taking up real estate in my head.

This seemed like a good time to call my brother and get an update.

I dialed the number for the law office, without thinking. And had a moment of absolute blankness when Darcy answered the phone. "Martin and McCall."

"Oh," I said. "Um..." My new half sister. I wasn't as upset as Mother, but it was still strange for me, too. "It's Savannah."

"Hi, Savannah." Darcy sounded equally leery. Hard to blame her for that. She had gone from being a sibling-less orphan to having two sisters, a brother, two brothers-in-law, a bunch of nephews and nieces, not to mention a step-mother and a biological mother, all in one morning. It was understandable that she was a bit overwhelmed, and—given Mother's reaction to the news—more than a little nervous about the whole thing. Darcy had always gotten along well with all of us. Dix had hired her for the law office long before he knew who she was. But this was tricky for everyone concerned.

"Is Dix around?" I asked. "I wanted an update on Mother."

"He's in with a client," Darcy said. "I can have him call you when he's free."

I told her that that would work. "Did he go over there this morning?"

He had. "He said your mother was sober but still angry."

I would hope she was sober, since it had been early. As for being angry... it would probably take her a while to get over that. More than twenty-four hours, at any rate.

"Is he going over there again later?"

"He didn't say," Darcy said, "but I assume so."

"Can you tell him to give me a call after he has?"

Darcy said she would, and an awkward, short silence

ensued.

"So how are you doing?" I asked.

She sighed. "I'm fine."

"You could have stayed home today, you know. Dix wouldn't have minded."

"It's better to have something to do," Darcy said. "At home I'd just sit and think. Even if it's a little weird to be here, now that things have changed, I'd rather be here than home alone."

I could definitely imagine that. "Dix and Jonathan aren't treating you any differently, are they? In a bad way, I mean?"

"No," Darcy said. "Although we're all tip-toeing around each other a little more carefully than usual, I guess."

"That's probably normal." Even if the situation wasn't normal at all. "It'll take us all some time to get used to this, I think. After twenty-eight years of having two siblings, suddenly I have three. And it's not that I mind. It's just... different."

"Definitely," Darcy said.

"Have you spoken to Audrey?"

Audrey, as we'd found out yesterday, is Darcy's biological mother. She's also been Mother's best friend for the past thirty-plus years.

"Not since yesterday," Darcy said.

"She's probably giving you time to get used to the situation."

She didn't answer, and I added, "This must be hard for her. Normally, she and my mother would go to lunch and Audrey would talk and Mother would listen, and they'd both feel better. But they can't do that now."

And unlike Mother, who had all of us around her to listen and take care of things, Audrey was alone. No parents, no spouse, no boyfriend. No children apart from Darcy. She and my mother had been inseparable since Mother married my dad and moved to Sweetwater thirty-three years ago. I couldn't imagine how hard this must be for both of them.

But since I couldn't order Darcy to go see her mother, not

until she was ready to do so on her own, I changed the subject. "Did Patrick Nolan call?"

Nolan was an officer with the Columbia PD, the nearest big town to Sweetwater. His partner was Officer Lupe Vasquez, with whom we'd had occasion to speak while we were trying to track down Darcy's biological parents. Nolan had barely been able to take his eyes off Darcy during the conversation, and she hadn't been much better.

But then he and Vasquez had gotten called out and had to go deal with a situation, and he hadn't had a chance to ask her for her number. And I had assured her that he'd get in touch with her in the next day or two—he knew who she was and where she worked—but if he didn't, we'd track him down and find out why.

"No," Darcy said and sounded depressed.

"I can contact Lupe Vasquez, if you want, and have her give him a nudge."

"No," Darcy said. "If he isn't going to call on his own, it doesn't matter."

I wasn't sure I agreed with that, but if she didn't want me to call, I wouldn't. And besides, it was early days yet. He might call today.

I said so. Darcy sighed. "I doubt it."

"Then maybe you should contact him. You know where he works. And it's easy to make up an excuse for why you need a cop."

"I'm not going to force him!" Darcy said.

"I doubt you would be. He seemed really taken with you on Sunday. He's probably just worried that you don't feel the same." Either that, or he, too, had something going on in his personal life he had to deal with.

"Anyway," I added, "it's up to you. He might call today. And if he doesn't and you want me to contact Lupe Vasquez and give him a nudge, let me know."

Darcy said she would.

"Tell Dix to call me later. After he's looked in on Mother."

"I will," Darcy said. "I'll talk to you later, Savannah."

She hung up before I could say anything else. I guess I was bothering her.

Lunch was over. I paid the check and headed out.

Four

The small town where Miss Harper lived, on Dickerson Pike north of Nashville, is called Goodlettsville. It was incorporated in 1958, with three thousand inhabitants, and named for A.G. Goodlett, pastor of the Cumberland Presbyterian Church. In 1963, when Nashville chose to merge with the government of Davidson County, Goodlettsville elected to remain autonomous.

In the interest of saving time, I took the interstate north. At Long Hollow Pike, I got off and headed west, and then north on Dickerson. A couple of minutes later, after a right onto Lickton Pike, I found myself in front of the old Harper homestead.

It was definitely antebellum. Early antebellum, at a guess. Smaller and a bit more squat than the house I grew up in.

The Martin Mansion was built around 1840, of red brick with tall, two-story pillars in the front. Your stereotypical Southern mansion: like Tara, but not all-white. A lot of the antebellum homes around here aren't. They're made of brick, and in a lot of cases, the brick is left exposed. In Middle Tennessee, Riverwood and the Belmont Mansion are stuccoed, white and blush respectively, while Two Rivers, Carnton, Rippavilla, Oak Lawn, and Rattle and Snap are all exposed brick. As is the Martin Mansion, a little further south. And they're just a fraction of the antebellum homes that are available in this area.

At any rate, the Harper place was older. Early 1800s, at a

guess. It sat close to the ground, and while the structure had two stories, the roof only came halfway up to what would have been the second story on the Martin Mansion. The ceilings must be much lower, and there was no wide and graceful staircase rising to an imposing double door. Here, there was a somewhat squat stoop in front of a single door. The windows were smaller than at home, and the front porch was narrow and only on the first floor. The house was built of wood, and was badly in need of painting. Even the pillars were unimposing.

It did look as if someone was getting started on fixing it up, however. Tim had told me that Miss Harper's attorney had sent the renovators packing yesterday. Today, someone was back. A tall ladder leaned up against one side of the house, and on top of it stood a young man with a scraper, pecking at the house to make flakes of old paint rain down on the overgrown lawn.

I pulled the car into the driveway and rolled down the passenger side window. "Hello!"

I'm fairly certain he heard me. In fact, I'm sure of it, because by the time I had parked the car in front of the stoop and gotten out—which took a little longer than usual these days, seeing as I almost needed a shoe horn to extricate myself from behind the steering wheel—the ladder was empty. And not because the guy had come around the corner to see who I was and what I wanted.

No, he was gone. Completely and utterly vanished.

I stood for a second at the corner of the house and looked around.

Out here, beyond Nashville, things were pretty rural. The Harper house sat back from the road, with a field of overgrown lawn in the front, and a tangled mess of bushes and trees in the back and on the sides. It had definitely been a while since Miss Harper had had anyone out to do landscaping.

The young man in the white T-shirt and jeans was nowhere to be seen. I walked around the back of the house to be sure, picking my way carefully across the pitted ground. There were rocks and hollows hidden by the ankle high grass, and every step was an invitation to disaster. One of these days I really would have to make good on my promise to myself and stop wearing shoes with heels.

Today was not that day, however. I had put on wedge sandals when I left the house this morning, and I wasn't about to kick them off and go barefoot. There could be all sorts of critters lurking in the grass. Snakes and frogs and salamanders, not to mention fleas and ticks and God knew what.

So I kept my shoes on and moved slowly past the ladder down to the corner, and along the back of the house.

No one was there. And whoever he was, he hadn't gone in through the back door. There was one, but it was boarded up, with a sheet of plywood screwed to the door frame. I pushed on it, just to make sure it was securely fastened, and it didn't budge.

It was a little eerie here on the backside of the house, between the dilapidated, peeling wall and the second wall made of tangled vines and branches. It was quiet. No buzzing of insects or chirping of birds.

Doesn't that usually mean that something has upset the wildlife?

The intruding presence might be mine, I suppose. Or it might be the young man from the ladder. The idea that he was hiding in the shrubbery, watching me walk by, was a bit creepy, to be honest.

I made my way to the next corner and around to the other side of the house. It looked the same as the first side, with the exception of the ladder. A tall sandstone chimney in the middle of the wall, with a window on each side, one set on the first floor and one on the second. They were smaller windows than I was used to: both the Martin Mansion and the Victorian house where I lived with Rafe had big, beautiful windows, as tall as me. This house was older, and built at a time when big panes of glass were harder to come by. The windows were small, six over six—

six small squares on the bottom sash, six more on the top. I tried to peer in, but they were just tall enough that I couldn't really get a good look. Besides, they were grimy.

Around the front, I climbed onto the worn stoop and tried the door. The knob turned, but the door didn't open. I both pushed and pulled, but it remained stubbornly shut.

Eventually, I ended up back where I had started, at the foot of the ladder next to the chimney on the right side of the house.

It was still empty. The ladder, I mean.

There was a window next to it, however, up on the second floor. I couldn't remember whether that window had been open or closed when I drove up to the house—I likely hadn't noticed one way or the other—but was it possible that the young man had climbed inside the house rather than, as I had assumed, climbed down and run away?

I contemplated the ladder and my shoes. And then I contemplated the stomach that currently prevented me from seeing my shoes, unless I twisted and lifted my foot, like a Charleston dancer from the 1920s.

Climbing that ladder to the second floor probably wouldn't be a good idea. If I fell off, Rafe would kill me.

But I probably wouldn't fall off. I'd climbed ladders before, after all. And if the guy was inside, getting up there would be worth it.

I grabbed the ladder and put my foot on the first rung. And stepped up.

So far, so good.

I did it again.

And again.

And then I made the mistake of looking down.

I was only about four feet from the ground, but it looked a long way off. And I couldn't get as close to the ladder as I wanted. My stomach was in the way, and although I could fit it between the rungs of the ladder between steps, I still had to lean back to take the next step. Take the stomach out of the current hole before I could gain a rung and fit it into the next one. And every time I leaned back, I felt like I was pulling the ladder away from the wall.

It took forever to get up to the top. And when I got there, I realized that the window was too far away to make for easy access. For someone who wasn't six months pregnant and wearing a skirt and high heels, maybe it wasn't. But it would take letting go of the ladder with one hand and moving one arm and one leg over to the window, two feet or so away. And then trust that I could hang on long enough to get myself through the opening.

I decided I wasn't brave—or stupid—enough to try. It was bad enough up here on the ladder. Letting go of the ladder and swinging through the air toward the window was beyond me.

But I did lean over that way and call out. "Hello? Anyone here?"

I could only see a sliver of the inside from where I stood. Dusty wood floors, faded wall paper with what looked like magnolias. Quite fitting, considering.

I could hear, though. And as soon as I called out, there was a scramble from inside. Rapid footsteps across the floor and then the clatter of feet on the staircase inside.

Shit! I mean... shoot. He was getting away.

I started making my way back down to the ground, one rung at a time, but it was no quicker going down than going up had been. I was still several feet from the ground when I heard the front door slam open and hit the wall. The whole house shook, and for a second I thought the ladder was about to part company with the wall and dump me in the grass. I shrieked and leaned forward with all I had, willing the ladder to stay against the wall.

It took me a few seconds to get moving again. When I hit solid ground, all I wanted to do was spend a full minute catching my breath. Instead, I headed for the front of the house. There was no one in sight. But on the other side of the house, I heard the sound of a motor revving.

I legged it in that direction, careful not to turn my ankle on the uneven ground. Beyond the trees, I could hear wheels turning and gravel spitting as someone did his best to get away as quickly as possible.

The trees were old and it was a long time since anyone had done any gardening around the Harper place. The grass and weeds reached beyond my knees, and vines festooned the branches like Christmas garland. By the time I had fought my way through the dense growth to the other side, my legs and arms were scratched to the point of bleeding, and I had taken a branch to the face that had caused my ears to ring. I was pretty sure I was working on a black eye.

And to add insult to injury, there was nothing to see. Just a dirt track behind the trees, going in the direction of the real road. Before it got there, it disappeared beyond another bank of trees. All I could see was a cloud of dust down at the end of the path.

As I stood there, trying to catch my breath, a yellow school bus came lumbering up the road past Miss Harper's property. When it drew even with me, I heard a squeal of brakes, and then the school bus came to a quivering stop. I imagined children inside falling like bowling pins.

A second later, a car rocketed down the road from the other direction.

I followed its passage from where I stood. Dark in color. It looked dark green, but that might have been a reflection of the trees above. It was boxy. A Jeep or Land Rover or something of that nature. An SUV type, but sporty. Something that looked like it wouldn't be out of place on the beach in Waikiki or creeping up a mountain in Yellowstone.

As the green vehicle disappeared out of sight, the school bus started moving again. I deduced that the SUV had shot out from the track I was standing on, right in front of the bus, and that's why the bus had stopped so abruptly. Hopefully no one onboard was hurt.

The bus lumbered away. After another moment I did the same. Slowly and carefully this time. I had enough scratches and chigger bites. I didn't want any more.

Miss Harper's old friend Mr. Peretti had his law office in a small row of similar businesses on the main road in Goodlettsville, just up the street from City Hall. There was a big antique shop on the corner, taking up half the building; a consignment boutique that looked like it specialized in children's clothing was on the other side of the law office, and then there was a yarn store at the end. Both looked interesting. The baby's birth was close enough now that I found myself looking at layettes and cute little baby booties whenever I went somewhere that had them. I'd have to stop into the consignment store after I'd talked to the lawyer. And then maybe go and fondle some yarn. I know how to knit, even if I don't do it much. But a baby blanket—soft and fuzzy and straight up-and-down—might be right up my alley.

But business before pleasure. There were two empty parking spaces right in front of the law office, and I slid the Volvo into one of them. Cut the engine, and sat for a moment peering out.

The building was whitewashed brick. The office was small: just a door next to a single, big window. *Peretti and Son*, it said on the window, in faded gold letters, *Est. 1928*.

Another family law business. I grew up in one of those, and almost ended up going into it. Until I dropped out of law school to marry, and then divorce, Bradley Ferguson.

I knew the buttons to push here. This was familiar territory.

I opened the car door and swung my legs out. And walked up to the door and twisted the knob.

Like at Miss Harper's place, the knob turned but the door didn't open. The lights were off inside. I pressed my nose against the window and blocked out the light with my hands. I could make out a small room with a single desk, filled with stacks of papers and an old-fashioned telephone, the kind where the ear piece is stuck to the phone with a curly wire.

Did those even work anymore?

There was no sign of life inside. The faded gold letters on the door announced that the office was supposed to be open another hour, but Mr. Peretti must have closed up shop early and gone home. Or somewhere else. Maybe to hold Miss Harper's hand while all this got sorted out. She had to be beside herself with worry.

I knocked, just in case Mr. Peretti was holed up somewhere out of sight and had locked the door for privacy while he was using the bathroom. But no one answered. After a minute, I abandoned the law office and made my way over to the consignment store instead.

It was nice and air conditioned inside. We were now well into August, but the late summer has the potential to bring killer heat to Nashville. And the more pregnant I got, the more the high temperatures bothered me.

At least by next summer I wouldn't be pregnant anymore. That was something to look forward to.

I spent a pleasant few minutes browsing the racks of baby clothes on consignment. There were some very cute things on display. A little strawberry-printed dress with matching bloomers and bonnet for a little girl; a little onesie with embroidered trains for a boy.

I didn't know what I was having. We were far enough along in the pregnancy that we could find out, but we hadn't yet. The first ultrasound had been a long time ago, too early, and the result of a fight I'd gotten into. We'd been more concerned with making sure the baby was OK than with figuring out what kind of parts it came with. And during the last ultrasound the baby had been stubborn in showing us its back, and had refused to move, no matter how much the ultrasound tech poked at it with the wand. I had some concerns about that stubbornness going forward.

Anyway, I didn't know whether I was having a boy or a girl. And since I didn't, there was no point in buying strawberry bloomers or trains. I ended up with some onesies and booties in unisex yellow and green, and took them up to the register. "Nice place."

"Thank you." The woman behind the register was maybe five years older than me, a little plump, with brown hair and freckles. Her hands were quick and capable as she sorted through the tiny clothes. "A couple of us got together when our youngest kids started school. We had all this kid stuff sitting around that we didn't think we'd ever use again. We decided to try to get some money for it. Kids are expensive. But there wasn't a consignment store in town we could take it to, so we started our own."

She looked up at me, and added, "What happened to you?"

"I ran into a bush," I said, as if that explained the scratches on my arms, and the legs she couldn't see below the counter. "I'll put something on it when I get home. That was smart of you. And your friends. Starting the store, I mean."

She nodded. "We're not getting rich, but it's something to do while the kids are in school. And it's nice to work with friends."

I bet it was. For the most part, everyone I worked with at LB&A had a somewhat contentious relationship with everyone else. It probably came from being competitors for the same clients and listings rather than working toward a common goal and trying to accomplish something together.

She rang up the clothes, and while I dug for my wallet, I told her, "I was actually looking for Mr. Peretti next door. The office is supposed to be open, but no one's there."

"He left about an hour ago," the shopkeeper said, as she ran the debit card and gave me the slip to sign. "Guess he didn't have any more appointments today."

Guess not. "Do you know Miss Harper? She owns a big

antebellum house up on Lickton Pike."

The shopkeeper nodded. "The Harpers have been around for generations. Miz Harper taught school until she retired. I had her myself, a long time ago. Is that where you got those scratches?"

"I walked around the house. It looks like it's been a while since anyone did any yard work up there."

She just shrugged, and I added, "I heard Miss Harper's thinking of selling. Do you know if that's true?"

She stuffed the clothes into a thin plastic bag. "To Magnolia Houston. You know, the country singer?"

I nodded.

"Some realtor from the city came up and talked Miz Harper into it." She pronounced 'realtor' 'reel-a-tor.' "It's kinda sad to see it go out of the family, I guess. The Harpers have been here for centuries. But maybe now the place'll get fixed up. It's looking pretty rough."

I picked up my bag. It crinkled as the contents settled. "There was a guy on a ladder chipping at the paint when I was there."

"Probably Magnolia's boyfriend," the shopkeeper nodded. "I've seen them together a couple of times. They tore past here a few minutes before you came in. I saw her hair flapping as they went by. His, too, if it comes to that."

"He has long hair?"

"Not as long as hers," my new friend said, "but he looks like a musician, you know?"

I nodded. I knew exactly. "Do you know if anyone around here was upset about her selling? Someone who didn't want Magnolia Houston moving in? Or just didn't want the house sold?"

"I can't imagine who. Miz Harper didn't have any family. The house would have gone to strangers anyway, when she died. Nobody else had a claim on it."

"The city didn't want it because it's historic or anything?"

"No money to fix it up or maintain it," the shopkeeper said.

"And it isn't especially historic. Just old. Nothing exciting happened there."

Right. "What about Magnolia? Are people upset about her buying it?"

She shrugged. "Some of us'll have to keep an eye on our husbands, I figure. But mostly, folks around here thought it was great. The place has been looking rough. Someone like Magnolia Houston has the money to fix it up right, I imagine. And when word gets out that she lives up here, we might see some more of the tourist types. That'll help all of us."

I must have looked blank, because she gestured to the bag I was holding. "You wouldn't have been here if not for Magnolia Houston. If there are more like you, I'll make more money."

True.

I shifted the bag into my other hand. "I don't suppose you know anything about Mr. Peretti?"

"I know a lot about Mr. Peretti," the shopkeeper said. "He's been in business next door for close to a century. Everyone in town knows Mr. Peretti."

"Surely he didn't start the business in 1928." He'd have to be more than a hundred years old if so.

"His father did. Oscar's been practicing since the 1950s. He never married, never had any kids."

"Like Miss Harper."

She nodded. "They grew up together. Friends their whole lives. I don't know what he'll do now that she's not right up the street anymore. Retire, maybe."

"Does he do a lot of business?"

"Not much anymore. I hardly ever see anyone go in next door. Just some of the old-timers who want a real, old-fashioned attorney and none of this new-fangled stuff." She grinned. "He still has a rotary phone."

"I saw it. Through the window."

"And no computer. Everything done by hand, just the way

it's always been done. If it was good enough for his father, it's good enough for him."

That probably took Mr. Peretti out of contention for having sent the email to DeWitts, then. No computer to send it from, and most likely not enough know-how to do it.

"I appreciate it," I said.

"No problem. You go home and put some ointment on those scratches. And come back and see us if you're in the neighborhood."

I promised I would, and took myself, my scratches, and my gently used onesies out of there.

Five

Like Mr. Peretti and Miss Harper, Rafe and I grew up together. Or rather, we grew up on opposite sides of the same small town. But we'd never been friends. Different schools, different circles. I was the princess from the mansion on the hill: Robert Lee and Margaret Anne Martin's perfect youngest daughter. Rafe was the son of a girl from the trailer park who got herself in the family way at fourteen by a colored boy. For a single year—his senior year and my freshman year—we went to the same high school. The summer after that, he went to prison. By the time I graduated and moved on to finishing school in Charleston and law school at Vanderbilt, he'd left Riverbend Penitentiary and gone undercover for the TBI.

We'd met again last August, outside his grandmother's house on Potsdam Street. Now we lived there together. Married, and with a baby on the way.

It's amazing how much things can change in a year.

When I pulled up in front of the brick Victorian, Rafe's big, black Harley-Davidson was parked at the bottom of the stairs. And I admit it, my heart skipped a beat. Not just because, after a couple of months of marriage, I'm still crazy about him and can't wait to see him at the end of each day, but because today was a special day.

That sounds sort of nice, but it really wasn't. I guess what I should have said, is that today wasn't just any day.

During the week or so I'd spent trying to help Darcy figure out who her biological parents were, we'd chosen to make a trip to the Tennessee Prison for Women on the north side of Nashville. Not because we had any reason to think Darcy's mother was there, but because a former doctor named Denise Seaver was a guest of the state. She's been incarcerated at the TPFW since last November, for two counts of murder and more than a few of kidnapping and selling babies. And thirty-five years ago, when Darcy's mother had been pregnant, Denise Seaver had been a newly-minted OB/GYN in Columbia, and we suspected she knew who Darcy's biological mother was.

She hadn't been willing to tell us anything, of course. I'd expected that, but we had to try.

Anyway, while we were at the prison, I'd seen someone else whose face I knew. Her name was Carmen Arroyo, and she'd been a guest of the state since December, when the TBI and the Metro Nashville PD, along with the Georgia Bureau of Investigation and the Atlanta police, had swept up the remains of the largest South American Theft Gang in the Southeast. The head of the SATG had been a man named Hector Gonzales, and Rafe had spent the past ten years infiltrating Hector's organization. He had also, on one or more occasions, infiltrated Carmen's bed.

Perhaps I should be upset about that. When I thought too hard about it, I was. But we hadn't been together at the time. Rafe had been laboring under the impression that while I'd been sleeping with him, I'd also been sleeping with Todd Satterfield. And since he'd always suspected I would end up with Todd anyway—mostly because he thought I lacked the guts to stand up for him with my family—it was hard to blame him. Especially when I considered that Carmen would have found it suspicious if he'd turned her down. And the last thing anyone would have wanted, was to make Carmen suspicious.

Anyway, he hadn't really cheated on me. But he had slept with her. And now she was pregnant. When I'd seen her at the TPFW last week, she'd looked ready to burst.

I'd told Rafe about it last night, the first chance we'd had to talk privately. He'd promised me he'd look into it today. So my skipped heartbeat wasn't just because I was happy to see him. It was also because I was afraid of what he'd have to tell me.

Climbing the steps to the porch and getting the key into the lock was hard. Part of me just didn't want to go inside. I had managed to avoid this issue all day. I hadn't called him to find out what he'd discovered, and whenever the thought of doing so had crossed my mind, I had squashed it. Tim's task had been helpful. It had given me something else to focus on. But now it was time to face the music.

I pushed the door open and closed and locked it behind me. And kicked off my shoes. My feet cheered, even as I staggered barefoot down the hall toward the kitchen.

I assumed Rafe would be there, but he wasn't. As I opened the fridge for something cold to drink, I heard a faint whooshing sound from the pipes behind the wall, and realized he was in the shower upstairs. He must have gotten home just before me.

Under other circumstances, I might have gone upstairs and joined him. The idea had appeal. But I was too nervous. And anyway, shower sex is more difficult these days. The baby gets in the way.

So I took a seat at the table, with my bottle of flavored water and a small bowl of nuts, and waited.

It didn't take long. It might be a holdover from those prison showers twelve years ago, but he never spends much time under the spray. Not unless we're doing something together aside from getting clean. Three minutes later, I heard his footsteps on the stairs, and then saw him come padding down the hallway toward me.

His feet were bare on the worn wood floors, and he was

wearing a pair of threadbare jeans hanging low on his hips and nothing else. My tongue got stuck to the roof of my mouth, and I had to peel it off. It took effort. When I could speak again, I told him, "That's low."

He grinned. "I didn't know you were home until I saw the car through the window. I didn't hear you come in."

I told him I'd only been there a few minutes.

"Feet hurt?" He went to the fridge and pulled out his own bottle of water. "I saw you kicked off your shoes as soon as you came in." He cracked the cork and leaned against the counter as he drank half the bottle.

I sipped my own while I watched his throat move. "I think I'm going to have to stop wearing heels soon. And I'm not sure I have ankles anymore."

He bent to peer under the table. "Still there.

"Good to know." I took another sip of water. "I had a run-in with a bramble bush, though."

"I can see that." He pulled out the chair on the other side of the table and sat. "Where'd you find a bramble bush?"

"Outside this house in Goodlettsville that Tim's trying to sell. Do you know who Magnolia Houston is?"

"Some kind of country singer, ain't she?" He reached for my nuts.

"Country Barbie. She wanted to buy a genuine antebellum home, so Tim found her one. And talked the seller into moving to an old folk's home. But now the money's gone missing."

He looked up from the nuts. "Scuse me?"

"The five hundred thousand dollars Magnolia Houston was going to pay for the house. It went astray between her closing attorney and Miss Harper's."

"Miz Harper being the seller?"

I nodded. "DeWitts was handling Magnolia's side of the transaction. Tim likes to use them. Or did. I don't think he will after this. And Miss Harper was using an old friend up in

Sumner County to close for her. Mr. Peretti. They signed all the paperwork on Friday. Tim didn't think anything was wrong. Until Mr. Peretti called him on Monday afternoon and told him the money never arrived. DeWitts say that someone at LB&A sent them an email changing the wiring instructions."

"And nobody did?"

"If somebody did, it wasn't Tim. The money's gone. DeWitts is on the hook for half a million dollars, because they didn't double-check the new wiring instructions with Tim. Their insurance company is probably refusing to pay. And they're trying to throw it back on LB&A."

"And Tim asked you to look into it." It wasn't a question.

I nodded.

"Any reason you didn't just say no?"

"I didn't think it would hurt," I said. "He's pretty freaked out. And it's not like anything happened to me. It's just scratches. I wouldn't even have had those if it wasn't for the guy on the ladder."

"I see." He leaned back and folded his hands across his stomach. Muscles moved smoothly under his skin, and I smiled. He smiled back. "Tell me about the ladder. And the guy on it."

"Oh." I explained about driving to Goodlettsville to look at the Harper house, and about the young man. "Angie at the consignment store said it was probably Magnolia's boyfriend. That she'd seen them together a couple of times. I have no idea why he'd avoid me. Unless he thought I was going to give him a hard time about being there. But he just vanished. By the time I got out of the car, he was gone."

"What were you thinking he'd tell you?"

"I'm not sure," I admitted. "But he was there. It seemed like a good idea to talk to him."

Neither of us said anything for a moment.

"So how was your day?" I added.

He winced. I took pity on him. "Did you finish up all the

reports after the gang war? And the meth lab that exploded?"

He nodded.

"Is Jamal OK? Still employed?"

Since he can't do undercover work anymore, after blowing his cover sky high before Christmas, Rafe's current job is training TBI rookies in the tricks of the trade. He's working with three of them, of which Jamal is one. The other two are Clayton and José. It was Jamal who got them both involved in a gang war a week and a half ago. And Jamal who disappeared in the middle of the operation, making everyone worry that the bad guys had gotten to him.

"He's employed," Rafe said grimly, "for now. But on warning. If he breaks protocol again, he's out."

"There were extenuating circumstances," I reminded him. "It isn't every day a man finds out he's knocked up a teenager."

And before you get the wrong impression from that statement, Jamal's only around twenty or so. Alexandra is seventeen. So really, the age difference between them isn't any bigger than the one between Rafe and me.

However, Rafe winced again. "I told Wendell that. He said it was hardly a point in Jamal's favor."

Wendell Craig was Rafe's handler during the undercover days. Now he's Rafe's boss. And the boss of the boys, as well. And I could see his point.

Maybe this conversation wasn't any easier than the one I was avoiding.

I took a breath. It went down hard, and the words took effort to push out. "Tell me about Carmen."

He didn't say anything, and I added, "You did go out there, right? To the prison?"

He had promised me he would. Although if Wendell had kept him busy at work all day, I guess I could understand it if he hadn't had the time, especially the day after a finished op, and one with complications. But I really wanted to know something as soon as possible.

He nodded. "Yeah."

"And was she there?"

"Where else would she be? Not like they're giving them time off to go shopping."

No, although Carmen would probably appreciate that. She was gorgeous, and knew how to dress. I had run into her at the Green Hills Mall once, and she'd been hauling more bags than I had.

"Did you talk to her? Or just to the doctor?"

"I started with the doc," Rafe said. "I figured, if she'd said something to somebody maybe I wasn't gonna have to talk to her directly."

Yes, I would prefer that, too.

"They got Denise Seaver working in the clinic over there. Did you know that?"

"No," I said, "how would I know that?"

"I thought maybe she mentioned it," Rafe said. "When you talked to her."

"Oh." No, she hadn't. "It wasn't a particularly friendly conversation." Although Denise Seaver had been acquainted with Carmen and knew when Carmen was due to give birth, so maybe I should have guessed that former Doctor Seaver was affiliated with the prison clinic. "It makes sense. I mean, she's an OB/GYN. It seems like a waste to have her peel potatoes in the kitchen. Might as well put her to use doing what she knows."

Rafe nodded. "Old witch."

That she was. "You two are related somehow, aren't you? Second cousins twice removed or something like that?"

"Something," Rafe said. "On my mama's side. She don't like me much."

I had gathered as much. "Did you talk to her?"

"Had to. When I asked about Carmen, the doc called her over. Seems she handles a lot of the female problems so he don't have to."

"You'd think they could have hired a female obstetrician in the first place, for a prison population of women."

Rafe shrugged. "He checked her chart. Carmen's. There was nothing written there about the father of the baby. That's when he called Doc Seaver over to see if Carmen had said anything to her."

"She recognized you, I'm sure."

His mouth twisted. "Oh, yeah. And knew why I was asking. The other doc thought I was there on official business. I made as if I'd known she was pregnant all along, and we'd been waiting all this time to find out about the daddy. But Seaver knew immediately. I could see it in her eyes."

No doubt. I knew that expression. Sly and knowing and a little amused. "Did she say anything to you?"

"Just that Carmen hadn't told her anything about who the baby's father might be."

Good. I wanted to know what Carmen knew, or thought she knew, but I didn't want her confiding in Denise Seaver. The less Doctor Seaver knew about anything, the better.

However— "That's too bad."

Rafe shrugged. "We'll figure it out. The doc asked Seaver about DNA tests. It's more her field than his, I guess."

I guess.

"Seems you can test the mother's blood for shreds of the baby's DNA, and then match that to the father's blood. You can also draw directly from the baby, and that'd be more accurate, but she's so close to the end of the pregnancy that Seaver said something like that could bring on premature labor."

And while it was late enough in the pregnancy that the baby would probably be OK if it was born now, nobody wanted to take that chance. I could certainly understand that. Besides, Carmen would probably have to agree to the procedure, and maybe it was best, at least for now, if she didn't know what was going on.

"So they're going to check her blood for the baby's DNA and then match it to yours?"

He nodded. "Seaver said she's due in for a checkup tomorrow anyway. That way, it'll just look like routine."

Excellent. "Who's doing the paternity test?" Not Denise Seaver, I hoped. If so, there was no way we'd be able to trust the results, either way they came out.

"The TBI forensic lab," Rafe said. "I'll go give'em my blood in the morning. They should have Carmen's by afternoon. Maybe the next day we'll know something. Or by the end of the week at the latest."

"It takes a lot longer on TV."

"Backlog," Rafe told me. "It ain't that the test takes all that long. It's that the lab has a lot of'em to do, and they take'em in order. If this was somebody else, it'd be a couple weeks, at least."

"I guess they do it faster for one of their own."

"That," Rafe said, "and it was a big case. She was part of it. And everybody wants to know if the baby's got anything to do with anything. Like, if it's Hector's baby, that'd be interesting."

"Do you think it might be Hector's baby?"

He shrugged. "Could be anybody's baby. Could be mine, but I doubt I was the only man she slept with that week."

"But if it is yours..."

"We'll figure something out," Rafe said and pushed the chair back. "Wanna sit there and watch while I cook dinner?"

Under normal circumstances, that sounded like a very nice pastime. Is there anything sexier than watching a half naked man cooking the dinner he plans to feed you?

However— "I'd rather have your help searching Heidi Hoppenfeldt's office," I said, and watched him arch a brow before he sat back down.

"You serious?"

"I couldn't search it earlier. Too many people around. So I

decided to come back when the place is empty."

"Why Heidi's office?"

I told him I had started my process of elimination by figuring out who needed the money and who didn't. "I know there could be other reasons why someone might want five hundred thousand dollars other than need…"

Rafe nodded.

"…but it's somewhere to start. Brittany makes less than anyone else in the office." Except me. "She went shopping for a trousseau today. She must have spent a nice chunk of change. Some of the bags she brought back were from expensive stores." Stores I had frequented when I was married to Bradley, and had his lawyer's salary to play with, but stores I didn't frequent any longer. "She and Devon are flying to Curacao to honeymoon this weekend, she said."

Rafe didn't say anything, just lifted the other brow.

"Interesting, right? And Heidi… she was Brenda's protégée before Brenda was killed. Brenda was teaching her to be a kick-butt realtor. And then Brenda died, and now Tim's mostly using her to do administrative tasks. He sent her to the office supply store today, for envelopes. And she didn't act like she minded, but I don't imagine she's very happy about it, either."

"So she's making less than she was expecting, and he ain't appreciating her."

I nodded. "If I were Heidi, I might not mind implicating Tim in the disappearance of half a million dollars."

"She strike you as somebody who'd steal?"

"She went to work for Brenda," I reminded him. "Brenda was a crook."

"She's worth looking into, then."

I thought so. "So you'll come with me?"

"I figure I'd better. There's no telling what kind of trouble you can get into on your own."

He pushed the chair back again, and got to his feet. "I'm

gonna go put on a T-shirt and some socks. And find something to put on those scratches of yours."

"I thought you were going to cook for me," I said.

"Tomorrow. If we're going snooping tonight, I want a burger."

I'd already had a burger today, but I was up for another. I'm pregnant. I get to eat what I want.

"I'm right behind you," I told him.

Six

By the time we got to the office, it was after eight, and the parking lot was deserted.

First, we'd spent thirty minutes upstairs. 'Resting,' as Rafe called it. We spent the time in bed, but it wasn't particularly restful. The hour following it had been, since I'd fallen asleep with his hand stroking my stomach and his voice cooing at the baby.

After I woke up, we went to this little hole-in-the-wall restaurant that Rafe likes and had greasy burgers and fries. I followed it up with Tums, since I figured I'd be paying with heartburn later. And by then, it was dark and Rafe decreed it was safe to go to the office. "It's prob'ly empty. Right?"

"Probably." Occasionally, someone will have late business to take care of, a quick run inside to pick up paperwork or scan something somewhere, but under most circumstances, the office is empty by six-thirty or seven.

We parked by the curb. "Might as well," Rafe said. "I know you work here and nobody'd wonder why your car'd be in the lot at night, but better safe than sorry." I opened the back door with my key and gestured him in.

We stood for a second and let our eyes adjust to the dark. Everything was quiet. I raised my voice. "Hello? Anyone here?"

Nobody answered.

We locked the door behind us. "Heidi's office is over there." I gestured through the dark.

"What're we looking for?"

"I'm not sure," I admitted as we walked in that direction, "but I figure I'll know it when I see it." Heidi's door was closed but unlocked. I pushed it open, into Stygian blackness. Heidi doesn't have a window in her office. "You think it's safe to turn on the light?"

"We're gonna have to," Rafe said. "Unless you brought a flashlight."

I hadn't, so I flicked the light switch. The brightness burned my retinas, and I squeezed my eyes shut as I went back to the conversation as it had been before the distraction. "We're looking for anything to do with Magnolia Houston or Miss Harper. Or Mr. Peretti, the lawyer. Or proof that the email to DeWitts came from Heidi's computer. Failing that, five hundred thousand in cash sitting in a file drawer would be nice."

"Somehow I don't think we're gonna get that lucky."

I didn't, either. Heidi wasn't stupid. She wouldn't leave half a million dollars in cash sitting around. And anyway, there had been no cash involved in this transaction. Just wire transfers. The money was sitting snugly in an account somewhere. Not in the bottom drawer of someone's desk.

"I'm not sure what we're looking for," I admitted. "We're just looking. And I don't expect to find anything. But we have to look."

"Then we'll look." He glanced around. "You want the desk or the filing cabinets?"

I chose the cabinets. "Do you know anything about computers?"

"Not much. But I can call José. He likes technology."

"Go ahead, if you think he can help. Just make sure you don't do anything you can't fix again. We don't want Heidi to realize we've been here."

I pulled out the first drawer in the filing cabinet while Rafe dialed.

He must have gotten voicemail, because all the said was, "It's Rafe. Gimme a call when you have a minute. I need some help with a computer."

With that done, he put the phone back in his pocket and started to go through the desk.

We worked in silence. This wasn't the time for small talk—we had to get done and get out as quickly as possible. Wasting time with sexy banter would only slow us down, and besides, there wasn't much to say. I certainly didn't come across anything pertaining to Magnolia Houston or Miss Harper or the house in Goodlettsville that I needed to share with him.

Which was a little surprising, come to think of it. If Heidi was Tim's assistant—and she was—shouldn't she have copies of his files?

Then again, maybe he had relieved her of the copy yesterday afternoon, when he found out about the wayward money.

I had a filing cabinet and a half to go when Rafe straightened.

I did, too, and put a hand to my back. Bending is harder than it used to be. "Done already?"

He put a finger to his lips, and then I heard it, too. A car engine at the rear of the building. Someone was pulling into the parking lot.

It might be someone who couldn't find parking on the street and who didn't want to pay for parking in one of the commercial lots, so he figured he'd park in the real estate company's lot for free while the office was closed. I'm sure it wouldn't be the first time.

Or it could be someone coming into the building. Another realtor, the cleaning crew. Or someone else.

Rafe had already moved, soundlessly, across the floor to the door and flicked off the light. "C'mere."

There was barely any sound behind the words. More air than

anything else.

I left the file drawer open and made my way toward him, doing my best to avoid running into anything, in the suddenly pitch black room.

He snagged me around the middle and pulled me up against the wall behind the door.

If it was Heidi, obviously she'd see us once she came into her office and turned on the light. But if it were anyone else, we stood a chance of escaping detection. Unless the newcomer was up to no good, he or she had no reason to search the place.

It was probably just one of the agents stopping by to pick up some paperwork. But better safe than sorry.

Outside, the engine had stopped running. I focused, but couldn't hear the sound of footsteps. Maybe whoever was out there was just on his way to the FinBar for a drink or late dinner, and was headed away from us.

Or maybe not. A jingling and a scratching noise was the sound of a key being inserted in the lock.

Rafe put his finger against my lips. He must be able to see me better than I was able to see him. I've always suspected he's able to see in the dark.

I nodded. I knew I had to be quiet.

The door opened, and then closed again.

There was a moment of silence. Whoever had come in, was just standing there, not moving.

That was a little suspicious. As if he or she was making sure the place was empty.

Or maybe that wasn't why, and it wasn't suspicious. Maybe the person in the hallway was able to sense that someone else was here and was wondering what the hell—heck—we were doing, standing here in the dark.

I opened my mouth, and Rafe's finger pressed harder. I closed it again.

Out in the hallway, someone moved.

By now, my eyes had gotten used to the lack of light, and I could see the outlines of things. The desk, the back of the chair, the computer monitor. There was a bit more light in the hallway, from the security light in the parking lot shining in.

Whoever was out there must have decided he was alone after all. Or at least he—or she—didn't bother to check the rooms lining the hallway for signs of life. I heard footsteps come closer and then pass the door, as a shadow brushed across the gap between the door and the jamb.

It was only a second. Too fast and too dark for me to get an impression of anything but a human figure. Average sized. Could be male or female. A tallish woman or a medium sized man. There was no distinctive click of high heels.

I'm five-eight in my bare feet. On the taller side for a woman. Rafe's six-three. Tall for anyone. And muscular. Whoever had just brushed past, was much smaller than Rafe, both in height and breadth.

Could be Tim. He's the slender and elegant type, around six feet tall.

Or it could be one of the other male agents.

We stood and listened while he—or perhaps she, but I was leaning toward male—continued up the hallway toward the front of the building. I expected him to turn into one of the offices along the way, but he didn't. After a few seconds—that felt a lot longer—we heard him go into the lobby.

"My office!" I hissed.

"Shhhh!" Rafe hissed back.

"What if he's going to my office?"

His breath tickled the hair in front of my ear. "Is there something in your office anybody would want?"

I couldn't think of anything. Unless it was Tim, and he wanted to know what, if anything, I might have discovered about the missing money.

Or unless he was hoping for nude photographs of Rafe. If so, he'd be disappointed.

But if he'd wanted an update on the investigation, Tim would have called me. He wasn't the type to sneak around the office in the dark. Not when he had every right to be here. Brittany wouldn't think anything of it—or at least wouldn't say anything about it—if Tim walked into my office tomorrow morning and started going through my desk. He was paying her salary. There was absolutely no reason why he'd need to sneak around now.

I felt Rafe move away from me. I reached for his arm. He twitched away, and just as he did, a shrill ringing cut through the air.

"Shit!"

He didn't stop to turn off his cell phone—José, calling back to offer help with the computer?—just ran, as a panicked scramble sounded from the front of the office. Whoever was out there must have realized he wasn't alone.

I took off after Rafe, as a thin scream cut through the air.

"Don't hurt me! Don't hurt me!"

I arrived in the front lobby to find Rafe looming over a smaller, more slender man who had his back against the wall and his hands up in front of him. Rafe had a hand fisted in the front of his T-shirt, and he was practically gibbering with terror.

"It's OK," I told Rafe after I had flicked on the light. "You can let him go."

He shot me a glance over his shoulder. "You know this guy?"

"His name is Devon. He's Brittany's boyfriend." Or fiancé. Or husband-to-be.

He looked the same way he always did. A skinny young man in his early twenties, with too-long, dark hair obscuring half his face, a nose ring, a couple of tattoos on scrawny arms, dressed in a pair of skinny, black jeans and a black T-shirt.

Good for burglarizing, but I'd seen him wear all-black before, too, so it wasn't necessarily a sinister sign of anything.

When Rafe let him go, he did his best to smooth out the wrinkles in the T-shirt, but without much success. The sneer wasn't very successful, either, since he was clearly terrified. Rafe had moved back a step, but he was still four inches taller and forty pounds heavier than Devon.

"What are you doing here?" I asked.

He gave me a hostile look through the strands of hair. "Looking for something."

"What?"

"Something Brittany forgot earlier."

"What was that?"

"None of your business." He flipped the hair out of his face. "I don't answer to you."

True. "Did you find it?"

"Yes," Devon said, and touched his pocket, "before your gorilla here attacked me."

Rafe growled. It was more panther than gorilla, and Devon turned a shade paler. When Rafe told him, "Then get outta here," he ran for the door. And knocked me back against the wall on his way past. I guess maybe he underestimated the size of the stomach.

Rafe took a step after him, and I put my hand out. "Never mind."

"You OK?" He put a hand on my stomach, warm through the fabric of my dress.

I nodded. "Fine. No harm done. Let him go. He has the right to be here." Sort of.

Rafe leaned up against the wall next to me. "Brittany's boyfriend?"

"The receptionist. They've been together at least a year. I've seen him a couple of times. Enough to know who he is."

"Wonder why she didn't come here herself to pick up whatever it was she forgot."

"Maybe she's outside in the car," I said.

Rafe shrugged.

"What was he doing when you came in here?"

"Booking for the front door as fast as he could." He nodded to it, next to the wall he'd had Devon up against. "He coulda been doing anything at all before that."

"No idea whether he was rooting around in Brittany's desk or mine?"

He arched a brow. "Any reason he'd root around in yours?"

"None I can think of."

"Take a look," Rafe said. "I'll check over here." He indicated Brittany's reception desk, sitting in lone majesty in front of the window. From where I was standing, I couldn't tell whether anything had been disturbed. Which meant that from this angle, at least, nothing seemed to have been.

I let him deal with it, and headed for the door to my own little office.

Nothing seemed too disturbed there either. I've had my office ransacked before, and nothing like that had taken place this time. The desktop was in a little bit of disarray, but I could have left it that way when Brittany went to lunch this morning. I couldn't remember whether I had or not. And the top desk drawer was open a crack, a Bic pen caught in the opening... but I could have done that myself, too. There was no proverbial smoking gun here. Nothing to say with certainty that Devon had been here. He might have been telling the truth about picking up something for Brittany.

I tried to imagine what that might have been, at close to nine o'clock at night. If they'd just waited twelve hours, she could have picked it up herself when she came to work in the morning. What was so important that they couldn't wait twelve hours for it, but had to come over here at night?

"I can't tell for sure," I told Rafe once I'd stepped through the door and was back in the lobby. "Nothing's missing, that I noticed. And there's no mess. He could have been in here, but if he was, I don't know what he was doing."

"Prob'ly nothing much," Rafe said, pushing the desk drawer shut before straightening. "He hadn't been here very long."

No, he hadn't. Enough time to find whatever small item Brittany had left behind—or so he said—but Rafe was right, it hadn't been more than a minute from when Devon walked past Heidi's office to when Rafe came into the lobby. Not a lot of time to find anything, to be honest.

"Do you think he was lying?"

He shrugged. "Dunno. Don't know him well enough to say. Mighta been."

"Can you think of anything Brittany might have left, that was important enough that they couldn't wait twelve hours for it?"

"Condoms?" Rafe suggested.

Maybe. If they were that desperate to have sex, there must be drugstores closer than this, though. I had looked up Brittany's home address earlier today, and it was in the Melrose area. Lots of stores around there. Including a Walgreens and a 24-hour grocery store, if memory served.

"Was it José who called?"

"I imagine so." Rafe pulled his phone out of his pocket and checked the display. "Yeah. You want I should call him back?"

I hesitated.

"Devon gonna tell his girlfriend we were here?"

"Oh, most definitely." He might even tell her—probably would—that we were skulking in the dark in someone's office. Not necessarily Heidi's—he might not know that's where we'd been when he moved past us down the hallway—but he knew we'd been somewhere between the back door and the lobby.

"You think she'd believe we snuck in here for a quickie?"

She might. And if it came down to it, I might trot out that explanation. It would be embarrassing, but it was better than the truth. "If Heidi had something to do with the missing money, I don't want her to think we're on to her. Or even that I'm looking into it. Someone who'd steal half a million dollars might not be above killing someone to keep it."

Rafe nodded. "Murder's been done for less. Maybe you shouldn't go to work tomorrow morning."

"I have to go to work. If I don't, I won't know what they're saying."

He shrugged. It looked like capitulation, but I figured we'd probably have this conversation again tomorrow morning. He was just abandoning it now because he had something else he wanted to talk about. "You still wanna try to get into Heidi's computer?"

I hesitated. If Devon told Brittany we'd been in the office at night, and Brittany told Heidi, and Heidi had something to hide—or for that matter if Brittany herself had something to hide—I could be in trouble.

Then again, the damage was already done. We'd been caught. Might as well do what we'd come here for. And finish the job.

"We're here. Let's just get it done. It's too late to worry about getting caught anyway."

Rafe was already dialing. "Gotta minute?" he asked when, presumably, José had answered. "I need some help tracking an email."

The phone squawked, and Rafe shook his head. "This is something else. Nothing to do with work."

José must have wanted to know what it was about, then, because Rafe glanced at me and said, "Something my wife's looking into."

"Just tell him," I said. "But without using any names, please. Just the situation."

Rafe laid out the situation in a nicely condensed manner. "Someone was buying a house. Money was wired from the buyer's account to the closing company and from there to the seller's representative. But he never got it. Turns out someone sent the closing company an email telling them to wire the money somewhere else. I'm looking for that email."

José spoke. At length. After about a minute, Rafe must have realized that it would be better to let me listen to what José had to say, than for him to try to paraphrase it later. "...compromised," was the first word I heard, "the email should be in sent mail or deleted mail. If it's been deleted from deleted mail, especially if it's webmail, it's hard to get it back. Easier if it's a desktop program."

"Can you unpack that a little more?"

"Gmail is webmail," José said. "Outlook Express is a desktop program. If you have OE, and you leave your computer, you can't access your email. But you can access Gmail from anywhere."

I nodded. I might not know much, but I did know that. "This email came from the LB&A email network. Or so I was told. I haven't seen it. But my broker said it came from his email address."

"That sounds more like someone spoofed it," José said. "It's easy to do with a server and a little knowledge. And you don't have to be onsite to do it."

That sounded promising. Or maybe not, since it sounded like anyone in the whole, wide world could have sent the email.

"It wouldn't show up in sent mail or deleted mail?"

José said it wouldn't. "It wouldn't have gone through the company servers. It would have been sent from somewhere else, but when it got to where it was going, it would have looked like it came from you."

"But if it wasn't actually sent from here, we can't find who sent it?"

"Not from your end," José said. "If I had the email, I could maybe backtrack and find where it originated."

That would mean getting DeWitts onboard. If they even had the original email still. They may not. Although it was worth trying to find out. If José could track it back to where it had come from, we'd have a pretty good idea who sent it.

"How close could you get to him?" Or her.

"The sender?" He sounded amused that I asked. "His living room. Or bedroom closet. Or basement. Wherever he keeps his server."

"You'd be able to find his address?"

"Should be," José said. "It might take a couple minutes."

I nodded to Rafe. "We'll get back to you," he told José. "Thanks for your help."

José said it was no problem, and hung up. Rafe dropped the phone in his pocket. "Still wanna check Heidi's computer?"

I shook my head. "If it's that easy to spoof an email address from somewhere else—and that's what he said, right? That it was easy?"

Rafe nodded.

"Then I don't think we have to. Whoever did it, probably didn't do it from here. And anyway, Heidi isn't stupid. Brittany might be, but I already checked her email program this morning. If Heidi sent the email, she would have deleted any evidence of it."

"So we're done here?" He looked around.

"I guess so." I did the same.

"Wanna have that quickie, just in case someone asks?" He quirked a brow.

"I appreciate you trying to help, but that would be weird."

"I don't see why," Rafe said, but he followed me to the door and out into the night.

Seven

Dix called just as we pulled up in front of the house on Potsdam. I'd forgotten all about him in the excitement. "Sorry," I told Rafe. "It's my brother."

He glanced at me. "Go ahead and talk to him."

"I called him earlier for an update about Mother." I pushed the appropriate button on the phone. "Dix?"

"Sis."

"Rafe's here, too."

Dix sighed. "Collier."

Rafe's lips twitched. "Martin."

I sighed, too. "The two of you are family. Why do you keep calling each other by your last names?"

"Habit," Dix said.

I glanced at Rafe. He shrugged.

"Fine. What do you want?"

"You called me," Dix reminded me. "For an update about Mother."

"Let me guess. She's drunk again."

"Not today," Dix said. "I think she probably learned that lesson yesterday. She felt pretty sick at the end of it. Although I think she's spiking her tea with whiskey."

Rafe made a noise. I think it was amusement.

"Of course she is." Although that was better than chugging

brandy straight from the bottle, so it seemed like a step in the right direction. "I assume she hasn't spoken to Audrey?"

"I didn't ask," Dix said. "I was afraid it would set her off. But I assume not."

"And she hasn't spoken to Darcy."

"No."

"What about Bob? Do you know if he's had any contact with her? Or is she shutting him out, too?"

Bob Satterfield is the Maury County sheriff, and my mother's gentleman friend. They were friends when their respective spouses were alive, too, and Bob's son Todd has been Dix's best friend since before kindergarten. Just one big, happy family, in other words. Until it came out on Monday morning that Bob knew that Audrey had been in love with my father before he met my mother, and had had a child by him. Now Mother felt betrayed by both of them, and who could blame her?

"I haven't spoken to him," Dix said. "I haven't seen him, either. He wasn't at Mother's either time I was there. And he hasn't stopped by the office."

Chances were she was still angry with him, then. He had known about it—Audrey's feelings for Dad, anyway; if not the pregnancy—and Mother probably felt betrayed by him, too.

"Should one of us call him?"

"I'm sure he's trying," Dix said. "More than likely, it's Mother who won't have anything to do with him."

Probably so. And it wouldn't do any good to tell him to contact her if she was the one who refused to see him. Dix was right: the sheriff was probably doing his best to talk her off the ledge.

"Is there anything I can do?"

Dix said there wasn't. "I'll check on her again tomorrow. If you want to come down this weekend, you can."

"I don't suppose she's mentioned me?"

Walking out had seemed like a fine idea on Monday

morning. But now that things had settled down, I was a little worried that I might not be welcome back.

"No," Dix said.

"I guess that means she's still angry?"

"You did take Darcy's side."

"So did you!"

He didn't answer, and I added, "She isn't trying to get you to fire her or anything, is she?"

"She's not talking about it," Dix said. "She hasn't mentioned Darcy. Or Audrey. Or Bob. Or even Dad."

That didn't sound good. "Maybe I will drive down this weekend. We can stay with you if we need to, right?"

"Sure. Or with Catherine and Jonathan. Or Darcy."

My other sister. Right.

"I'll let you know," I said. "Call me tomorrow, OK? And let me know what's going on."

Dix said he would, and we hung up. And sat for a moment, still in the car, while the cicadas kept up their racket in the trees on the other side of the driveway.

"That doesn't sound good," Rafe said eventually. He hadn't been in Sweetwater with me when all this went down, so he had it all second-hand.

I shook my head. "Really not. I'll probably have to drive down there this weekend. If for no other reason than to show solidarity with Darcy. And to show my mother that I'm not afraid of her."

"Better you than me."

I glanced at him. "You could come, too. She likes you."

My mother, who had been against my relationship with Rafe from the beginning, had had a change of heart just before the wedding. Now she seemed to like him better than me.

"Unlike you," Rafe told me, "I *am* afraid of your mother."

"Really?"

He shrugged. "Maybe we can take David with us. She seems

to like him."

"What's not to like?" Even if, honestly, it had been a little surprising how quickly my mother had taken to Rafe's biological son, who lived with his adopted parents on the other side of Nashville. He looked pretty much just like Rafe did at that age—thirteen—and I had thought for sure that Mother would be rude to the boy, but instead she had taken one look at him and melted. It was seriously weird, and not like her at all. Not that David isn't adorable; I just wouldn't have thought Mother was susceptible.

But Rafe was right. She did seem to like David. Maybe seeing him would make her happy.

"Can you call Sam and ask?"

"Sure," Rafe said and opened his door. "Ready to go in?"

I guess I was. It had been a long day.

"So tomorrow you'll get Carmen's blood sample to the TBI lab, so we can start the process of figuring things out?"

"Bright and early," Rafe confirmed as he put his hand under my elbow to give me a boost up the stairs. "The doc at the clinic said she's got her checkup first thing in the morning."

"Are you going out there to pick up the sample?" I watched as he inserted the key in the lock and twisted the knob.

He shook his head. "Don't want nobody to say nothing about the chain of evidence."

He pushed the door open and gestured me inside.

"That makes sense." I kicked my shoes off on the floor of the foyer again. "So someone from the prison will drive it there?"

He nodded, as he closed and locked the door behind us. "They do that a lot anyway. Both to us and to the medical examiner's office."

The Nashville medical examiner's office is on Gass Boulevard, just down the road from TBI headquarters. I'd forgotten that.

"And you'll go to the lab in the morning and have your

blood drawn?"

"That's the plan. I have to do that regularly anyhow. All of us do. Specially those of us doing undercover work. They wanna make sure we don't get too fond of the merchandise."

"Drugs? You didn't have anything to do with drugs. Did you?"

"Hector had his fingers in a lot of things," Rafe said with shrug. "But I've never had a bad drug test, if that's what you're asking. I don't use. Never did."

I didn't think he had. He'd told me once that he'd smoked cigarettes for a short time in high school, and gave it up because he didn't want anything to have that much power over him. These days, he'll have a beer or two, but that's about the extent of it. I wasn't surprised that he didn't touch illegal drugs.

"They probably have your DNA on file already, then. Don't they?"

"I'm sure they do," Rafe said. "And have for a while. Just in case they had to identify what was left of me."

During the old undercover days. Yes, I could see why that might have been necessary. And I was terribly glad it hadn't turned out to be. "But you'll give them a new sample anyway?"

"I'm gonna be there anyway. Might as well make sure it's fresh."

Might as well.

"I'm kind of tired," I said. "I know it's early, but it's been a long day. I think I'll go up to bed. And maybe read a book or watch some TV until I fall asleep."

Rafe nodded. "I'll be there in a minute. Just wanna make sure all the doors and windows are locked."

"I appreciate it."

He grinned. "Why don't you slip into something comfortable?"

"Like bed?"

"Like that," Rafe agreed, and headed down the hallway

toward the kitchen to make sure we were safe for the night.

The next morning dawned the way most mornings did. Rafe got up and out early, and left me to sleep, since it takes a lot of effort to make a baby. It's a rare day that I'm able to drag myself out of bed much before nine.

So also today. I dragged myself out of bed around nine, and made it to the office by ten o'clock or so.

The first thing that happened, was that I noticed Brittany wasn't at her desk. Then Tim showed up, just as I was hanging my purse on the hook by the door. "Thank God you're here."

I blinked. "Is it Groundhog Day?"

He blinked back. "What?"

"Isn't that what you said yesterday?"

"Maybe." He shook his head. "I need you to cover the front desk for a while."

"Again? I sat at the front desk for most of the day yesterday."

Tim lowered his voice, and glanced over his shoulder to make sure we were still alone. We were. "Did you learn anything?"

I hated to admit I hadn't. So I didn't. "A few things. Nothing conclusive. I couldn't find any evidence that the email originated here, but that doesn't mean anything one way or another, it seems. It didn't have to, to come from someone here. Or it could have come from somewhere else. Someone I talked to said that for someone with an email server, it isn't hard to spoof an email address and make it look like it came from practically anywhere. That's probably what happened. He said, if he can get access to the original email, he might be able to trace it back to the source."

Tim looked nauseous, maybe at the thought of talking to Lane DeWitt.

"I went to Goodlettsville," I continued, "and tried to talk to Mr. Peretti, but he wasn't at work. The woman in the store next to his office told me he doesn't have a computer, though. So this wire fraud business is probably beyond him. And I stopped by Miss Harper's house. The only person there was a guy scraping paint, but he didn't want to talk to me. Maybe because he wasn't supposed to be there. You said Mr. Peretti told you the renovators had to cease and desist, right?"

Tim nodded.

"Brittany is spending money hand over fist. She took a four hour lunch yesterday, and came back with hundreds of dollars worth of packages. Maybe more. She says she and Devon are getting married this weekend, and going to Curacao for their honeymoon."

Tim winced. "Right. About that..."

I continued quickly, before he could ask me to take over Brittany's job all of next week. "And speaking of Devon, when Rafe and I were here last night—"

"Rafael was here last night?"

"Just about where you're standing now," I said, and watched Tim's nostrils quiver.

"About Devon..."

"Right. When Rafe and I were here last night—"

"No," Tim said. "He's the reason Brittany isn't here this morning. He was shot and killed last night."

"What?"

The question was sort of automatic. I'd heard what he said. I didn't think I'd misunderstood him. 'Shot and killed' isn't the kind of thing you mishear. They're short, simple words, not really open to interpretation. But it didn't seem possible. We'd seen Devon last night. Right here in the office. How could he be dead?

"Your Detective Grimaldi went to Brittany's apartment at seven this morning. Brittany recognized her from when she was here last year, after Brenda was killed."

"She isn't *my* Detective Grimaldi," I said. "What happened?"

"Brittany didn't say. Just that he was shot and killed. In the parking garage under their condo."

"Mugging gone wrong?"

Tim said he had no idea. "But she won't be in today. Can you sit the front desk? At least until Heidi gets here?"

"How about I take the first half of the day," I suggested, feeling a bit guilty now that I knew the reason why Brittany wasn't here this morning, "and Heidi can take the second. That way I'll have some time this afternoon to work on your problem. If I'm stuck at the desk all day, I can't."

Tim allowed as how that sounded fair. "Do you want me to contact DeWitts?"

He sounded like he'd rather have a root canal, and it was tempting to tell him yes, but I refrained. "Not yet. I have to coordinate with José first. See what he wants to do and when he might have time to do it. I'll let you know."

Tim nodded and took himself off. I did the same, over to the front desk.

The first thing I did, of course, was call Tamara Grimaldi. "Detective."

"Ms...." She's been calling me Ms. Martin for a year, and can't quite wrap her brain around me being Mrs. Collier. So she has, reluctantly, come around to calling me by my first name. "Savannah. Make it quick. I'm in the middle of something."

"I know," I said. "I just got to the office. Tim told me that Brittany won't be in today. Our receptionist. Her boyfriend was killed last night. Devon... um..."

"Knight," Grimaldi told me. "And it was very early this morning. TOD is estimated at around two-thirty."

"Any idea who did it?"

"Not so far," Grimaldi said.

"Tim said he was shot in his parking garage. Mugging?"

"That's what it looks like. Phone and wallet are both gone."

"What about the car?"

"The car's still here," Grimaldi said.

"What kind of car?"

"Jeep Wrangler. A few years old."

Maybe the age explained why the car had been left behind. Then again, it was strange. The car had to be more valuable than both Devon's phone and his wallet. And if he was coming home, he must have had his car key with him. No need to hotwire it, or anything like that. Just grab the key, turn the car on, and go.

Why take the phone and wallet and leave the car?

"How long before he was found?"

"A couple of hours," Grimaldi said. "Nobody heard the shot. Your friend was asleep."

Brittany wasn't really what I'd call a friend, but I let it go.

"911 got the call just after five this morning. An early riser had gone into the garage to take his car out for the day, and found the victim."

I winced. I didn't envy him, whoever he was. I've seen my share—some people would say more than my share—of dead bodies, and there's nothing fun or exciting about it. "Do you have any suspects?"

"If I did, I couldn't tell you. But so far I don't. It looks like a crime of opportunity. Someone saw him drive into the garage and decided to make a quick buck."

Or not. "We should talk," I told Grimaldi.

"We are talking."

"Not on the phone." And not in the office, where God knew who was listening. Tim had told me he didn't want the police involved in the wire fraud issue, but what if Devon had been involved, and that's why he was dead? "Can you take thirty minutes for lunch?"

She hesitated. "Is this general nosiness, or something more?"

"Just meet me," I said, "and I'll tell you. Surely you have to eat?"

"If you see what I see every day, you may not wanna eat, either."

Maybe not, but I didn't have a choice. "If I don't eat, the baby starts gnawing on my stomach lining. It hurts. Noon?"

"Twelve-thirty," Grimaldi said. "And you'll have to come and meet me somewhere down here. I'll still be working."

Assuming 'down here' meant Melrose, I suggested a diner on Granny White Pike in the 12 South neighborhood, four or five blocks from the crime scene. Grimaldi said she's see me there at twelve-thirty, and hung up.

I took a quick look around Brittany's desk, just to see if anything had changed since the last time I looked. I was still trying to figure out what Devon had been doing here last night, and what it was Brittany had asked him to pick up.

But everything looked the same as it had when I left for lunch yesterday. The small changes were likely made by Brittany herself after I'd gone.

I'd have to find out from Detective Grimaldi what Devon had had in his pockets when he was found. Maybe he'd still had whatever it was. And if he hadn't, maybe someone else had been after it, too.

If there'd been something here worth killing for, I sure hadn't noticed it.

We'd seen him at eight-thirty, or maybe closer to nine. It would take me maybe twenty minutes to drive to Melrose later. That was for lunch, when there were more cars on the road. At nine o'clock last night, he might have gotten there in fifteen. If time of death had been estimated around two-thirty in the morning, he hadn't gone straight home from here.

So where had he gone? And to do what?

Eight

At noon, I packed up and let Heidi know I was going to lunch and that she had to come take over the front desk.

She had walked in around twenty minutes after me, and had seemed suitably shocked to hear about Devon. And no reason why she wouldn't be. He hadn't been in her office last night, so whatever was going on, if Devon was involved in it, Heidi didn't seem to be.

She also didn't seem to notice that her office had been searched last night. Or if she did, she didn't say anything about it.

Of course, it had been searched by a pro. I wasn't worried about my part: there's nothing much involved in pulling out and pushing in filing drawers. The only thing that would reveal my presence, was someone looking for fingerprints, and there was no reason why anyone would bother. No, where she'd notice the search, would most likely be the desk. But it was Rafe who had searched Heidi's desk, and he knows what he's doing. There was no reason at all that she'd notice he'd been there. She treated me the way she always did, with a mixture of hostility and malice. Nothing new there.

"You're on the desk for the rest of the afternoon," I told her as I headed for the door, bag over my shoulder. "I have some things I have to do."

She glanced down the hallway. "Tim..."

"Knows about it. And said it would be all right. I'll see you tomorrow."

"I haven't had lunch yet!" Heidi shouted after me.

I didn't slow my steps. "I think I left a Lean Cuisine in the freezer last week. You can have that if you want. It's chicken pot pie."

"Grrr!" Heidi said. And if she said anything else, I didn't hear it. I was already gone.

Twenty minutes later, I was sitting across from Detective Tamara Grimaldi in a booth in an old-fashioned 1950s style shiny diner on 12th Avenue South, just up the street from Sevier Park. The tables were speckled Formica with chrome edges, and the seats were red Naugahyde, as were the chairs grouped around the tables. The walls sported black-and-white photographs of Marilyn Monroe, James Dean, Marlon Brando, and of course Elvis, all in their heyday.

The detective looked the way she always did: businesslike in a dark suit—pants, not skirt—and low heels. She has short, black, curly hair and an olive complexion, and she's a few years older than me, at a guess. I've never actually asked.

She doesn't always look like someone has died. I've seen her casually dressed, drinking beer on my brother's deck in Sweetwater. I even got her into a dress for my wedding two months ago. But when she's working, this is pretty much her default mode of dress and demeanor. Dark and strong and grim.

Probably because, when she's working, it *is* because someone died.

She was already there when I arrived, sitting on one side of the booth looking at something on her phone. I squeezed in on the other side. It was a tight fit, and since the table was bolted to the floor, there wasn't much I could do to help accommodate the baby.

Grimaldi watched my efforts. "Would you prefer a table

instead of a booth?"

I shook my head. "This is good. I'll be OK once I get situated."

The detective already had a glass of sweet tea in front of her. I ordered a milkshake. Dairy is good for the baby. And also because I was getting to that dangerous time when the baby was eyeing my stomach lining and salivating. I needed something semi-solid in my stomach, stat.

Grimaldi asked for a patty melt, and I ordered a club sandwich. After two burgers yesterday, I was all burgered out. The waitress—dressed in a striped uniform with a little white apron and her hair in a ponytail—withdrew on squeaky, white Keds and left us alone.

There was a moment of silence.

"So," I said. "Devon's dead."

Grimaldi nodded.

"Are those pictures of the crime scene?" I eyed the phone.

"Yes." Grimaldi dropped it in her pocket. "And I'm not showing them to you."

"That's OK. I didn't want to see them anyway."

"Sure," Grimaldi took a sip of tea.

I grimaced. "Fine. I'm curious."

"I know you are. But I'm still not going to show you my crime scene photos. They're none of your business."

"They might be."

She arched her brows. "How do you figure that?"

"I'll tell you. It started yesterday morning, when I got to work. Or actually, it started a couple of months before that, I guess. Technically. Do you know who Magnolia Houston is?"

"Yes," Grimaldi said with a sneer.

"Well, after making all that money, she decided she wanted to buy herself a mansion."

"Of course she did."

"And she hired Tim to help her. My broker, Timothy Briggs.

You remember Tim, don't you?"

"Who could forget?" Grimaldi said.

"Right. Well, anyway..." I went through the whole story: how Tim had found Miss Harper and convinced her to sell Magnolia the house, how Tim had waylaid me yesterday morning and told me about the missing money, and what I had done since then to try to figure out what was going on. And eventually, I got to Rafe's and my visit to the office late last night. "We were snooping in Heidi's office when we heard a car outside."

Grimaldi nodded.

"We didn't know who it was, and we thought us being there might look bad, so we turned the light out."

"Naturally," Grimaldi said drily.

"We waited a bit, and then someone came in. And went past us to the lobby. When Rafe went after him, he turned out to be Devon."

"Let me guess. Your husband scared him into confessing to some horrible crime?"

"Nothing all that horrible. He said he was there to pick up something Brittany had forgotten. It might even be true."

"Did he tell you what it was?"

I shook my head. "He said it was none of my business. And it wasn't. But when I asked him if he'd found it, he said yes and patted his pocket."

Grimaldi looked interested. "Which pocket?"

"Front left," I said, and watched as Grimaldi pulled out her phone again and punched buttons.

She shook her head. "Nothing in his front left pocket when he was found."

"What about the other pockets?"

"Car keys in his hand," Grimaldi said. "It happened pretty much as soon as he got out of the car. He only had time to close the door, but not lock it. And judging from the way he fell, between his own car and the one next to it, he was still facing the front of the car when he was shot."

"So someone came up behind him. He probably never even saw them." It wasn't a crime scene photo, but it painted a picture nonetheless.

Grimaldi nodded. "It didn't look personal at all. Whoever shot him probably didn't even say anything. No evidence he turned around to face his assailant. The guy—or woman—just came up behind him, gave him two quick pops—one to the back, one to the head—and left again."

"Yikes." I made a face. The picture was becoming clearer than I wanted it to. I could imagine the scene a bit too well.

"Have something to drink," Grimaldi instructed, as the milkshake made its way across the floor toward me. "Try to settle your stomach. You're turning green. We don't have to talk about this anymore."

"I want to talk about it." I nodded thanks to the waitress for the shake and stuck the straw in my mouth. After a swallow or two, I started to feel better. "I'm just constantly hungry. And if I don't eat regularly, I get nauseous. And like I said, it feels like the baby starts gnawing on my insides. I'm sure that's not actually true, but it feels that way."

"Too much information," Grimaldi said. "To continue, he had his keys in his hand. They were found next to him. He dropped them when he fell. The car was still where he parked it, with the driver's side door closed but unlocked. There was nothing in his front pockets, although we surmise he regularly kept his keys there, because the front right pocket had a small hole in the lining, as if he kept something pointy there. Keys are a logical guess."

I nodded, and focused on my milkshake.

"His phone was missing, and so was his wallet, assuming he carried one. The wear on his back pockets indicated he did. Phone on the left, wallet on the right. When he fell forward, the shooter must have helped himself."

"But he wasn't rolled."

Grimaldi shook her head.

"So chances are nobody checked his front pockets. If it was a robbery, the thief had already gotten what he came for."

"Presumably," Grimaldi said.

"So if Devon had picked something up at the office and put it in his front pocket, it should still be there. And since it wasn't, he must have given it to someone."

Grimaldi nodded. "Unless he lied, and he didn't pick up anything at all."

Unless that. "What was he wearing?"

"Black jeans and boots," Grimaldi said. "Black T-shirt with the name of a rock band on the front."

"The same thing he was wearing when I saw him. He hadn't been home to change."

Not that that meant anything. He could have gone home, but without changing. Why would he change, after all?

Although it did imply that he might have been somewhere else between the time we'd seen him at the office and the time he was shot, and was only getting home at two-thirty in the morning.

"Have you asked Brittany?" I asked.

Grimaldi's face darkened. "I had to do the notification."

"She's not his next of kin, is she? They aren't married. She told me they were going to tie the knot this Friday."

Grimaldi winced. "She didn't mention that. But no, she isn't. I also had to call his parents in Virginia."

"I don't envy you your job," I said.

"Times like that, I don't either."

"I don't envy you your job at any time. I wouldn't want it. I'm just nosy."

It would have been nice if she'd told me I wasn't nosy, just endearingly curious. She didn't. "If you're wondering how she took it, she got hysterical. Worse than you used to get, whenever you thought something had happened to Mr. Collier."

"I had good reason to worry about Rafe," I told her, even as I remembered, vividly, falling into a dead faint once when the detective showed up at my door with what she called 'bad news.' The news hadn't turned out to be about Rafe, as it happened, but about my sister-in-law Sheila. But by the time she told me that, it was too late: I had already fainted. "And I didn't say anything. Or suggest anything. I have no reason to think she wouldn't be genuinely upset if her boyfriend died."

Grimaldi grunted.

I squinted at her. "Do you?"

"The significant other is always the first person we look at," Grimaldi said.

It was my turn to arch my brows. "That wasn't a very straight answer."

"But you know it's true. We always look at the spouse first. Or in this case, girlfriend." She waited for me to say something, and when I didn't, she added, "She was there. Upstairs. She had access to the garage. She knew where he parked. And she was alone. That gives her opportunity, if nothing else."

I suppose.

"What can you tell me about their relationship?"

"Not much," I said, as I watched my club sandwich and Grimaldi's patty melt come across the floor. "They've been dating for as long as I've been working at LB&A, so more than a year. But I've only met Devon a handful of times. The annual Christmas party the last two years, and the couple of times he's stopped by to talk to Brittany about something. Other than 'hello' and 'nice to meet you,' last night was the first time I'd actually had a conversation with him."

The sandwiches arrived, and were arranged on the table. The waitress asked us if we needed anything else. We said no, and she withdrew. Grimaldi picked up the conversation. "No arguments that you've heard of?"

"They've certainly never argued in front of me. And Brittany and I aren't exactly best friends, so it isn't something she'd confide in me, if they did." I pulled the little cocktail spear out of one of my sandwich quarters and put it on the edge of the plate. "Yesterday, she told me they were going to go on their honeymoon this weekend. To Curacao. She was buying her trousseau."

Grimaldi got a funny look on her face as I bit into the sandwich. "Trousseau?"

I chewed and swallowed. "Old-fashioned word for wedding wardrobe. We talked a lot about trousseaus—or trousseaux—in finishing school."

"I bet you did." She shook her head. "So they were planning to go to the Caribbean this weekend. She didn't mention that."

"Maybe she didn't think it was any of your business. Or maybe she just didn't think of it. She had just been told her boyfriend was dead, so she must have had other things on her mind."

Grimaldi nodded. "I'll have to have another talk with her when she's calmed down. I asked whether she wanted me to call someone to come stay with her, but she said no."

"Maybe I should stop by," I said, "and pay my respects."

Grimaldi rolled her eyes, but didn't tell me not to. "Let me know if she says anything that might apply to the shooting."

"Of course." I licked a smear of mayonnaise off my fingers and lifted the next triangle of bread, turkey, lettuce, tomato, etc. "Anything else I should know?"

"I can't think of anything," Grimaldi said.

"I don't suppose there were security cameras in the garage? Even at the entrance, so maybe you've got the shooter coming or going?"

"That would be too easy," Grimaldi said. "But there are cameras on some of the buildings in the area. There's a traffic cam on the light down at the corner. We might get lucky there.

And the liquor store across the street also has a camera on the parking lot. We might be able to see a car going by."

It sounded like tedious work.

Grimaldi nodded when I said so. "A lot of police work is tedious. Talking to people and checking alibis and sitting through hours of camera footage. The same kind of things you did yesterday."

"You'll figure out who did it, won't you?"

"We usually do." She sounded calm. "Nine times out of ten, it was someone the victim knew. It just takes time to sort through all the relationships and reasons someone might want to do away with him. Although if it was random, maybe we won't. If someone happened to be walking by, and saw him pull into the garage, and thought it looked like a fine way to make a buck..."

"You said he drove a Jeep Wrangler, right? That doesn't sound like it would say 'loaded' to anybody."

Grimaldi shook her head. "It was seven or eight years old, and a little dinged up. He'd probably had it since he got his license at sixteen. And you're right, nothing about it said 'the owner of this car is carrying a lot of cash.' But we have to consider every angle. Someone might have followed him inside and robbed him. If nothing else, I have to rule it out."

Understood. I ate a couple of French fries and washed them down with milkshake while Grimaldi chewed and swallowed.

"Anything you want me to find out from Brittany when I go there? Something she might be more likely to tell me than you?" Not that she was necessarily likely to tell me anything at all. We weren't close. Although between me and the police, she might consider me the lesser evil.

"Just anything suspicious," Grimaldi said. "You know what to look for."

The compliment made me feel ridiculously good about myself. I grinned. "Thank you."

"Don't let it go to your head." She put what was left of the patty melt on her plate and reached for the iced tea. "And of course keep in mind that if she killed her boyfriend, and you show up asking questions, she might shoot you, too."

Theoretically, I knew that. In reality, the idea that I had to be afraid of Brittany because she might shoot me was ridiculous. "Does she even have a gun?"

"She says not," Grimaldi said. "I'll check, of course. I'll also check the alarm system on her apartment, to see if the door was opened during the time in question. But until I do, just keep in mind that you don't want to piss her off. Don't say or do anything stupid until we're sure she isn't involved."

Chances were Brittany wouldn't even invite me in, so it was most likely a moot point, but I nodded.

Grimaldi leaned back against the red Naugahyde. "So what else is new?"

I did the same. "What isn't? My mother's drinking, I have a new sister, and Rafe may have knocked up Carmen Arroyo."

So much for Grimaldi's relaxed demeanor. She straightened so fast I feared for her spine. "What?"

"I thought Dix might have called you. Remember Darcy?"

She and I had visited Grimaldi at police headquarters the week before, to take a look at some files the police had removed from St. Jerome's Hospital concerning the adoption ring that had operated there. It was what had given us our first loose thread to start unraveling the mystery of Darcy's birth.

"Of course," Grimaldi said. And then she caught on. "Darcy is your sister?"

"Half sister. She's Audrey's daughter. Audrey and my dad had a fling before he met my mother."

Grimaldi looked overwhelmed, and granted, it was a lot to take in. "I thought Audrey was your mother's best friend."

"She was. Until yesterday. Now Mother's drowning her sorrows in whiskey and tea and refusing to leave the house. Dix and Catherine drive over there several times a day to check on her."

"That doesn't sound good," Grimaldi said.

"It isn't. I'll probably have to drive down this weekend. Rafe suggested we should bring David. She likes him."

"It couldn't hurt," Grimaldi agreed. "What's that you were saying about Carmen Arroyo?"

"Oh." I winced. "I guess I didn't tell you. When Darcy and I went to the Tennessee Women's Prison on Sunday, to talk to Denise Seaver, I saw Carmen Arroyo. The woman who managed Hector's nightclub, remember? Back in December?"

"I remember her very well," Grimaldi said.

Yeah, me too. "Well, she's pregnant. Due in a couple of weeks, according to Doctor Seaver. Which would make the time she got pregnant right around the time she was sleeping with my husband."

"Who wasn't your husband then," Grimaldi reminded me. "He wasn't even your boyfriend then. Not according to you. Every time I called him that, you corrected me."

I grimaced. "I know. I don't blame him for sleeping with her." Much. "We weren't together. He could sleep with anyone he wanted to."

"I don't think he wanted to," Grimaldi said. "It was more that she wanted him to, and saying no would have made her suspicious. Jorge Pena had a reputation for liking the ladies."

And Rafe was pretending to be Jorge Pena, while Jorge was in the morgue. I nodded. "I was mostly over it, you know? I didn't think about her anymore. We worked things out between us, and then we moved in together, and then I got pregnant again, and then Rafe got abducted, and then we got married. Carmen wasn't really a blip on my screen for months."

"No reason why she would be," Grimaldi agreed.

"Exactly. But then I saw her on Sunday. And she was pregnant. And she might be having my husband's baby. And now it's all I can think about."

"I suppose you're going to tell me that's why you're getting involved in my case? Because it'll give you something else to think about?"

"I wasn't going to say that," I told her, "but it's true. On Sunday and Monday morning, I had Darcy to worry about. And Mother. Then on Monday afternoon, there was that incident with the gang-banger at Alexandra's house."

Grimaldi nodded. She had stopped by to pick up said gang-banger, but being busy, we hadn't had a chance to speak.

"Monday night," I continued, "I had to tell Rafe about Carmen. And Tuesday morning, Tim told me about the money. It gave me something else to think about all day yesterday. Which was helpful."

"No doubt," Grimaldi said. "Can you tell me what's being done?"

"About Carmen? At the moment we're just trying to figure out whether the baby is Rafe's or not. Until we know that, there's nothing we can do, and no reason to do anything."

Grimaldi nodded.

"The TBI lab is rushing through a paternity test. She was scheduled for a checkup today anyway, so the doctor out there— not Doctor Seaver—said they'd get a blood sample over to the TBI. And Rafe stopped by to have his own blood drawn, as well. It's apparently not quite as conclusive as testing the baby, but they can't do that without Carmen's consent, and at the moment, Rafe doesn't want to alert her to what's going on."

"If the baby is his, though..."

"Then she'll have to know. Of course."

"What will happen?"

"I don't know," I said honestly. "Doctor Seaver told me that Carmen's sister is taking the baby. It can't stay in the prison with Carmen after the first few weeks. But that was before. If it's Rafe's baby..."

"He'll have more of a claim on it than Carmen's sister."

I nodded. "And if it is his baby, he'll want it with him. He lost his chance with David because Elspeth never told him she was pregnant—"

"He might have lost that anyway," Grimaldi pointed out. "He was in prison when David was born."

True. "He's not going to lose it this time. If that baby is his, he'll want it. If he's the father, he'll probably get it. And that means I'll have to bring it up. Along with my own baby. And I'm not sure how that's going to work out."

What if I couldn't treat them the same? What if I favored my own? Or what if I favored Carmen's, because I was so afraid of favoring my own?

"It'll work out just fine," Grimaldi said firmly. "You're a lot stronger than you think you are."

While I stared at her, mouth open, she added, dryly, "Of course, you'd have to be, to marry your husband."

I closed my mouth. And opened it again. "I'm not sure what to say. Thank you?"

Grimaldi waved it away. "If that baby is his, you'll love it. It won't matter that it isn't yours. If it's his, you'll love it just as you would your own."

I wished I could be as sure. "I hope so," I said.

"I know so." She looked around for the waitress. "And on that note, I should get back to work."

So should I. "Will you let me know how it goes?" I asked as I dug for my wallet.

She waved it away. "It's on me. Get me something good. Something that'll help me figure out what happened to Devon. Right now it looks like a random mugging, and if that's the case, this could be one of those unsolved mysteries. So find me something I can use to prove that it wasn't."

I nodded. "I'll do my best."

Nine

I followed Grimaldi over to Franklin Road and the crime scene. She disappeared into the garage, and I went around to the front of the building and looked for Brittany's name on the doorbells.

It wasn't a terribly big place. Four stories tall, with what looked like six apartments on each floor. Brittany's apartment seemed to be on three. Closer to the top of the list than the bottom.

I pressed the bell and waited. And waited some more. And pressed the bell again. And held it, for good measure.

It took a couple of minutes before Brittany answered. "Yeah?" She sounded tired and angry. Maybe I'd woken her.

"It's Savannah," I said. "Can I come up for a minute?"

"Why?"

"I brought you lunch." A late brainstorm, just before we left the diner. It seemed like a nice gesture, since she probably didn't feel much like cooking, and I thought it might gain me entry.

"I'm not hungry," Brittany said.

"There's a milkshake, too."

She hesitated. "What kind of milkshake?"

I glanced at it. "Chocolate. With whipped cream and little chocolate shavings."

If it had been me, that would have done it. Brittany hesitated. But then the buzzer on the door sounded. I juggled the food and drink containers and pushed it open.

"Third floor," Brittany said as I headed in.

There was an elevator, and I took it. On a full stomach, with a baby on board and things to carry, I didn't feel like climbing the stairs. So sue me; I'd worry about losing the baby weight after the baby was born.

When the doors opened on three, Brittany was waiting, leaning on her door jamb like she couldn't quite keep upright on her own.

She looked horrible. And I'm not just saying that because I feel more and more like a small hippopotamus with every day that goes by, and I envy everyone who still has a waist.

Nor is it because deep down, I don't really like Brittany.

The truth is, she looked awful. Pale, haggard, and at least ten years older than I knew her to be, with dark shadows under her eyes that a medium-sized burglar could hide in.

"I'm sorry about Devon," I said, as I handed her the milkshake. "Tim told me what happened."

Rather than asking if I could come in—there was a chance she'd say no—I just maneuvered myself and the bag of food past her and into the apartment. "Are you hungry? I brought you a sandwich and fries from the diner on 12th."

"I'm not hungry," Brittany said, pivoting slowly to watch me look around for the kitchen.

The place was small. Just a one-bedroom, judging from the layout. Open concept living, dining, and kitchen just inside the front door, with a single door on the opposite wall. Similar to the apartment I'd lived in, between my divorce from Bradley and when I moved in with Rafe.

It was decorated in IKEA minimalist modern, with a royal blue couch the only splash of color. Everything else was white, black, and shades of gray. It looked good, but I wouldn't have wanted to live in it. Too cold.

I turned to Brittany, who had taken the time to close and lock the door. "Would you like me to put this on a plate for you?"

"I'm not really hungry," Brittany began, although her nostrils quivered.

"Just try a little." I moved past her into the kitchenette, where I put the bag on the counter and started opening cabinets looking for a plate. "You have to eat. It's important to keep your strength up."

"I don't know why," Brittany said. "It doesn't matter, now that Devon is dead." She put the milkshake on the counter and buried her face in her hands.

"I know how you feel," I told her, as I transferred the sandwich and fries onto a blue plate I'd found in the cabinet. "My sister-in-law was murdered last November, remember? I know what it's like, having someone you care about die violently." And it wasn't too long before that, that Rafe had been shot and Dix told me he had died. For eight interminable hours, I had believed the man I loved was dead. I'm sure Brittany's hysterics had had nothing on mine. Grimaldi had been very kind in not mentioning that little incident, when I had showed up in her office at police headquarters, screaming like a banshee and accusing her of lying to me.

"Why don't we have a seat?" I picked up the plate and snagged the milkshake on my way past. And put them both on the pub-height dining table between the kitchen and the living room. "If you can't eat, at least sit down."

I took the chair on the other side of the table, and waited. It took a few seconds, but then Brittany climbed onto the chair across from me. "Why are you being so nice to me?"

"I'm always nice to you," I said. More commonly, she was the one being snooty with me. "And I told you, I know what you're going through."

"No one knows what I'm going through!" Brittany wailed and buried her face in her hands again.

I refrained from rolling my eyes, just focused on making *there-there* noises. "Do you want to talk about what happened?"

"I don't know what happened," Brittany said, lifting bloodshot eyes to glare at me. "Not until that detective came and knocked on my door this morning."

I nodded. "Detective Grimaldi's good at her job. She'll figure out who did this."

Brittany sniffed.

"At least have something to drink," I said and nudged the milkshake closer to her. "You probably haven't put anything in your stomach today. It isn't good for you."

Brittany stuck the straw in her mouth and slurped. My mother would have been horrified. In the interests of obtaining information I decided to ignore the uncouthness.

"So you didn't know anything had happened until Detective Grimaldi rang the doorbell this morning?"

Brittany shook her head, still sucking up milkshake. I guess maybe she'd decided she was hungry after all.

"Why was Devon out so late?"

"Rehearsal," Brittany said.

"Rehearsal?"

She gave me a superior look. I deduced she must be feeling better. "He's a musician. Musicians rehearse."

Of course they do. But they don't do it in our real estate office.

"When did the rehearsal start?"

"Seven," Brittany said and reached for the sandwich. "Every Tuesday."

"Do they always rehearse so late?"

"Seven o'clock isn't late," Brittany said, around a bite of BLT.

"Maybe not." But two-thirty was. And that was when Devon had come home from 'rehearsal.'

Brittany shrugged. "Most of them have day jobs. They have to finish work first."

"What's Devon's day job?"

"Troubleshooting," Brittany said.

Troubleshooting? "Does that have something to do with computers?"

Brittany gave me a look down her nose. It couldn't have been easy, when we were both sitting down. "Yes."

"But what he really wanted was to be a musician?"

Brittany nodded. Her eyes started filling with tears again. I guess the past tense had reminded her that he was gone.

"I saw Devon last night," I said, in an effort to stem the flow. I had been planning to keep that tidbit to myself, but it just sort of slipped out.

Brittany stopped chewing. After a moment's silence, she swallowed. "Where?"

"At the office. He said he was picking up something you'd forgotten."

Brittany blinked.

"Was he picking up something you'd forgotten?"

Brittany shook her head.

So he'd lied. "Do you know why he was there?"

"No," Brittany said.

"I don't suppose you have any idea who would want to kill him? Or why?"

Brittany's eyes flickered. She shook her head.

I got to my feet. "I should let you finish your food in peace. Call me if there's anything you need."

Brittany didn't answer, but when I glanced at her on my way out the door, she was snarfing down French fries. Once she got going, the tragedy didn't seem to have affected her appetite all that much.

I made my way out through the garage, where Grimaldi was observing a crew of white-clad techs combing what I assumed was the crime scene for evidence. There were three of them, and they were picking up what looked like specks of dirt and putting them in small baggies. I'm sure they were gathering more than specks of dirt, but everything was so tiny, and held in the points of tweezers, that I had no idea what it actually was. Some form of evidence, undoubtedly.

Grimaldi was standing a few yards away, her hands on her hips, watching.

"Is that Devon's car?" I asked, as I stopped next to her.

Among the area the crime scene crew was combing was a dark green Jeep Wrangler with a cloth top.

Grimaldi nodded.

"Have you looked inside?"

She glanced at me. "I took a quick look."

"Did you find anything that looked like it might have come from the LB&A office?"

"I have no idea," Grimaldi said. "What would something like that look like?"

"No clue. But Brittany said she hadn't asked him to go pick up anything for her. So he lied about that."

"Interesting," Grimaldi said. "How is she?"

"Not hysterical anymore. When I left her, she was sitting in the dining room shoveling in French fries."

"Did she tell you anything?"

"Not much," I admitted. "She said that Devon was at a rehearsal yesterday. From seven until he came home and got shot. When I told her I'd seen him at the office, she seemed surprised, so I don't think she knew what he was doing there."

Grimaldi nodded. "I'll have to find out who he rehearses with and talk to them."

"Brittany could probably tell you that. She also says he has a day job. Troubleshooting."

Grimaldi's brows rose. "Computers?"

I nodded.

"That's interesting."

"Interesting for me, given the spoofed email. He'd probably know how to do that. According to José, it isn't difficult."

"It's interesting to me, too," Grimaldi informed me, "since the fact that he had the skills to embezzle half a million dollars from his girlfriend's workplace makes for a nice motive for murder."

I guess it did. "I asked Brittany if she could suggest someone who might have wanted to kill him. She said no, but I can't say I believed her."

"I'll make sure to ask," Grimaldi said.

I eyed the Jeep again. "You know, I saw a car like that in Goodlettsville yesterday."

"Did you?" Her tone said that she figured I'd probably seen several. And I probably had. Except I was talking about one car in particular. One I hadn't just passed on the street.

"The guy I told you about? The one on the ladder outside Miss Harper's house? He drove away in it."

Now I had her attention. "This car?"

"I don't know if it was this car," I said. "I only caught a glimpse of it, since I had to climb back down the ladder and push through the trees, and by then it was almost gone, but it looked like this."

"Green?"

"It might have been green. I think it was. I can't swear that it was this car. I didn't see the license plate—" and there were no identifying bumper stickers or anything like that on the back of the Jeep, "—but I'm pretty sure it was this kind of car."

"Interesting," Grimaldi said. "So the man on the ladder... was it Devon?"

I blinked. I should have followed that corollary to its logical conclusion, but somehow I hadn't gotten that far. I sounded surprised, even in my own ears. "I'm not sure."

"Think back," Grimaldi ordered. "To the first time you saw him. On the ladder."

"I only saw him once." And for only a moment. I'd been halfway up the driveway by the time I noticed the ladder, and almost to the house by the time I saw the man on it. It hadn't occurred to me that he looked familiar, so maybe he hadn't.

I closed my eyes and tried to recall the picture. Coming out of the shade of the trees into the sunshine surrounding the house. It was blinding for a second. I saw the ladder, and followed it up. To faded blue jeans and a white T-shirt, topped by shaggy, dark hair.

The hair fit, anyway.

So did the physique. Devon was built like Brittany, straight up and down. More boy than man. Same as the guy on the ladder, who'd had long, thin legs inside the jeans and skinny arms holding the scraper.

Had he turned to look at me?

I thought he had, but not for long enough to be recognizable. I had an impression of a pale oval of a face below and behind the dark hair, but that was all.

"I'm not sure," I told Grimaldi. "It might have been him. But I honestly can't tell you for sure. Every time I've seen Devon, he's been wearing black. Jeans, T-shirts, boots. This guy was dressed in a white T-shirt and blue jeans. It didn't even cross my mind that I might know him."

"No reason why it would," Grimaldi said. "But clothes can be changed."

Of course they could. "Let me put it this way: I looked at the guy for a second, and I didn't think, 'this guy looks familiar.' But that might have been because he wasn't wearing what he's always wearing."

"I get it," Grimaldi assured me. "It looked like this car, though?"

"Looked like it. But it was a ways away. I didn't get a really good look. It could have been this car. Or it could have been one like it. Or something similar."

Grimaldi nodded.

"It doesn't make a whole lot of sense, though," I added.

"Angie, the woman in the consignment store, said the guy on the ladder was probably Magnolia's boyfriend. She'd seen them together before. She even said she'd seen them driving away together a couple of minutes before I came into the store. You could ask her for a description of the boyfriend and the car. She'd probably do a better job than me."

"And I might do that," Grimaldi said. "But for now, go on."

"Well, Devon couldn't have been Magnolia's boyfriend. He was marrying Brittany on Friday."

"Or so she said."

"Right. But why lie about it? I mean, they've been dating for a long time. It wouldn't be surprising if they decided to get married."

Grimaldi nodded.

"And he has—or had—the skills to spoof Tim's email address and reroute the money. So maybe he did that. And maybe someone killed him for it. But that's no reason why he'd be on a ladder outside Miss Harper's house scraping paint. It was probably someone else."

"Most likely," Grimaldi nodded. "But we'll look into it. For now, I'll go upstairs and have another talk with your friend."

"She's not my friend." My response was automatic. "Will you tell me if she says anything that might have something to do with the missing money?"

Grimaldi said she would. "One question. Why isn't Mr. Briggs calling in the authorities on this? Five hundred thousand dollars is a lot of money to go missing. You'd think he'd want some help figuring out what happened."

"He did. He wanted *my* help."

"Other than you," Grimaldi said. "You won't even be able to trace the money to the account it's in. I'd need a subpoena for that, so there's no way you could."

I wasn't so sure about that, actually. It was possible José had the hacking skills to get me that information, but naturally I didn't say so. "I guess it's because, until I started looking into it, we thought the email had to have originated from inside the firm. Until I found out about spoofing, I didn't realize that someone unrelated to LB&A could have done it."

"Devon isn't exactly unrelated to LB&A," Grimaldi pointed out.

"I know. But he isn't one of the agents. I guess maybe that would make it a little better." I hesitated. "I guess it's too soon to tell Tim that Devon might be the guilty party?"

"Much too soon," Grimaldi said firmly. "We have no proof that he had anything to do with it. He had a background in technology, and now he's dead, but that's not enough to accuse him of grand larceny. I'll have to check his electronics and his bank accounts, to begin with. If I come across anything that seems like it might have a bearing on your problem, I'll let you know."

I told her I appreciated it.

"Where are you off to?"

I wasn't entirely sure. "I guess I could go back to Goodlettsville. If the guy on the ladder is there today, we'll know he isn't Devon."

Grimaldi nodded. "Let me know how it goes. And keep me updated on your mother and the Sweetwater situation."

"You could just call Dix," I said.

She turned away. "I'm busy here. If your brother wants to talk to me, he knows where to find me."

Fine. "I'll see you later," I said, and walked out to my car.

Thirty minutes later, I was back in front of Miss Harper's house on Lickton Pike.

It looked much as it had yesterday. Still decrepit, still set against the same backdrop of tangled vines and trees. The ladder still leaned against the east wall, but today it was empty. And the front door hung wide open.

I eyed it speculatively for a moment, before getting out of the car.

To be honest, it might have been doing that since yesterday afternoon. After my encounter with the chiggers, ticks, and brambles, I'd limped back to my car, moaning and swearing—in a ladylike fashion, of course. But I hadn't paid any attention to the house. Perhaps I should have.

At any rate, the door stood open. The man on the ladder—Devon or someone else—must have climbed in through the window when I showed up. And then, when I climbed the ladder and it seemed as if I might be coming in, he hightailed it down the stairs and out, through the brambles over to his car.

I should have asked Detective Grimaldi whether Devon had sported any scratches. Unless he knew of a different way to go—and he might—the man from the ladder couldn't have taken the path I took through the trees without getting torn up.

But that was for later. For now, the door that had been locked yesterday hung open. I made my way up on the stoop and peered around the door frame. "Hello? Anyone here?"

No one answered.

I carry a little canister of pepper spray in my purse. It looks like a lipstick. I have another that holds a tiny knife, that also looks like a lipstick. In this case, I figured the pepper spray would be the most useful, and fished it out. Thus armed, I made my way across the threshold into Miss Harper's house, and looked around.

It was old, no question. Older than the Martin Mansion, and less ostentatious. At home, the front door opens into a big, two-story foyer with a graceful, split staircase leading up to the second floor.

There was nothing like that here. The front door led directly into a living room, with a big stone fireplace on one end, with wide plank floors and lower ceilings than I was used to, both from the mansion and Mrs. Jenkins's Victorian.

A few pieces of furniture remained. An ugly flower-upholstered sofa of 1970s vintage sat in front of the fireplace, while an old secretary—the desk, not the person—stood against the back wall, next to the door to the dining room.

It was the same in the next room. The table and chairs were gone, but an oversized breakfront stood against the wall: probably too heavy and cumbersome to make the trip to the retirement home with Miss Harper.

So far I had seen no sign of life, and heard no indication that anyone was in the house with me. But I kept the pepper spray clenched in my now sweaty hand as I made my way from room to room.

It all looked the same. Old, unkempt, with abandoned furniture and a lot of dust. The kitchen had Formica counter tops, similar to the tables at the diner on 12th, and the appliances must have been thirty or forty years old. I opened the fridge—it smelled—but it was empty.

The dust on the stairs was scuffed. I looked around for footprints, and saw some, a bit bigger than mine, that looked like they might have come from tennis shoes. I dug my phone out of my bag and took a picture of one, making sure to zoom in as close as I could. Maybe Detective Grimaldi could match the sneaker to something of Devon's. He'd died with his boots on, no pun intended, but he probably had a pair of sneakers somewhere. Most people do. Even me.

The second floor was all bedrooms, same as in the Martin Mansion. Most of them were empty, but one—the one with the faded magnolia wallpaper and the open window with the ladder outside—had a big steamer trunk sitting under the window. I walked over and hauled on the lid.

It was heavy, and for a second it crossed my mind that maybe I shouldn't be trying to lift it. But then it popped up. I looked down on a paint scraper on top of a stack of what looked like old curtains and table cloths.

The scraper must be the one the guy on the ladder had used yesterday. If I got it to Grimaldi, maybe she could pull fingerprints from it. That would tell us, one way or the other, whether the man on the ladder had been Devon.

I took a picture of the scraper *in situ* before folding the top curtain panel—stained damask—around it carefully. I was just about to lift it when my phone rang.

I had dropped it back into my purse after using it for the photograph, since I wanted both hands free for the curtain and paint scraper. Now I dug it out again. "Rafe."

"We have a problem," my husband said grimly.

My heart gave a single, heavy thud. "You got the DNA results back already?"

"No," Rafe said. "Carmen had her checkup this morning. They drew blood and did whatever other stuff they do to a pregnant woman almost ready to give birth."

Things the two of us would be dealing with within a couple of months ourselves. But now didn't seem the right time to mention that. From my own checkups, I knew the doctor would have listened to the baby's heartbeat and probably done a pelvic exam, though.

"And?" I said.

"They sent her back to her cell," Rafe answered. "A couple hours later she went into labor."

Uh-oh.

"The doc at the prison doesn't like to handle births when he doesn't have to, so he sent Carmen to the hospital. Denise Seaver volunteered to go with her."

My heart sank. "I have a feeling I know where this is going."

"I'm sure you do," Rafe said. "They didn't get there. Cops just found the van abandoned halfway between the prison and the hospital. The driver was dead. Stabbed multiple times. Carmen and Denise Seaver are in the wind."

Ten

For a second or two, I just couldn't think. Couldn't breathe, either. It felt as if someone had sucker punched me in the stomach and knocked the wind out of me.

Rafe must have realized it, because he waited patiently until I found my voice again. "What can I do?"

"Dunno that there's much any of us can do. The cops are out looking for them. They haven't asked the TBI for help, but—"

"It's your baby," I said. And between you and me, it wasn't easy to get the words out. Nor, for that matter, to keep my voice even. "Or it might be your baby. You're going to want to look for them."

He waited a second. "You have a problem with that?"

"No." It didn't sound very convincing, not even in my own ears, so I repeated it. "No, of course not. I understand. It might be your baby. And even if it isn't, she's out there, in labor, with only Doctor Seaver to help her. I'm sure Denise Seaver has delivered babies before. But that was in a hospital, with all the necessary equipment. What if something goes wrong?"

Rafe didn't answer.

"What can I do?" I asked again. "Can I go with you?"

"Where?"

"Wherever you're going. I might be useful."

"How d'you figure that?"

"I'm another woman," I said. "If you find them, and Carmen's in labor, or... or... ill, and you have to deal with Denise Seaver, I can deal with Carmen and the baby. Because I can tell you right now that Denise Seaver isn't going to go quietly. This is her doing. She probably planned the whole thing. Maybe she gave Carmen something to induce labor when she was in the clinic this morning, and offered to go with her to the hospital. She didn't just stumble upon whatever she used to stab the guard. She brought it with her. Somehow. I guarantee it."

Rafe thought it over. "Dunno if it's a good idea to drag you into this. Denise Seaver has good reason to wanna hurt you."

"I'm not worried," I said robustly, even though, to be honest, I was. But I was more worried about being left behind. "You'll protect me."

"The best way I can do that is keep you outta harm's way."

Hard to argue with that. So I didn't try. I begged instead. "Please take me with you. I'd rather be with you than by myself. I'll go crazy if I have to sit around and wait to hear something."

"Where are you?"

"Goodlettsville," I said.

"I'll meet you at home in ten minutes."

Ten minutes?

I wanted to tell him that unlike him, I'm a defensive driver who tends to go the speed limit. There was no way I could get home in ten minutes. But he'd already hung up. And anyway, I couldn't spare the time to argue. If I wasn't there in ten minutes, he'd probably leave without me. So I gathered up the paint scraper inside the curtain and clattered down the stairs and out to the car, where I peeled off with a spatter of dirt. The green Jeep had nothing on me.

I didn't make it home in ten minutes, but it was close. Not close enough for Rafe, though. He was pacing the front porch when I pulled into the driveway, looking like a caged puma. By the time

I pulled up to the bottom of the stairs, he was waiting, and he had the door open and himself inside before I'd even come to a full stop. "Drive."

I drove. "Where?"

"What the hell is this I'm sitting on?" He drove a hand underneath his excellent posterior and dug around.

I glanced over. "Be careful with that. It's a paint scraper the guy from yesterday was using on Miss Harper's house. I was going to take it to Grimaldi for fingerprints, to see if the guy on the ladder was Devon or someone else."

"Devon?" Rafe said, digging the scraper out from under himself and tossing it and the curtains into the back seat. "The kid from the office last night?"

"He's dead. Someone shot him this morning around two-thirty. In the parking garage underneath his condo."

Rafe was silent for a moment. "Sounds like you've had a busy day."

"You have no idea. After you left, I went to the office. Tim told me that Brittany wouldn't be in, because Devon had been shot. Tim said Brittany had recognized Detective Grimaldi, so I called Grimaldi and asked her to lunch."

"Trying to solve her case again?"

"It might have something to do with the missing money," I said. "Turns out Devon's day job was troubleshooting computers. He'd know how to spoof an email address."

Rafe arched his brows, but said nothing.

"I saw his car. He was driving a green Jeep. And the guy I saw yesterday, who was scraping paint from Miss Harper's house, drove off in one of those. So I went back up to Goodlettsville to see if he was back today, or whether it might have been Devon."

"Don't you think you woulda recognized Devon?"

"Not necessarily. I don't—didn't—know him well. And anyway, the place was empty today. No guy, no Jeep. But the paint scraper was upstairs, so I took it. I figured Grimaldi could test it for fingerprints. That way we'll know one way or the other if the guy on the ladder was Devon or someone else."

Rafe nodded. "Makes sense."

"But it can wait. The paint scraper's not going anywhere. Neither is Devon." People don't check out of the morgue. "Right now, finding Doctor Seaver and Carmen is more important."

We drove in silence a minute. Since he hadn't answered my question about where to go, I'd taken a right out of the driveway, and another right from Potsdam onto Dresden. At the moment, we were on our way toward Dickerson Pike and the interstate.

"Where do you want me to go?" I asked.

"The abandoned van is between mile markers 22 and 23 on Briley Parkway eastbound. Why don't we start there."

Sure thing. It meant I'd gone in the wrong direction—I should have taken a left out of the driveway onto Potsdam—but it was easy to fix. I navigated the light at Dickerson and headed for the entrance to the interstate. We'd go north and pick up Briley Parkway up there.

"So tell me about your day," I said, as we wended our way onto the entrance ramp to I-24.

He gave me a quick look. "I went in and gave blood in the morning. Worked with the boys after. José says anytime you can get access to that email, he'll take a look at it for you."

"I appreciate it."

"The lab called when the sample from the prison got there. About ten-thirty or eleven. After that, I worked with the boys some more. Until I got the phone call from the doc out there at TPFW that the transport never made it to the hospital. And then the call thirty minutes later that they'd found it and the guard."

He shook his head. "I gotta do something, Savannah. It don't much matter whether it's my baby or not—"

It seemed to me it mattered rather a lot, but I didn't say so.

"—it's somebody's. And the two of'em are out there

somewhere, walking around, or holed up in some shack in the woods, and you're right. What if something goes wrong?"

"Women spent a lot of centuries giving birth before we had modern hospitals," I told him, as we headed north on the interstate. "Most of them were fine."

"But some weren't. A lot of 'em died. So did the babies."

True. Let me put it this way: I wouldn't choose to have my baby in a shack in the middle of the woods. Not if there was a well-equipped hospital available.

But I wasn't incarcerated. No one would take my baby away from me and give it to someone else after I carried it for nine months and gave birth to it. And that's what Carmen was looking forward to. Whether it was Rafe or her sister, she wouldn't be able to bring up her own child.

I wondered whether she had chosen this, or whether the whole thing was Denise Seaver's doing. And if it was, was she just using Carmen as a way to get herself out of prison, or did she think she was helping?

"Exit's coming up," Rafe said.

I nodded. "I see the sign. What do you want to do once we get there?"

He shrugged. "Have a look around, I guess. Figure out where they were, and then see if we can figure out where they went from there."

That might be easier said than done. But I didn't say so, just flipped on my turn signal and took the exit for Briley Parkway.

We hit mile marker 22 first, going toward the prison rather than away from it. I slowed down, and we started looking around. Less than twenty seconds later, we saw the DOC van—white, with *Tennessee Department of Corrections* spelled out in black letters along the side—down in the grass beside the road on the other side of the median. A vehicle from the morgue was parked next to it—I've seen them before, so I recognized it—and several white-clad crime techs were moving around.

There was no way to get across to the other side. We had to drive past, down to the next exit, and then turn around and come back in the same direction the DOC van had been driving: away from the prison toward town. Just as we approached, the morgue vehicle pulled off the grass and away into traffic. I drove off the road and into the space it had vacated, behind the Metro PD crime scene unit van that had been parked in front of it.

No sooner had I come to a stop, than a uniformed officer jogged in our direction, hands up and out. "This is a crime scene! You can't stop here!"

Rafe brandished TBI credentials at him, and he scowled. "Nobody told me the feds would be coming."

"They're not," Rafe said. "I was part of the team that took Hector Gonzales's theft gang down. I did too much work to have Carmen Arroyo walking away like this."

The cop bent down to peer into the car. I twiddled my fingers at him. I'd personally taken Denise Seaver down, with a shot of pepper spray, but it was probably best not to mention that. I had no official standing here. And besides, it was Sheriff Satterfield who had arrested her. I'd just incapacitated her first. And managed to get myself shot in the process, I might add.

"Any word on where they've gone?" Rafe asked.

The cop shook his head. "Might have walked off into the hills."

Briley Parkway on the north side of town runs through a pretty rural area. Where we were standing right now, there were hills in all directions. In the distance, I could see the rooftops of the subdivision at Eaton's Creek, but right here, there was nothing. Just a dirt road below the interstate, running up the holler between two small knolls, and a big sign advertising a dressing service.

Dressing as in cutting up deer and other animals that people had hunted, not dressing as in putting on clothes.

"Is anyone following the trail?" I asked. When they both turned to me, I added, "If they walked away. Up the road, say. Or into the woods." The hillside was thickly crusted with trees and bushes. "Is anyone looking for them?"

The cop glanced at Rafe, maybe to ascertain whether he should answer or not. When Rafe didn't tell him not to, he said, "A couple of guys with tracking experience went up that way. I don't know if they've found anything."

If they had, they would have called, I assumed.

"Mind if I take a look?" Rafe gestured to the van.

The young cop looked mutinous, but also looked like he didn't quite dare refuse. I guess he wasn't quite sure how Rafe fit into this case, and erred on the side of not offending him. My husband has that effect on some people. "Go ahead. Just don't touch anything."

Rafe promised he wouldn't. And turned to me. "Stay here."

I nodded, and watched him walk away; long legs in faded jeans eating up the distance between the Volvo and the van.

As soon as he was out of earshot, the young cop turned to me. "Was he really part of the team that took down Hector Gonzales?"

"Ten years undercover," I said grimly, as I watched him approach the van and peer inside. "He wasn't just part of it. He was the guy on the inside. Without him, they wouldn't have had the evidence to take anyone down."

The cop stared at me.

"But yes. He took Hector down personally." With a blow to the throat that made it questionable whether Hector would ever be able to talk again.

In justice to him—and I was there, tied to a chair at the time—Hector had had a knife and been hell bent on killing him, so it was hard to blame him for the use of force.

Also, Hector did eventually talk. It took a couple of days, but he got there. And now he's in a Georgia prison serving a nice, long sentence.

The young cop gazed at Rafe with something like awe. "That was him?"

"In the flesh." And very nice flesh it was, too.

I watched as Rafe leaned into the back of the van, hands carefully behind him. One of the crime scene techs was working inside, and said something to him. I could see her teeth flash when she smiled.

He has that effect on women. And on some men, too. Even here, in this setting.

"Wow."

"I know."

We stood there—or sat, in my case—and watched him walk back. This time he came to my side of the car and opened my door. "C'mon."

"What are we doing?" I accepted the hand he extended, and let him pull me out of the car. "I don't have to look at the body, do I?"

He shook his head. "The body's gone. I wanna drive. You couldn't outrun a funeral procession."

"Could so," I said, but I walked around the car anyway. "And I wasn't aware we had to outrun anyone."

The young cop gallantly held the door for me, and closed it once I was inside.

"You never know," Rafe said, and started the engine. He gave the cop a nod. "Appreciate it."

The young man nodded back. "It's no problem." He looked a bit star struck still, and when we peeled away from the gravel and took off down the road like a bat out of hell—Rafe's usual mode of locomotion—he gazed after us until we were gone.

"Need you to do something for me," Rafe said, as we made our way back toward town.

"What's that?"

He glanced at me. "You knew Denise Seaver."

"I don't know about knew," I said. "I mean, we weren't friends or anything. She was my gynecologist. But I dealt with her. So I suppose I knew her. A little."

"I need you to think about where she mighta gone. The cops have trackers up in the hills. They got a head start, but two women—one of'em pushing sixty and outta shape, and the other ready to give birth—they ain't gonna be able to walk far before they need to shelter. If they're out there, the cops'll find them."

I nodded. That made sense. If Doctor Seaver and Carmen had walked away from the DOC van, and Carmen was in labor, they couldn't have made it more than a mile or so. Even if Denise Seaver had given Carmen something to stop the contractions—and we didn't know that she had—labor might have been too far advanced for the medication to work. And if it did work, it would take time for it to kick in. If they were on foot, they'd be rounded up pretty quickly.

"Do you think they hitched a ride? Would anyone pick up two women in prison uniforms standing next to a Department of Corrections van?"

"A pregnant woman giving birth on the side of the road?" Rafe said. "Some good Samaritan's bound to stop."

He had a point.

"Or they mighta arranged for a ride."

"Planned it?"

He shrugged.

I thought about it. "It's possible, I guess. Depends on when either of them figured out what was going on."

"Couldn'ta been before yesterday," Rafe said. "That was the first time I was out at the prison."

Yes, but... "I was there on Sunday. And I know that Denise Seaver saw me notice Carmen. She told me Carmen's due date is in a couple of weeks. I didn't think Carmen saw me, but Denise Seaver might have asked Carmen about me later. Or about you, since she knows we're married now. She could have asked

Carmen about you and found out that there's a chance you're the father of Carmen's baby. She isn't stupid. And she knows about David. She's the one who took him away from Elspeth. So she knows you've already lost one child. She might have figured that you'd do whatever you had to, to keep this one. And if she told Carmen..."

"Shit," Rafe said.

I nodded. "The other alternative is that she didn't realize it until you showed up yesterday. She might have told Carmen about it this morning, and gotten the OK to induce labor so both of them could try to escape. Or she did it without telling Carmen."

"Not sure which would be worse."

I was pretty sure. If this was all about Denise Seaver getting out of prison, and Carmen and her baby were just the means to achieve that, that would be worse. That meant Denise Seaver didn't care whether they lived or died.

"I hope Carmen knew," I said. "At least that she knew what to expect. I hope she isn't out here with no idea what's going on."

Rafe nodded, his hands tight on the wheel, the knuckles showing white under the skin. The car took the curves on two wheels on our way back toward town.

"You knew Carmen," I added. "Probably better than I knew Denise Seaver." Or at least more intimately. "If she's part of this, do you have any idea where she'd go?"

"Her sister's house? Or the mother's?"

Good thinking. "They were both there on Sunday, visiting her. I saw them. I realize none of this had been cooked up then, either way you look at it, but we should definitely check that out. They both seemed to really care about her."

"And why not?" Rafe said grimly, as the car sailed over a bump in the road and went airborne for a second or two. "Her being so loveable and all."

Better not to touch that one, I thought, and kept my mouth firmly closed.

Eleven

Carmen's mother lived in a small house on the south side of Nashville, near Nolensville Road. The drive took us past the *Havana*, the nightclub where Carmen had worked for Hector Gonzales last year. It was his club, and it did a little illegal gambling—not allowed in the state of Tennessee—as well as a lot of money laundering and other things. Rafe had spent a few weeks there playing bouncer, while he pretended to be a South American hitman by the name of Jorge Pena. This was after those eight interminable hours I mentioned earlier, during which word went out that Rafe was dead, so he could come back as Jorge. Everyone in Hector's organization knew that Jorge had been sent after him. Nobody thought for a moment that Jorge would miss. And when he did—almost—Rafe, Grimaldi, and Wendell Craig cooked up a plan in which Rafe would become Jorge and weasel his way into Hector's organization that way. Since ten years of trying to do it the other way hadn't worked.

But I digress.

As we zoomed down Nolensville Road, I glanced over at the cinderblock building that had housed the *Havana*; dark and closed now, with a For Rent sign out front. "Where did Carmen live? With her mother?"

Rafe gave me a sideways look. "Townhouse out by the lake."

"Fancy."

He shrugged.

"Didn't you like it?"

"It was fine. Not my taste."

OK, then. "Any chance she'd go there?"

"I figure she prob'ly lost it," Rafe said. "But we can check. After we're done down here."

"Does the sister live in this area, too?"

"Couple miles east."

So between here and the lake.

"Can you think of anywhere else she might have gone?"

"To her baby daddy," Rafe said grimly, "less'n that's me."

"Any idea who it might be? If it isn't you?"

He shook his head. "Far as I saw, she wasn't doing nobody else at the same time she was doing me. But who knows?"

Right. A bit of anger there. And probably time to change the subject.

"Denise Seaver still owns her house in Sweetwater. Darcy, Dix and I broke in there a couple of nights ago, looking for medical records."

He nodded, his mouth relaxing a little. "You told me."

"It's a long distance from here, though. I mean, we could make it there in an hour, the way you drive. But they're two women on foot—unless they planned it beforehand and arranged for a ride. And if they're dependent on the kindness of strangers, it could take them all day to get to Sweetwater."

Rafe nodded. "Not sure Carmen has all day."

I wasn't, either. "We should keep it in reserve. If we don't get any leads anywhere else, we could head down there. Or I could call Dix and ask him to go take a look."

"Safer to call the sheriff," Rafe said. "They've got a gun."

"How?"

"Took it off the guard they killed." He moved into the right lane and flipped on the turn signal. We must be getting close.

"With that, they could flag someone down and force them to

drive to Sweetwater. Or anywhere else they wanted to go."

Rafe nodded. "Call Bob Satterfield, please."

I dug out my phone and dialed. "Do you want to explain?" I asked while I listened to the ringing on the other end.

He shook his head. "You do it. You can ask him about your mama and Audrey at the same time."

I could. I settled back into the seat and waited for the phone to be answered while I watched a neat and tidy neighborhood of small, mid-century ranch houses move past outside the car.

"This is Bob," a voice said in my ear, and I straightened.

"Hi, Sheriff. It's Savannah Martin. Collier." After more than two months, you'd think I'd have gotten my new name down, but I've been Savannah Martin for twenty-eight years, and habits are hard to break. It isn't just Tamara Grimaldi who's struggling.

The sheriff's voice got a degree warmer. "Afternoon, darlin'."

"Same to you. How are you?"

"Been better," the sheriff said, while Rafe gave me a sardonic sideways look.

I rolled my eyes. So I've been trained to be polite. Sue me. "Have you seen Mother?"

"Not since that scene in your brother's office on Monday morning. I figure when she's ready, she'll call me."

Maybe so. "What about Audrey?"

"She's holding up," the sheriff said. "Tough situation for her, finding her daughter and losing her best friend all in the same day."

No kidding. "She hasn't spoken to Mother, I assume?"

"Not as I've heard."

"What about Darcy? Have they been in touch?"

"Not yet. But they're getting there. Less baggage between the two of them."

Couldn't argue with that. Darcy's only crime had been being born. She had some resentment toward her biological mother for giving her up for adoption, but I believed she'd be able to get past that, now that she understood the circumstances. But Audrey and my mother had been friends more than half their lives. It was no wonder Mother felt betrayed.

"I need a favor," I said, as Rafe came to a stop outside a tidy little bungalow with yellow shutters.

"I ain't pushing your mother, darlin'. When she's ready to face this, she'll let me know."

"This doesn't have anything to do with Mother," I said. "Denise Seaver escaped from prison this afternoon."

"What the hell?"

That thought had crossed my own mind. "Another inmate went into labor. I think Doctor Seaver probably induced it. While the two of them were on their way to the hospital in a Department of Corrections van, somehow they managed to kill the driver and take off."

"In the van?"

"No." And now that I thought about it, that was strange. They had a vehicle at their disposal. Why not use it? "The cops found the van abandoned a few miles from the prison, with the dead guard inside. People are out combing the hills to see if they've sheltered there. Carmen probably couldn't walk far. But they might have flagged down another car."

"And you think they might be coming here?"

"Denise Seaver still has her house," I said. "It's sitting empty."

"So it is."

"Any chance you could run by once or twice in what's left of today and see if anyone shows up?"

"How come you're the one asking me this, darlin', and not the police? Or that husband of yours?"

"Rafe is sitting next to me," I said. "If it'll make you feel better, he can tell you the same story."

I handed off the phone without waiting for the sheriff's response, and sat there while Rafe confirmed everything I'd said.

"Appreciate it," he said after a minute or so. "Let me know if you see'em. Or if you'd rather deal with the cops, you can call Tammy Grimaldi. You need her number?"

The sheriff must have informed him he had it, because Rafe didn't read it off. "Thanks, Sheriff," he said, and handed me the phone.

I dropped it in my bag. "So this is the place?"

Rafe looked at it and nodded, his jaw tight.

"Have you been here before?"

"Dropped Carmen off once. Didn't go in."

"Does her mother know that you... um..."

"Was sleeping with her daughter? I imagine she mighta guessed."

"I was thinking, does she know that you arrested her daughter?"

Rafe grimaced. "I imagine so. Yeah."

Great. This should be fun. I opened my car door. "What do you want to do? Knock on the door and ask her about the last time she saw her daughter? Or sneak around the house and peer in the windows?"

"Both," Rafe said. "She don't know you. You go to the front door and knock. Pretend to be a reporter or something. You look like you could be on TV."

Awww. "That's so sweet," I said, and felt tears well up in my eyes. "Sorry. Hormones." I flapped a hand in front of my face.

He grinned, and grabbed it to pull toward him so he could kiss the back of my hand. Then he turned it over and kissed the palm, which always makes me a little short of breath.

I closed my hand around the kiss. "I love you."

He smiled. "Love you, too. And while you take your gorgeous self up to the door and keep her there as long as you can, I'll go around the house and see what I can see."

It sounded like a plan. All I had to do now was figure out what to say.

As I swung my legs out and headed up the driveway, I decided that pretending to be a reporter probably wouldn't work. Where was my camera? And my camera man? So maybe I could simply ask her whether she'd seen her daughter lately. Chances were nobody else had been here yet, and if I was the first person to give her the news that Carmen was on the run, that ought to give Rafe enough time to walk the perimeter of the house.

He was already crossing the lawn. I waited on the bottom of the two steps until he'd ducked behind the corner, and then I stepped up in front of the door and pressed the buzzer.

The sound cut through the house like a siren.

I waited, then, when nothing happened, pressed the buzzer again.

Rafe came walking around the corner from the other side of the house. "No answer?"

I shook my head. "I don't think she's here. Anyone in their right mind would answer the door just so whoever is out here wouldn't buzz again. What a horrible noise."

He smiled. "I didn't see nobody inside. Looks like the place is empty."

"Are any of the curtains closed?" Because if so, someone might be in that room.

He shook his head. "I looked in every window. Nothing but empty rooms."

"It's just as well." I started to step off the porch, and took his hand to help me down. Not because I needed it, but because it was nice of him to offer. "If I'd told Mrs. Arroyo that her daughter's escaped, the first thing she'd do, I'm sure, is call her other daughter. And if Carmen's there, she'd be gone before we could get there."

Rafe nodded. "Let's just go take 'em by surprise."

That had a vaguely ominous ring to it, and I told him so as we walked hand in hand down the driveway toward the car.

He chuckled. "I ain't talking about an ambush, darlin'. Besides, in her condition, Carmen prob'ly couldn't run very fast."

Probably not. Whether that condition was pregnant and in labor or just post-birth by the time we caught up with them.

He took the driver's seat again, and I climbed into the passenger side. We drove a couple miles east, closer to the lake. The neighborhood out here was less manicured, probably a bit less affluent—young married couples with kids versus retirees—and the houses were bigger. Rafe checked the address on his phone and pulled up in front of a 1960s split level. The driveway was cracked and the wooden parts of the house could do with a coat of paint. It looked old and sort of tired, even with the colorful big wheel and assorted toys strewn across the grass.

I glanced at him. "Have you met Carmen's sister?"

He shook his head.

"But you know this is her house?"

He nodded.

"Am I still going to be a reporter while you go around back?"

He shook his head. "This time we'll just knock. There are a lot of cars here."

There were. A beige mini-van. A big truck, one I recognized from Sunday. I'd seen it parked outside the women's prison when we arrived. I recognized it from the painted beach scene with the buxom young woman in a bikini on the tailgate.

Finally, there was a shiny, red Mercedes, just a couple years old. I recognized that, too. Last time I'd seen it, Carmen had been behind the wheel.

Rafe lips tightened.

"Carmen's car?"

He nodded.

"You think that means she's here?"

He glanced at the house and shook his head. "She prob'ly signed it over to her mama when she went to prison."

That made sense. However— "Wouldn't they have sold it to get money to pay the defense lawyer?"

"No point in a defense lawyer," Rafe said, his eyes back on the car. "Besides, she had plenty of other money."

"Didn't they—you—freeze her accounts? Ill-gotten gains, and all that?"

"The prosecution offered her a deal if she'd testify against Hector," Rafe said. "She took it, and got off with a lighter sentence. They didn't charge her with any of the murders. Just the financial crimes."

I blinked. "Did she murder someone?"

"Personally?" He shrugged. "Maybe not. But she knew it was going on. Accessory."

Right. I looked back at the house. "So we just walk up to the door and knock?"

"That's the plan. You can stay in the car."

I shook my head. "Absolutely not." If he was going, I was going.

"It ain't gonna be pretty."

I hadn't supposed it would. "Does she know you... um..."

"Arrested her sister?"

"That. But I was thinking more, 'does she know you slept with her sister and may have knocked her up?'" If she hadn't told her mother, she might have told her sister. I had told Dix about Rafe before I'd told anyone else. He and I have always been closer than Catherine and I.

"Guess we'll find out." He opened the car door. I squared my shoulders and did the same.

The walk up to the front door took forever, and if it felt that way to me, I could only imagine how it felt to Rafe. This had to be hard for him. He didn't say much, and I would guess that was in direct proportion to how much he felt. I could see him brace himself before he reached out and knocked on the door.

The woman who opened it was the same one I had seen on

Sunday, visiting Carmen in prison. Mid-thirties, shorter than me by several inches, a bit broader in the beam—or so I'd like to believe. She had straight black hair pulled back in a ponytail, and while I could see a resemblance to Carmen in her features, she wasn't as pretty.

Behind her stood an almost exactly replica, twenty or twenty-five years older. This was how Carmen's sister would look when she got to be my mother's age. A little older, with touches of gray at her temples and wrinkles around her eyes, with traces of Carmen in her features, as well.

Neither of them seemed to even notice me. They were both staring at Rafe, with expressions like Old Nick himself had materialized on the doorstep.

He was the one who broke the silence. "We need to talk."

Carmen's sister's eyes narrowed. "We have nothing to say to you."

She made to slam the door, and couldn't, when Rafe stuck his boot in the gap. I've tried to do that, and it hurts. He didn't flinch. Just pulled out his badge and showed it to them. Without a word. I guess just the reminder that he was law enforcement was supposed to be enough.

Carmen's mother said something in Spanish, and her daughter turned to answer her. Before she could, Rafe had rattled off a sentence or two. I didn't catch any but the most common words. This form of street-Spanish was far removed from the upscale Castilian I'd been taught.

Ten years of infiltrating a South American organized crime syndicate had done wonders for his language education.

Mrs. Arroyo said something back, and then the two women got into it. The back-and-forth was so rapid I didn't understand a word. "What's going on?" I asked Rafe.

He spared me a quick look. "Mrs. Arroyo wants to hear what I have to say. Bianca's angry."

"And Mrs. Arroyo isn't?"

He shrugged.

This exchange had put me on their radar, possibly for the first time, and now they both looked at me. "Who are you?" Bianca demanded.

I lifted my hand. The one with the wedding band on it. And no, I didn't raise my middle finger.

Bianca looked at it. The ring, not the finger. Then she turned back to Rafe and let loose with another irate spate of Spanish. It ended with a wad of spit. Luckily, she spat on the ground in front of his feet, and not directly at him. Even so, her mother expostulated, and the two of them went off on another back-and-forth.

"What did she say?" I asked Rafe.

"I had her sister arrested. I seduced her. I played with her affections. I betrayed her. Take your pick."

His face was impassive and his voice even, but he was just a shade or so paler than usual.

"This is bullshit," I said bluntly, and managed to surprise him. For a second, his eyes widened and his mouth dropped open. "Sorry," I added, "but it is. Let me talk to them."

The corners of his mouth twitched, as he took a step out of the way. "Be my guest."

"Thank you." I moved closer to him, in front of the door, and raised my voice. "Listen. Listen!"

They both shut up and turned to me.

"My name is Savannah," I said. "Rafe and I got married two months ago."

They didn't say anything, just looked from me to him and back.

"He wasn't married when he knew Carmen. But he had to arrest her. It's his job. And she was breaking the law."

Bianca's face darkened, and her fists clenched. Her mother didn't speak, though.

"That doesn't matter right now. Your sister—" I moved my

attention to Mrs. Arroyo, "your daughter, is missing. She went into labor this morning, and—"

"The baby?" Mrs. Arroyo said, her Spanish more deeply accented than her daughter's. Than either of her daughters'. I had spoken to Carmen back in December, and she hadn't had any more of an accent than I did. "Carmen's baby is coming?"

"They left the prison to go to the hospital. They never got there. They stabbed the guard who was driving them, and left."

Both Bianca and her mother turned pale, and Mrs. Arroyo crossed herself.

"We need to come in and search your house," Rafe said.

They looked at each other, and Bianca started to look mutinous. Her mother, however, said something, and she took a step back.

Rafe turned to me. "Wait—"

...*here?* I shook my head. "Wither thou goest." And not only because we were married, but because I wasn't about to have him walk inside with the two of them, and perhaps with Bianca's husband, while I was locked out. They could kill him in there, while I stood on the step like a dutiful wife and waited.

"I'd feel safer if you stayed outside."

"I'd feel safer if I came in," I said, and that was the end of it. He shrugged and crossed the threshold, and didn't say anything when I slipped in after him.

The front door opened into a foyer, with stairs on the left going up and down to the other levels. Rafe headed down the stairs, hand on his gun, and I followed. After a quick glance at each other, so did Bianca and her mother.

The back of my neck felt creepy all the way down the stairs.

At the bottom, there was just one big room. It looked like a combination TV room and play room, with a big screen TV on one wall, above the gaping maw of a fireplace, and with sofas and recliners arranged in a semi circle for viewing. Behind the sofas was an open area where two children played. A boy and a girl, maybe two and four years old, with their mother's straight, black hair and broad, brown face.

They gaped at Rafe when he came into sight, but they didn't seem nervous. After a moment, they just went back to playing.

We went back upstairs, with Mrs. Arroyo first this time. She had been whispering worriedly to Bianca, but I didn't get the feeling that we were in any immediate danger. And if Carmen was here, they made no move to get to her and get her away from us.

The first floor boasted the usual common areas: living room, dining room, and kitchen, plus a bathroom for guests. It was all pretty open concept, with no sign of life other than the four of us.

"Bedrooms?" Rafe gestured with his thumb up the second staircase.

Bianca nodded. "My husband's up there. He works nights." She sounded hostile, but at least she was somewhat polite. Or if nothing else, she was answering questions.

Rafe didn't answer, just took the stairs two at a time. They ended in a little hallway with two doors on either side. The first on the left opened into a bathroom. It was shabby, but clean. Across the hall from it was the open door to what might have been the smallest bedroom I'd ever seen. Hardly bigger than the bathroom, it only had room for a big crib and a chest of drawers. The bedding was blue, and someone had painted a race car above the crib. Perhaps the same person who had painted the beach scene on the back of the truck.

The second bedroom was hardly bigger, and sported a pink bedspread with a Disney princess on it. Bianca's daughter would have gotten along well with my brother Dix's kids. They like Disney princesses, too.

The last door was closed.

"My husband—" Bianca began when Rafe reached for the knob.

He gave her a look over his shoulder, but it didn't stop his momentum. He turned the knob quietly, though. I felt my heart beat faster. If Carmen was anywhere in the house, this would be where she was.

Although to be honest, I didn't expect we'd find her. A woman in the middle of giving birth doesn't tend to be quiet, nor does the baby once it's born. This house was too quiet to have two escaped convicts in it.

Rafe slipped through the door. The entire second floor was carpeted, just like the basement, so he moved silently. I crept up to the door and peered in. The master bedroom was burgundy, with what might have been the ugliest bedspread I had ever seen, and what looked like a dozen pillows strewn across the floor. I wondered if the kids enjoyed having pillow fights with those?

But no, if Daddy worked nights and slept during the day, they probably weren't allowed upstairs. That's why their playroom was in the basement.

Rafe moved silently across the floor to the bed, stepping over and around pillows on the way. He stopped at the edge of the bed and peered down. After a few seconds he straightened, hands on his hips, and turned in a slow circle, surveying the room. There must have been a closet over on the other wall, because he headed in that direction. After a moment, I heard the sound of doors opening. But Carmen must not have been there, because another few seconds later, he came back.

"Thank you," he told Bianca after closing the door behind him.

She wasn't about to tell him he was welcome, I guess, because she just nodded.

"Let's go downstairs and talk," I said. Carmen wasn't here, but it was just possible they might think of somewhere else she could be. And if we played up the danger she might be in, giving birth in some hole somewhere without the necessary medications or equipment, maybe they'd share what they knew with us.

Rafe gave me a look. Bianca gave her mother one. Then we all traipsed downstairs and into the dining room, where we took seats around the table.

"Here's the thing," I said when we were all seated. Properly, I guess this was Rafe's deal, but I didn't think they'd be too willing to help him. Not only was he the law, but he was the man who had arrested Carmen. They might respond better to me. "Your daughter—your sister—is out there somewhere. She's nine months pregnant, and as far as we know, she's in labor. We have to find her. Not just because she escaped from prison, but because she needs to be in a hospital, with doctors and equipment and drugs. Her life, and her baby's life, could be in danger otherwise."

Mrs. Arroyo said something to Bianca, and Bianca answered.

"We've already been to your house," I told Carmen's mother, "and we didn't see her. We're going to check her old townhouse out by the lake. Someone's checking the area around where the van was left, in case they just walked off. But after that, we don't know where else to go."

We still had Denise Seaver's house in reserve, and maybe St. Jerome's Hospital, although I didn't think she'd go there. But I didn't want them to know that Carmen had a trained OB/GYN with her. That might make them think there was nothing to worry about.

"Can you think of anywhere Carmen might go? Any friends she has, who might be willing to help her? Other family?"

They looked at one another. Like one, they shook their heads.

I didn't bother to sigh. It was what I had expected, but I had hoped for better.

We got to our feet.

"If she calls here," Rafe said, and dug out a business card from his wallet, "call me."

He put it on the table. They both nodded, but I think we both knew they wouldn't. If Carmen called, they'd tell her we'd been here, and then they'd find out where she was and go help.

Someone would have to stick around and follow them if they left, I guess.

Rafe caught my eye, and I knew he was thinking the same thing.

We headed for the door. It wasn't until we were outside and Bianca had her hand on the door, ready to close it, that Rafe broached the subject I'd been waiting for. "Did Carmen tell you who's the father of her baby?"

Bianca looked at him. For longer than was strictly necessary. Her eyes were flat and black, giving nothing away, and her face was impassive. Just when I wanted to grab her and shake an answer out of her, she shook her head. "No. She never said."

She closed the door with a thud that sounded very final.

Twelve

We walked back to the car in silence. Rafe was already digging for his phone, but he didn't dial until we were both inside the car with the doors closed. The first words out of his mouth told me everything I needed to know about who he was calling.

"I need the boys. Tell'em it's a surveillance assignment."

Wendell—for it was him on the other end of the line—must have asked for clarification, because Rafe explained where we were and what we were doing. "Tell them to bring their own rides. One of'em follows Mrs. Arroyo, one of'em follows Bianca's husband when he leaves, and one of'em stays with Bianca. They can decide who wants to do what, but I wanna know where everybody goes and what they're doing there."

Wendell must have approved of the plan, because the next thing Rafe said, was, "I'm gonna go check the townhouse out by the lake where she used to live."

That must have passed muster with Wendell, because they hung up. Rafe started the car.

"Don't you think we should wait until the boys get here?" I asked.

He glanced at me. "Not right outside the house. We don't want'em to think the boys have anything to do with us. We'll park around the corner."

"But it'll take your boys the best part of twenty minutes to get here. And we only have one car right now. If Mrs. Arroyo thinks were gone, and she leaves, we'll have to follow her. And as soon as we're out of sight, Bianca might leave too, and we'll never know it. If we can keep them together and in one place until reinforcements arrive, wouldn't that be preferable?

Rafe turned the car back off. "Maybe we should just sit here awhile."

Maybe we should. We had plenty to talk about, after all, and it wasn't very likely that Carmen was in the townhouse by the lake, if someone else lived there now.

"They aren't here," I said.

Rafe shook his head. "No sign of 'em. And the mother and Bianca were angry, but not afraid. Not of us."

"Afraid for Carmen, though."

He nodded. "Seemed that way."

"Did you get the impression that they knew where she might be?" He's a much better liar than I am, and more adept at picking up on other people's lies, too. And besides, he spoke their language.

He shrugged. "Hard to say. I didn't get a buzz, but by now, they mighta thought of something."

They might have.

"Do you think Bianca told the truth about Carmen's baby daddy?"

"No," Rafe said. "I think Carmen talked to her. But there ain't nothing I can do about it. Not like I can beat the truth outta her."

No. And anyway, it might not be the truth. "I guess it's too early for the DNA results?"

He nodded. "Tomorrow or Friday."

"I guess we'll just sit here and wait, then."

Which we did, for a few minutes. Rafe was watching the house, and I was staring straight ahead, out the window.

It wasn't all that long before I couldn't stand the silence anymore. What came out of my mouth wasn't particularly *a propos* to the situation, however.

Or maybe it was.

"Were you in love with her?"

He took his eyes off the house to look at me. Unblinkingly. After a few seconds, the look became a stare. I squirmed. "I have a right to know, don't you think?"

He took his eyes off me and went back to looking at the house. "This is about Carmen? You're asking if I was in love with Carmen when I—maybe—knocked her up?"

I nodded.

"No."

I waited. When he didn't say anything else, I said, "You slept with her. You must have felt something for her."

"It wasn't love. Mostly I was feeling that if I made a wrong move, she'd tell Hector I wasn't Jorge Pena, and then I'd be dead."

That was understandable. "She's just so pretty. Even nine months pregnant, she was glowing. And I feel fat and blotchy and like I don't have any ankles."

His mouth twitched, and he took his attention off the house to focus on me. His hands came up to cup my cheeks. "I've wanted you since I was seventeen. Once I got you—even if I wasn't sure I totally had you—I wasn't gonna want nobody else."

That was so sweet. My eyes filled with tears and my lips trembled. "Sorry," I managed. "Hormones."

He chuckled. "No problem. And you're not fat and blotchy with no ankles. Your ankles are fine. And you're gorgeous. You're having my baby."

One hand dropped to my stomach. The other moved around my neck, into my hair. He pulled me toward him as he leaned in. My eyes fluttered closed as his lips descended.

The moment was interrupted by the tooting of a horn and a loud voice. "Get a room!"

I felt Rafe's lips curve before he pulled away. Out of the corner of my eye, I saw a big pickup zoom off down the street. The Virgin Mary was glued to the rear window. José must have flown to get here so fast. And had let us know he had arrived without drawing attention to the fact that we knew each other.

Rafe grinned and put the car in gear. "Let's get outta here."

I settled back in the seat and crossed my ankles primly. "Let's."

We passed Clayton's Camaro and Jamal's old Buick on the way out of the neighborhood. Since we were out of sight of the Arroyo residence, Rafe slowed down to greet them both. "Wendell tell you what to do?"

They both nodded, heads hanging out of their respective windows. "José's parking down the street from the house," Jamal said. He tended to be the spokesperson for the group when they were together. "Clay and I are gonna stay up here. He's got the husband, I've got Mrs. Arroyo. If either of'em leaves the house, José'll call."

They both brandished their phones.

"And José's staying in sight of the house unless Bianca leaves?"

Jamal nodded. "That's the plan. If somebody shows up, we'll call you. How long do you want us on the job?"

"Until we find Carmen," Rafe said. "You stay with'em until I tell you otherwise."

They both nodded.

"Call me if anything happens."

"Will do." They both retracted their heads back into their shells, and drove off. Clayton continued down the street, while Jamal made a U-turn at Bianca's street and parked just beyond. As we prepared to leave the subdivision, I saw the Camaro appear in the rearview and come to a stop on the other side of the intersection.

"You've trained them well," I told Rafe.

"They're good kids. And they'll make good agents."

He turned the wheel, and we rolled out of sight.

Carmen's townhouse on the lake was in a subdivision called—appropriately enough—Lakeview. I could see glimpses of water between the trees in the backyard when we drove in. The house itself was on the end of a row of five, and there was a white SUV parked in the driveway.

Rafe pulled the Volvo to a stop across the driveway, parking the SUV in. "Just in case they're here and think they'll make a break for it."

I nodded.

The SUV's doors were locked, so he shined his flashlight app through the windows. "No sign of blood."

I shifted from foot to foot. "Would there be blood?"

He glanced at me. "No idea. I figured there would, but maybe not."

Maybe not. I didn't know, either. "If her water breaks, there's fluid. That can happen before or after labor starts, though."

"No sign of liquids," Rafe said, "except for a Starbucks cup in the cup holder."

"I don't think that would be it."

He shook his head and turned the flashlight off. "Let's go knock on the door."

There was a doorbell, actually, and a few moments after ringing it, we heard steps inside. Then came the rattling of the locks and security chain. A young woman in a skirt and blouse and bare feet peered out. Her eyes widened at the sight of Rafe, before she noticed me. "Yes? Can I help you?"

Rafe pulled out his badge and introduced himself. "How long have you lived here?"

She glanced from him to me again. "Six months?"

"Do you know the woman who lived here before you?"

She shook her head. "I never met her. The place was for sale and I bought it."

She sounded sincere. She also didn't sound like she was harboring two fugitives inside her tidy townhouse.

Rafe pulled up a photo on his phone. "This is what she looks like. If she shows up, would you call 911 and let them know?"

The girl's eyes—hazel—widened, and the door closed a few inches. "911?"

I smiled reassuringly. "She escaped from prison this afternoon. And she's pregnant and possibly in labor. We're trying to find her before she does harm to herself or the baby."

Strangely, my reassurance didn't seem to help at all. "Sure," the young lady said through the now two-inch gap between the door and the door frame. "If I see her, I'll call it in."

"Thank you," I managed, before the door shut entirely. The rattling of locks and chains went on for a while. Maybe her hands were shaking.

I turned to Rafe. "Do you think they're here?"

He shook his head. "She didn't seem worried until I mentioned 911. She just don't wanna get mixed up in anything."

"So what do we do now?"

"Not sure," Rafe admitted, as we walked slowly back to the car. "Maybe we shoulda stopped at the *Havana* on the way past. Maybe they went there."

Maybe. Although it didn't seem like a particularly comfortable place to give birth. I'd prefer somewhere with some furniture, if it were me. A bed, or at least a sofa or a fluffy carpet. Although I guess beggars can't be choosers.

He opened the car door for me and I slid in. No sooner had my butt hit the seat, than my phone rang. I dug it out of my bag while Rafe walked around the car and got behind the wheel. "It's the sheriff."

"Answer it."

I pushed the appropriate button. "Hi, Sheriff."

"Savannah." I had put the phone on speaker so we could both hear what he had to say, and his voice sounded a little hollow. "I'm here at the Seaver place. It's empty."

That explained the hollow sound.

"No sign that anyone's been there?"

"Not since you and your brother and sister broke in three days ago," Sheriff Satterfield said.

I had my mouth open to tell him that Catherine hadn't been part of the expedition when I remembered that I had two sisters now. And Darcy had definitely been there.

"Can you spare someone to sit there for the rest of the day?" Rafe asked. "Just in case they haven't gotten there yet?"

"Sorry," the sheriff told him. "We don't have the manpower to put someone on guard duty like that. But I can have someone drive by every hour or two for the rest of the day. And night."

Rafe made a face, but it didn't affect his voice. "Appreciate it. We'll keep on looking up here. I'll let you know if we find'em."

"I'll do the same," the sheriff said, and hung up. I dropped the phone back in my bag and buckled up.

"I guess they're not going to Sweetwater."

Rafe shook his head. His hands clenched into fists, and I reached out and put my hand on his arm. The muscles were hard as granite. "We'll find them. The baby will be OK."

He gave me a sideways glance, but didn't say anything. The look said plenty, though. *You can't know that.*

And I couldn't. But it seemed better to be optimistic than the opposite. I cast about for something to say that might distract him. "When you and Carmen did your thing..."

He arched a brow. "Thing?"

"Horizontal mambo."

The other brow followed.

"Was it just once?"

"No," Rafe said.

No. "You obviously knew where the townhouse was, so at

least once must have been here."

He shrugged, but I thought I saw a faint smirk.

I swatted his arm. "I'm not asking because I want to imagine you making love to someone else." I had imagined that plenty, and my imagination didn't need any more fodder.

"I didn't."

"Didn't what?"

"Make love to her. It was sex. Nothing more."

"Fine." But something inside me unknotted a little. "To continue. Did you ever make... have sex anywhere but here?"

"The nightclub," Rafe said.

I winced. "I didn't need to know that."

"You asked."

"Anywhere else? Where were you living while you were pretending to be Jorge?"

"Motel," Rafe said. "Jorge wasn't local."

"She wouldn't have gone there, then. Anywhere else? You didn't take her to the duplex, did you?"

He shook his head. "Never. And anyway, it isn't habitable anymore. It blew up this weekend, remember?"

I remembered. "She wouldn't have known that, though. Not until she got there."

"She wouldn't know where to go," Rafe said. "I never took her there."

"Then I don't know where else to go. Denise Seaver worked at St. Jerome's, but I don't think she would have gone there. They all know what happened to her. If she suddenly showed up, I think someone would call the police."

Rafe nodded. "Maybe one of the boys'll get lucky."

Maybe. Although I hadn't gotten the impression that either Bianca or her mother knew where Carmen was. Then again, a phone call from Carmen could easily change that.

"So what do we do now?"

He leaned back against the seat with a sigh. "Dunno."

We sat in silence a moment or two.

"No point in going to Sweetwater, I guess?"

"Not unless the sheriff calls."

"Would you like me to contact Tamara Grimaldi? Maybe she has heard something new."

That was if she even knew what was going on, of course. She was busy with Devon's shooting, so no one may have informed her.

"If I wanna talk to Tammy," Rafe said, "I can call her myself."

"Grumpy."

He rolled his head on the seat to look at me. One eyebrow arched.

"Maybe, if we don't have anywhere else to go right now—if you can't think of anywhere else where Carmen and Denise Seaver might be—we could call Grimaldi and arrange to drop off the paint scraper?"

He didn't answer, and I added, "I realize that finding Carmen is more important. But we can't drive around expecting her to be walking down the sidewalk somewhere. She won't be."

He sighed. "Fine. Call Tammy. Maybe you're right. Maybe she's heard something."

I was already dialing. A few seconds later, Tamara Grimaldi was on the line. "Ms.... Savannah."

"Detective," I said. "Has anyone told you that Denise Seaver and Carmen Arroyo escaped custody?"

Her voice went directly to extra-grim. "Yes."

"We've been checking out the places we thought they might be. Mrs. Arroyo's house, Carmen's sister's house, the last place she lived. We called Sheriff Satterfield in Sweetwater, and he went by Denise Seaver's house. We didn't find them anywhere."

"We?" Grimaldi said.

"Rafe and I."

"Your husband's there?" She didn't wait for an answer. "Put

him on."

I made a face, but handed the phone over. "She wants to talk to you."

Rafe took it, his face impassive, and put it to his ear. "Yeah."

Grimaldi quacked.

"No," Rafe said.

Grimaldi quacked again.

"Who the hell knows?"

Grimaldi quacked some more.

"No idea. You have anything to do with this case?"

They continued to talk. Since I could only hear Rafe's side of the conversation, it was kind of boring. I gathered that Grimaldi did have something to do with the case, though—she had been involved in both arrests, so it made sense that she'd be kept abreast of things—and there was nothing new.

When it sounded like they were winding down, I said, "Don't forget to ask her about the paint scraper."

He did, and listened to the answer. "She'll meet us for dinner," he said when they'd disconnected and he was handing the phone back to me. "The FinBar in forty-five minutes."

Was it that time already?

I looked at the phone, and yes, it was. Or would be by the time we got to the FinBar. At rush hour, it would take us every minute of that forty-five minutes to get back to our own neighborhood.

"No news on Carmen and Denise Seaver?"

He shook his head and turned the key in the ignition.

"Any news on Devon's murder?"

"I didn't ask." He gave me a quick glance. "Sorry."

"No problem. I know finding Carmen's more important. And I'll be able to ask her when we get there."

Rafe nodded and put the car in gear. We rolled away from Carmen's townhouse on the lake and headed back toward town.

Thirteen

We didn't speak much on the drive. Nobody called, and there just didn't seem like there was much to say. I didn't know how to make him feel better. His mind was fully occupied with Carmen—or more likely with Carmen's baby, and its chances of survival out there in the wild, in the company of two criminals who had just escaped from prison.

I wanted to help. I really did. I just didn't know how. I couldn't think of anywhere else they might have gone. And while the fact that Denise Seaver was an OB/GYN, was in Carmen's favor, it was pretty well canceled out by the fact that Denise Seaver's history with pregnant women and children wasn't precisely encouraging. It was difficult to find anything positive to say.

So we sat in silence while Rafe battled his way back to town, through rush hour traffic and his no doubt dark thoughts. I concentrated on my own, which weren't any better.

Detective Grimaldi's unmarked sedan was parked in the lot when we got there, easily identified by the government plates. I got out of the Volvo and opened the door to the back seat.

"Leave it until we're done," Rafe said as I reached for the curtain-wrapped bundle lying there. It sounded a little impatient, and when I looked up at him, he added, "The less you handle it, the better. You don't wanna smudge the prints."

No, I didn't. I closed the door again and we headed inside.

Grimaldi had snagged a table in the back of the restaurant, facing the door. That would leave Rafe with his back to the room, and I knew it wouldn't make him happy. They both liked to sit with their backs to the wall, where no one could sneak up on them. Every time we went somewhere together, it was a battle between the two of them as to who would get the preferred seat.

This time, however, Grimaldi took in Rafe's expression as we walked toward her, and got up. "You take this side. I'll sit with your wife."

Rafe's eyebrow arched, but he didn't say anything, just slid into the booth with his back to the wall and did an overview of the room. Meanwhile, Grimaldi waited for me to scoot in first, before she slipped in beside me.

"You look like hell," she told him bluntly.

He nodded. There was no point in arguing the fact. I mean, he did.

Oh, he's always good looking. Tall, strong, muscular. Handsome face, great body, power in motion. Several women had turned to look at him as we walked through the restaurant. But for us who knew him, the strain was obvious. The set of his mouth was tight and the look in his eyes grim. He looked like Atlas, forced to carry the heavens on his shoulders.

He probably felt that way, too.

"Any news?" I asked, as the waitress approached the table. "I'll have sweet tea, please."

"Same," Rafe said.

Both Grimaldi and I blinked. Usually he has a beer with his burger. I guess maybe he thought he couldn't risk that today.

Grimaldi already had her drink, and the waitress took herself off, telling us she'd be right back to take our orders.

"On the escape?" Grimaldi said when she was out of hearing. "Nothing I've heard."

"What about Devon's murder? Did you talk to Brittany again

after I left?"

"For a minute. She has no idea why her boyfriend would have been at your office last night. She didn't send him there. She also doesn't know why he would have been at Magnolia Houston's house in Goodlettsville. She says it's possible they may know each other, since they're both involved in the music business, but that Devon never mentioned Magnolia to her. She doesn't own a gun, and he didn't either. She didn't leave her apartment after she came home last night, and she says she can prove it. There's an alarm system tied to the front door, and if the front door was opened, it would be on the log. She even called the security company and requested the log so I could look."

"And did you?"

"They're sending it to me. But if she says it'll prove she didn't go out, I'm sure it'll do just that. No need to mention it to me otherwise."

"So Brittany couldn't have shot him."

"That's the way it looks," Grimaldi nodded.

We sat in silence a moment. The waitress made her way back with the two glasses of iced tea. She put them down and pulled out her notepad. "Are you ready to order?"

We were. Rafe had his usual burger and fries. So did Grimaldi. I opted for a salad, since I was still a bit burgered out from all the red meat yesterday. The waitress left again.

"So if he wasn't at the office to pick something up for Brittany, and she doesn't know why he was there, what was he doing?"

Grimaldi shook her head. "It seems only he would be able to answer that. And maybe you."

"We?" I glanced at Rafe. He wasn't looking at me, just kept staring at the spoon he was turning between his fingers. "We have no idea."

"Well, where was he when you saw him? What was he doing?" She looked from me to Rafe. Rafe had seen him first, so I gestured to him. It took a second for him to answer.

"Scrambling through the lobby on his way to the door."

"Could you tell where he'd come from?"

Rafe shook his head.

"Brittany's desk is there," I said, "with the petty cash box and the check book and everything else. But Rafe looked at the desk after Devon left, and as far as we could tell, it was all there."

Rafe nodded.

"Is your office still on the other side of the lobby?" Grimaldi asked. "Any chance he'd been in there?"

"I checked it," I said. "I didn't notice anything out of place. But he didn't have much time to look around. I think he was alone for less than a minute before Rafe went after him."

Grimaldi nodded.

"What makes you think he'd be interested in my desk?"

"You said you saw his car in Goodlettsville yesterday. Or at least a car that looked like his."

I had.

"And he saw you, and ran away from you."

He had.

"Do you think he recognized you?"

"He might have." I hadn't recognized him—if indeed it had been Devon—but that didn't mean anything. He could still have recognized me. And might have decided to take a look at my desk, just in case there was something there to tell him what, if anything, I knew.

"I don't suppose there's any way to know for sure?" I asked.

"I can fingerprint your office tomorrow morning," Grimaldi said. "Unless he was wearing gloves, he would have left prints."

"I didn't see any gloves." I glanced at Rafe, who shook his head.

"Then I'll put that on the schedule. Has anyone used your office since last night?"

"I went in there this morning, just for a few seconds. Then

Tim showed up and told me Brittany wouldn't be in, so I had to sit at the front desk until lunch. And then I left to meet you. So no, nobody should have been in there." Unless someone else had taken it upon themselves to search my office. If so, Grimaldi would find their fingerprints, too.

She nodded. "Meet me there at nine tomorrow."

I said I would. By then, hopefully Carmen and Denise Seaver would be back in DOC custody, and Rafe and I wouldn't be driving all over creation looking for them.

His phone chirped, and he pulled it out of his pocket to look at the message. "Bianca's husband's on the move."

"Probably heading in to work," I said. "Bianca said he worked nights."

Rafe nodded, without looking at me. "Clayton will let us know if he doesn't."

"Of course."

We lapsed back into silence.

All in all it was a weird meal. Grimaldi and I tried to keep things going, but Rafe had very little to contribute. And while he's never really the life of the party, the fact that he wasn't even following the conversation was unusual.

Of course I knew why. But that didn't make it any easier to deal with. In fact, it made me worry a bit. I could usually count on him to give me his full, undivided attention when we were together. Before, even when he'd been in the midst of work-related stress and issues preying on his mind, I'd never felt like an afterthought. And again, while I understood why, it was still a strange feeling.

It also made me wonder again what would happen if Carmen's baby turned out to be Rafe's baby, and he expected me to take it in and raise it with my own. I had considered what might happen from my perspective. The fear that I wouldn't be able to love it as much as the child I'd carried and given birth to, and the fear that I'd favor one over the other; either my own, or

Carmen's, out of guilt.

I hadn't considered how Rafe would feel. They would both be his children, along with David. I'd never worried that he'd love David more—or less—than a child I gave him, although David might well worry about it. Then again, Rafe was just an exciting sort of uncle/big brother/recently discovered dad distraction to David. His real mother and father were Ginny and Sam. Neither of them had brought him into the world, but until a year ago, they'd been the only parents he'd known. He'd be sad if Rafe disappeared—he'd worried enough about him to run away from camp and get himself in trouble when Rafe was abducted over the summer—but I didn't think it could compare to how he'd feel if something happened to Sam.

The thoughts were all pretty unpleasant. Thankfully, my phone rang and tore me out of my reverie halfway through the meal. I fished it out of my bag. They were both looking at me: two pairs of dark brown eyes surrounded by black lashes.

"It's Dix," I said, after checking the display. Rafe went back to eating, no longer interested, while Grimaldi's face stayed impassive. "Do you mind?"

She shook her head. I answered the phone. "Dix."

"Savannah. I'm just calling to update you. Mother is mostly sober, but still angry."

"I figured," I said. "I spoke to the sheriff earlier this afternoon. He said she hadn't tried to contact him, or as far as he knew, Audrey."

"What did you call the sheriff for?"

Ungrammatical, but fair. "Denise Seaver escaped from prison," I said. "We thought she might be on her way down there, so Rafe had me call the sheriff to put him on alert."

"Why is Collier involved? He had nothing to do with Denise Seaver's case."

Other than the fact that Rafe's son was one of the babies Denise Seaver had sold to a waiting couple, Dix was right. Rafe had only been involved in the adoption case—which also included Dix's wife Sheila's murder—because of me.

"Another woman also escaped," I said. "Her name is Carmen Arroyo, and she's someone who was part of Rafe's case back in December."

If we had been alone—or rather, if I had been alone with Dix on the other end of the phone—I might have given him the rest of the details. As it was, I didn't. "The sheriff said he'd drive past her place a few more times tonight. But if you happen to see her—or a very pretty Hispanic woman with a very large stomach—let him know."

There was a second's pause. "Very large stomach?"

"She's pregnant. Almost nine months. They were on their way to the hospital when the van either broke down or they figured out a way to get the guard to stop it." My money was on option two, but I was sure the police would check both scenarios. "They stabbed him and ran." Or in Carmen's case, waddled. "Now they're out there somewhere, either on foot or in another car."

"Collier can't be happy about that."

I glanced at him across the table. "He isn't."

Rafe arched a brow but didn't speak.

"Tamara Grimaldi is sitting next to me," I added. "Would you like to say hi?"

Grimaldi gave me a look. "Sure," Dix said, sounding happy.

I handed over the phone and picked up my fork, hoping for something good.

I didn't get it.

"Yes," Grimaldi said. She didn't sound happy. She didn't sound anything. Except maybe a little annoyed. With me, I figured. "Yes. Having dinner. Yes. Fine. OK."

She handed the phone back. "Don't do that again."

"Do what?" I dropped it in my purse.

"If I want to talk to your brother, I'll call him myself."

Uh-oh. "Trouble in paradise?"

Grimaldi gave me another look. "Your brother and I are friends. Nothing more. Now stop it."

Fine. I pouted and went back to eating.

Nothing exciting happened during the rest of the meal. Rafe's phone dinged, with the message from Clayton that Mr. Bianca had arrived safely at work, at the Mountain Dew manufacturing plant on Murfreesboro Road. In case you aren't aware, Mountain Dew originated in Tennessee: the original recipe was created by beverage bottlers Moses and Ally Hartman in 1940. The Tip Corporation bought the rights in 1958, and Pepsi-Cola acquired them from Tip in 1964. We still make Mountain Dew right here in town.

At any rate, Carmen's brother-in-law went inside the plant, and Clayton wanted to know whether he should stay in the parking lot and wait, or go back to the house in Antioch.

"It might not be a bad idea to send him back there," I said, without being asked. "What if Bianca and her mother both leave the house, and Jamal and José follow them? Then the house will be empty, with no one keeping watch."

Grimaldi nodded. "Ms. Arroyo and Doctor Seaver might show up as soon as the house is empty. Chances are that Mr.... um... Bianca's husband is at work and will stay there. He's no kin to Ms. Arroyo. If he's law abiding, he'll want her away from his children. If anyone's likely to help her, it'll be either her sister or her mother."

"I agree with that," I said. "It was the mother and sister who were there on Sunday, visiting. Not the brother-in-law."

Rafe looked from me to Grimaldi and back. After a second, he nodded.

We finished the meal mostly in silence. Grimaldi was irritated with me because I'd forced her to talk to Dix—what was going on there?—while Rafe just couldn't seem to keep his mind on anything that was going on. It was easier just to be quiet and eat.

We walked out together, and I took the curtain-wrapped paint scraper from the back seat of the Volvo and handed it to Grimaldi. I also showed her the photograph I had taken, of the footprint on the stairs. She wanted a copy of that, as well, so I forwarded it to her phone.

"I'll get this checked tonight." She lifted the bundle. "I'll let you know what I find out tomorrow morning."

"I'll be there," I said. It would take effort to drag myself out of bed early enough to be at the office by nine, but I'd manage. And anyway, there was a good chance Brittany wouldn't make it in to work again. I'd probably have to handle the front desk tomorrow, too.

Grimaldi said she'd see me then. She got into her car and took off. We got into ours and did the same.

"Where are we going?" I asked Rafe, after a few minutes' silence.

He glanced over. "I'm gonna take you home. Then I'll probably go back down to Antioch and check in with the boys."

"I can come with you," I said.

He shook his head. "No offense, darlin'. I know you wanna help. But there's nothing nobody can do right now. We're all just sitting around, waiting for something to happen. And while we do that, I'm driving you crazy."

It seemed to me it was the other way around, if he wanted to take me home and leave me there. I must be the one driving him crazy if he wanted to get rid of me.

As he often did, he read my mind. "I gotta find that baby. I gotta find Carmen and Doc Seaver and get 'em behind bars again, too. But that baby's out there with two women who wouldn't think twice about dropping it off a bridge if it was slowing 'em down."

I put a hand on my stomach. "I'm sure Carmen wouldn't do that."

Rafe arched a brow.

"I realize I don't know her..."

"No, you don't."

"But she's been carrying that baby around inside her for nine months. If she didn't want it, why not just have an abortion?" A thought struck me, and I added, "Don't women in prison have the right to have abortions?"

"They do. But when you're in prison, things don't always work the way they should."

Imagine that. And since he'd spent a couple of years behind bars himself, I figured he knew what he was talking about. "So she might have wanted an abortion but not gotten one?"

"She might could. Somebody coulda blocked it. They're not supposed to, but things happen. Or her mama coulda refused to pay for it. Somebody woulda had to. The prison ain't gonna pay. Not for something like that. And if her mama said no..."

I nodded. There'd be nothing Carmen could do about it.

"I gotta find that baby," Rafe said again. "Before something can happen to it. I don't trust either of'em with it. And if I'm too late..."

I winced. He glanced at me. "I don't want you there if I am."

Finding a dead baby that might be his own would be worse for him than for me. But I understood that he was trying to protect me. I nodded. "I'll go home. You'll call me if you hear anything, right?"

"Sure," Rafe said, and that's when the phone rang.

He fished it out if his pocket and glanced at the display. And put it to his ear. "Collier."

Someone on the other end spoke for a second.

"Where?" Rafe said.

The person on the other end spoke again.

"I'm on my way." He dropped the phone to make a highly illegal U-turn before stepping on the gas. The car jumped forward with a squeal.

I braced myself with both hands on the dashboard. "What happened?"

He shot me a look. "They found her."

Fourteen

'Her' turned out to be Carmen. It also turned out that she and Denise Seaver hadn't flagged down a car after they escaped from the DOC van. They'd walked off the road and into the woods instead.

Rafe didn't tell me any of that. I let him concentrate on driving, while I concentrated on hanging on. We got to mile marker 22 in record time. He'd probably managed to shave seven or eight minutes off the time it had taken me to get there. And we pulled off the road with a squeal of tires that kicked gravel in a thirty yard radius, and left the air smelling like burning rubber.

No one was around. The van was gone, and so was the crime scene crew and the young cop who had been directing traffic. Rafe turned off the car and got out. "C'mon. We gotta go on foot from here."

I made my own way out of the car. "Is that what Carmen and Doctor Seaver did?"

He nodded. "The cops tracked them up the hill. They said it ain't far. Half a mile, no more."

I could manage half a mile, even in heels. But my determination to start considering sensible shoes grew stronger.

We hopped the guard rail—or Rafe hopped, while I clambered, with a little help—and then we started off into the trees.

It felt a lot longer than half a mile. It could be the gathering dark. The sun hadn't set yet, but it was behind the hill, and I couldn't really see where I was going. The ground was uneven, and I kept running into bushes and trees.

Rafe had no such problems. He could see in the dark, and was wearing boots with heavy soles. Even so, he managed to walk quietly. I was the one stumbling through the trees like a heroine in a horror movie. I'm sure I frustrated Rafe. I'm sure he wanted to get to where we were going as quickly as possible, and I was slowing him down. After a couple of minutes, he reached back and took my hand. "You doing all right?"

"I'm fine," I panted. "But maybe I shouldn't have come."

"I didn't give you a chance to say no. And I want you here." He squeezed my hand.

I pushed on, feeling a little better.

Eventually—and it felt like a small eternity—we got to the other side of the hill, where there was a little holler. Too small to be a valley, but a depression between two other small hills. A track led up through the middle of it.

"C'mon." He pulled me through the tall grass onto the dirt surface. "This'll make it a little easier."

It did. However— "You know, I'm only six months pregnant."

Rafe nodded.

"Carmen was a lot farther along. And a lot smaller than me. And in labor. This must have been agony for her."

"That's prob'ly why they didn't get farther," Rafe said, and pointed.

Up ahead, on the side of the road, sat a little shack. It looked like it was at least a hundred years old, and on its last leg. I could see it pretty clearly, since it was lit up like a bonfire. The crime scene van from earlier was parked outside, along with a squad car, and a gray sedan. People were milling around in the glare of flood lights. The crime scene techs in their white coveralls, a patrolman in uniform, with the light reflecting off his badge, the gold lettering on his patch, and his name tag.

As we got closer, they all turned to look at us. The young patrolman—the same one from earlier—took a few steps forward, and then seemed to recognize us. "Sir." He came quite close to saluting Rafe, or so it seemed.

"I appreciate you calling me," my husband said.

"Yessir." The cop nodded multiple times. "I told Detective Mendoza you'd asked to be notified, and he said it'd be OK."

"Is this Detective Mendoza's case?"

The young cop turned to me. "Yes, ma'am."

Rafe turned to me too, with a scowl. I hid a smile.

Jaime Mendoza is a colleague of Grimaldi's, and from what I had seen, he's a good detective. He was also one of the best looking men I had ever seen, and let me assure you, after Rafe, that takes some doing.

In addition to that, he was the man my mother—jokingly, or so I told myself—had suggested should marry me, on the very day Rafe didn't show up at the courthouse for our wedding.

Mendoza, bless him, had handled Mother beautifully. He had turned me down without making me feel bad, and without making Mother feel like he didn't appreciate the offer of her daughter's hand in marriage. However, since Grimaldi had wasted no time in telling Rafe what had happened, my husband was—understandably—a little miffed. And prone to scowling whenever Mendoza's name came up.

"Is he inside?"

The cop nodded. "You can go in. Just don't touch anything."

We headed for the door to the shack.

Up close, it turned out to be a small log structure with weather-beaten plank walls. It looked like someone had put it up long before the Great Depression, and like no one had done a lick of work to it since. The plank walls had gaps in them big enough to fit my hand through, and I'm sure the roof leaked.

If Carmen and Denise Seaver had stopped here, it had to be because Carmen couldn't walk any farther.

The door was low. I had to duck my head to fit through, and Rafe had to bend almost double. The inside was garishly lit, even more so than the outside, where the surrounding woods seemed to absorb some of the light. I had to blink a few times before my eyes adjusted. Then I wished they hadn't.

I hadn't asked. I had suspected, but I hadn't asked, because I had wanted Rafe to be able to concentrate on driving. But part of me already knew what we'd find. I'm sure he did, too.

She was lying on her back on a narrow bunk attached to one of the walls. Her prison top was still on, covering her breasts and most of her upper body, but she was naked from the waist down. Her legs were spread, with one foot resting on the rough plank floor, and between them was a pool of blood. Some of it—a good amount of it—had dripped over the edge of the bed and onto the planks.

I heard Rafe swallow. He couldn't quite control the tremor in his voice, either. "The baby?"

Carmen's stomach no longer rose toward the ceiling, but looked flabby and sunken, like a deflated balloon.

Mendoza was standing by the bunk, his elegant designer suit at odds with his surroundings. Now he took a step forward, and managed to put himself between us and Carmen's body. I couldn't see the expression on Rafe's face, but I could imagine, and I was grateful to Mendoza for caring enough to provide a barrier. Even though he'd probably have questions about the necessity for it later. "Not here."

"Denise Seaver must have taken it," I said, and he glanced at me. "That's a good thing, in a way. It's alive."

"For now," Rafe said.

I shook my head. "If she didn't have a reason, and something she wanted it for, she wouldn't have bothered. She left Carmen here."

Rafe turned back to Mendoza, still standing in front of Carmen's body. "What happened?"

"The M.E. will make the determination. For now, it appears she died from lack of medical care. I'd guess a hemorrhage. If she'd been in a hospital when it happened, they might have saved her."

Postpartum hemorrhage kills three women in a hundred thousand in the industrial world. In the developing world, that number can be as high as a thousand in a hundred thousand. It was one of the many little pieces of trivia that had stuck with me from my pregnancy reading. And yes, if a woman is in the hospital, they can usually stop the bleeding and save her.

I looked past Mendoza to Carmen. With him standing where he was, all I could see of her was her head. Her hair was lank, lying in sweaty strands around her face, and her eyes were bloodshot. Birth isn't kind to a woman. Nor is death.

"Can't you at least close her eyes?"

"The M.E. has to see her first. He's on his way." He turned back to Rafe. "What's your status here?"

Rafe managed to drag his attention off Carmen and back to Mendoza. "Officially I don't have one. But I was involved in the case."

Mendoza nodded.

"And my wife was involved in the case against Denise Seaver."

Mendoza turned his attention to me. "The woman who's still on the loose?"

I nodded. "She was an OB/GYN in my hometown. Until she started killing people. One of them was my sister-in-law."

"I'm sorry for your loss," Mendoza said.

"Thank you." Sheila and I had never been close, but Mother had liked her better than both Catherine and me, or so it seemed. She'd been quite upset when it happened. And of course Dix had been devastated. "She ran a baby-selling operation. Illegal adoptions. Newborns whose mothers thought they had been stillborn. At least once she stole a baby out of a baby carriage and gave it to someone else."

"Detective Grimaldi told me about the case," Mendoza nodded.

"I'm concerned about this baby. Carmen's baby."

"You don't think she took it because she was afraid it'd die here on its own?"

"I doubt that," I said. We were less than a mile from the parkway. Chances were the baby would have been safe here for the couple of hours it had taken the police to find this small building. And it would be extra baggage for her. Not because it was all that heavy, but because a woman alone can move a lot faster than a woman carrying a newborn. It would need diapers. It would need food. And while Doctor Seaver might not care if it starved, it would cry if it wasn't fed and dry. And that would draw attention to her. She wouldn't want that.

No, she had a reason for taking it. Maybe she thought she could trade it for money.

Rafe's lips tightened when I said that, and I wished I'd censored my words better. "I could be wrong. When she took someone's baby away and gave it to someone else, it was always because she thought the baby would be better off. Maybe she's taking it to a hospital."

"We've already put out an APB," Mendoza said. "Hospitals, medical clinics, churches, food kitchens, homeless shelters."

She probably wouldn't go into a food kitchen or homeless shelter. Nowhere where she'd run the risk of being seen. More likely, if she wanted to get rid of the baby and she actually cared what happened to it, she'd find a convenient church. "It's Wednesday. A lot of churches have midweek services. That would be a good place to leave a baby. Someone would be sure to find it."

Mendoza nodded. "If she drops it off somewhere, we'll find it."

"She'll need diapers and formula. The baby will cry if it doesn't get changed and fed. And she won't have any milk to give it."

"I'll extend that notice to grocery and convenience stores, big box stores, and drugstores." He brushed past me to get to the door, where he gestured for his minion to approach. The young cop came at a trot. Mendoza relayed directions for how to extend the search while I turned to Rafe.

Mendoza and I had both pretty much just ignored him for the past minute or two. I'd wanted to give him a little time alone to process the fact that Carmen was gone—even though he'd probably already known that when we got here—and that the baby was missing. I don't know what Mendoza was thinking about the whole thing, but I'm sure he suspected something was going on, in addition to the offered explanation. It wouldn't take genius to figure out what, since most of the MNPD had been involved in the final assault on the *Havana*, and they'd all known not to shoot Rafe since he was undercover. Mendoza wasn't stupid, so he had probably figured out from Rafe's demeanor that there was more going on here than just a missing prisoner he'd once been a part of arresting.

I slipped my hand into his—it was cold—and leaned my head against his shoulder. "Let's go. There's nothing we can do here."

He looked down at me. For a second, I wasn't sure he recognized me, but then he nodded. He didn't move toward the door until I tugged on his arm, though. And when we got to the door, he glanced over his shoulder at Carmen one last time, and shuddered. I practically had to push him through the door and outside, and I wasn't surprised when he gulped a lungful of air like a man who'd been holding his breath for several minutes.

"Seen enough?" Mendoza said. He was standing just outside

the cabin in conversation with the young policeman.

I nodded. "There's nothing we can do here. We're going home."

"I'm gonna go give her family the news," Rafe added.

I looked at him—we all did—but it was Mendoza who spoke. "You want to do the notifications?"

There was a mixture of surprise and disbelief in his voice. Clearly, this wasn't something most people volunteered for.

"I told'em she'd escaped. I need to finish it."

Mendoza hesitated. Rafe had admitted that he had no official standing here. As lead detective, it should be Mendoza notifying the family that Carmen was dead. But he must be busy with all the other aspects of the case—like notifying the family of the dead guard—and being the bearer of bad news is never any fun. "Give me a call tomorrow. I have some questions."

Rafe nodded, and we trudged back through the woods toward the car. It was darker now than before, so the trip took even longer. Between looking out for obstacles and dealing with the ones we stumbled into, there was no time to talk. By the time we made it out of the trees at the bottom of the hill, and saw the headlights zoom past on the interstate up ahead, I was so glad to be out of the woods—no pun intended—that I could have bent and kissed the blacktop. If I could bend that far, anyway.

Rafe had to drag me the last few feet from the ditch onto the shoulder of the road. "I'll drive." He helped me into the car and closed the door before walking around to the driver's side. We pulled off the shoulder and into traffic, going back toward town.

It was another mostly silent trip. I think we were both in shock, both by the scene in the cabin, like something out of an Appalachian horror story from a hundred years ago, and by the fact that while we'd found Carmen and she was dead, her baby—maybe Rafe's baby—was still out there.

Part of me had no desire to go with Rafe to do the

notifications. I understood why he felt he had to, but I wasn't sure I did. At the same time, I wanted to give him what support I could. And finally, there was a part of me that couldn't wait to get home and go to bed. Both because it had been a long day, and the baby was tired, and so was I, and because oblivion sounded really good. Hopefully the image of Carmen and all the blood would go away eventually, but right now it was all I could see, and I really wanted some peace from it. Selfish of me, no doubt, but there it was.

"I didn't want her dead," I said.

Rafe glanced at me, and I added, "I had a problem with her. For obvious reasons. And I wanted her back behind bars. She belonged in prison. But I didn't want what happened to her to happen."

Rafe nodded.

We ended up around the corner from Bianca's house in Antioch, where all three of Rafe's boys were still on guard. We pulled to a stop across the street from Clayton and Jamal, and waited a minute for José to join us from the next block.

The three of them crowded around the Volvo. "What up?" Jamal wanted to know.

Rafe's voice was heavy. "You're off duty. Go home and get some rest."

They exchanged a look. "What happened, boss?"

"Police found her," Rafe said.

There was a beat, then— "She dead?"

Rafe nodded.

"You gonna do the notification?"

Rafe said he was.

"You want some company?"

"I've got Savannah," Rafe said, and the boys all peered in at me. I smiled and wiggled my fingers.

They straightened. "How 'bout the other lady?" Jamal wanted to know. "The baby dead too?"

"No. The other lady—" Rafe's voice had a fine undertone of irony, "took it and left."

"Man." The boys exchanged another look. "That's cold."

Yes, it was.

Usually, it was Jamal doing the talking for all of them. But now Clayton spoke. "You going home and getting some rest after this, too, boss?"

Rafe looked at him for a second before he answered. "No. I gotta do the notification. And then I'm gonna keep looking for that baby. Not like I can sleep while it's out there."

I had been afraid of that.

The boys looked at one another. Jamal spoke for all of them again. "You want some help?"

Rafe hesitated. I could sense the struggle between doing the responsible thing, telling them to go home and crash for the night, and the desire to have their company. He needed them more than he needed me tonight, I thought.

"I ain't gonna tell you what to do," he said eventually. "This is personal. Not business. Officially, I ain't involved in the case. If you wanna go home, go home." His gaze brushed over José, who had a fiancée waiting for him. Giving José tacit permission to leave, and letting him know that there would be no hard feelings if he did. "If you don't, there's a place a couple miles from here, called the Short Stop. It's kind of a sports bar, down off Nolensville Road. I'll go there after I'm finished with the notifications. If you're there, great. If not, I'll handle this on my own."

The boys looked at each other. "See you there, boss," Jamal said.

They scattered to their respective cars. Rafe put ours back in gear, and we rolled down the road to Bianca's house.

The red Mercedes was still parked in the driveway, along with the minivan. Maybe Mrs. Arroyo hadn't been able to face going home, after hearing the news about Carmen. Or maybe this was what they did on evenings when Bianca's husband worked. For all I knew, Mrs. Arroyo was babysitting while Bianca had taken advantage of her husband's absence to go out with friends.

We parked in the driveway behind the Mercedes. With the pickup truck gone, there was plenty of space.

The curtains in the living room twitched as we got out of the car, and before we were halfway to the front door, it had opened. Mrs. Arroyo stood in the opening, outlined by light.

She didn't say anything, just watched us come closer. If I had to guess, I'd say she'd probably guessed we wouldn't be back so soon unless there was bad news.

We stopped at the foot of the stairs, and for a second, nobody spoke. Then— "Is your daughter home?" Rafe asked.

Mrs. Arroyo nodded. And swallowed before she answered. "She's putting the children to bed."

"Would you mind if we came in?"

Mrs. Arroyo hesitated. Part of her probably wanted to tell us to spill the reason we were there right now, on the front step. Another part of her, I guessed, was trying to put off the inevitable.

After a few seconds she took a step back. Rafe gave me nudge up the stairs.

"Thank you," I told Mrs. Arroyo on my way past.

She didn't answer. She also didn't look at me. She was looking at Rafe, and I could see the fear in her eyes.

We ended up in the dining room again. Mrs. Arroyo invited us to sit, and then stood for a moment wringing her hands. After a glance up the stairs, to where Bianca must be reading her kids bedtime stories, she asked if we'd like something to drink.

I opened my mouth to decline, but Rafe got in ahead of me. "Coffee?"

Mrs. Arroyo nodded, looking relieved. She scurried off into the kitchen.

"It'll give her something to do while she waits," Rafe said softly. He reached for my hand under the table, and twined his fingers through mine. I held on to him, his fingers still cold as ice, and waited.

Mrs. Arroyo, the coffee, and Bianca arrived at the same time. There was a cup of coffee for me too, although of course I couldn't drink it. Not only did I not want to stay up all night the way Rafe did, but I was pregnant.

Bianca and Mrs. Arroyo sat down on the other side of the table. I could see Mrs. Arroyo reach for Bianca's hand at the same time as I let go of Rafe's. He wrapped both of his around the coffee mug, while I folded mine in my lap.

No one said anything. Finally—and it felt like a long time, but I don't think it can have been more than ten seconds—Rafe lifted his head. "I'm sorry to be back with bad news. Carmen was found dead this evening."

Mrs. Arroyo gasped and crossed herself. Bianca started babbling in Spanish. It went much too fast for me, although it seemed like Rafe followed most of it. He responded back, and they went like that for a minute or two, until Mrs. Arroyo had gathered herself. There were tears running down her cheeks. "*El bebé?*"

"Gone," Rafe said.

They exchanged a look, and the tears dried up like magic. "*Desaparecido?*"

Rafe nodded, and glanced at me. I gave him what I thought was an encouraging smile and got a grimace back.

"Where?" Bianca demanded, and Rafe turned back to her. "Where is my sister's baby?"

"The other woman—the one who escaped with Carmen— took it."

"She killed my sister?"

Rafe hesitated. I said gently, "We think Carmen died from complications from the birth. Um... *sangrar?*"

Mrs. Arroyo moaned and crossed herself again. Maybe this was something it was impolite to talk about. Or maybe she was just sad about the way her daughter had died.

"The police is looking for the baby," Rafe said. "After I leave here, I'm gonna look, too."

They both nodded. After a glance at me, Rafe got to his feet. I did the same. "We're sorry for your loss," I told them.

It was inadequate, but all I could say.

Bianca looked at Rafe, with tears swimming in her eyes. "Will you let us know what happens?"

He nodded.

"What will happen to the baby when they find it?" Mrs. Arroyo wanted to know.

Rafe hesitated. He glanced at me.

"It depends," I said, without going into the possibility that the baby may not survive. "Someone from DCS will take it first. The Department of Children's Services." They wouldn't just hand it off without first making sure it was going to the right place. "They'll find a temporary home for it. Unless it has to go to the hospital. Then it will stay there until it's well. Eventually, they'll decide who gets permanent custody."

"I was supposed to take care of it for Carmen," Bianca said.

I nodded. "You can tell DCS that, and unless there's a problem, that's probably what will happen. If there's family, and unless the family is unsuitable, they usually get custody. Unless the baby's father wants custody." I avoided looking at Rafe. "If he does, chances are he will get it, since his relationship with the baby is closer than yours."

Bianca didn't look at Rafe, either. I tried not to read anything into that, one way or the other.

"Did she ever tell you who the father is?" We'd asked before and she'd said no, but maybe the answer would be different this time. "Any chance he's involved? That Denise Seaver would take the baby to him?"

They exchanged a look. Then both of them shook their heads. "She wanted me to take the baby," Bianca said. "She didn't want him—the father—to know about the baby."

"Was she afraid he'd try to get custody?"

Bianca shrugged. Could be yes, could be no. Could be she'd been talking about Rafe; could be someone else.

We took our leave not much wiser than we'd come. When we walked outside in the cool air, Rafe stopped again and took another deep breath, like he had outside the cabin in the woods. "Shit."

"It's tough." It wasn't even twelve hours since Grimaldi had told me she had had to notify Devon's parents of his death, and I had told her I didn't envy her her job. "You didn't have to do this, you know. It was Mendoza's job. He would have done it."

Rafe looked at me for a second. "I guess I feel responsible. I put her prison."

"You and a lot of other people. And anyway, she's the one who broke the law."

He lowered his voice. "If it's my baby, she's dead because of me."

"Like hell she is!"

He frowned, and I added, in a much lower voice and with a guilty look over my shoulder, "She escaped on her own. If she'd gone to the hospital, she would have given birth surrounded by doctors and drugs and equipment. The chances that she would have died are close to zero. I don't mean to sound cold, but she made her own bed."

"That don't mean she deserved to die."

"Did I say she deserved it? I said it was her own fault. All she had to do was go to the hospital, and she would have been fine. Now she isn't."

"Maybe she didn't have a choice," Rafe said. "Maybe it was Denise Seaver who stopped the car and stabbed the guard."

"I'm sure it was." Carmen likely hadn't been in any kind of

shape to do much of anything. "But she could have refused to leave the van. She could have waited for Doctor Seaver to walk away, and then she could have radioed for help. She didn't, so she made her choice. And either way, you had nothing to do with it. You can't blame yourself for this."

He smiled, ever so faintly. "I think I prob'ly can."

"Well, you shouldn't. Just find the baby. That's all you can do now. Find it and make sure it's safe. I don't trust Denise Seaver."

"No shit," Rafe said and led the way to the car. When we were inside and pulling away from the curb, he added, "I'm gonna drive to the Short Stop. You can leave me there. One of the boys'll give me a ride home. Or to work tomorrow, if we're still looking by then."

I nodded. "They're good boys."

"The best."

"You'll be careful, right?"

"Always," Rafe said, in flagrant disregard of the truth.

I dropped him off at the Short Stop, and headed home. There was nothing more I could do for him. He didn't want me there, they'd probably get more done without me, and anyway, I needed to take care of myself and my own baby. I was pretty much dead on my feet, if you'll excuse the terrible pun. It had been a long day, and a busy day, not to mention a very stressful day, both mentally and physically. I needed to get home and to bed.

So I drove home, through the dark, and parked the car behind the Harley in the driveway. The house loomed somewhat threateningly. It's an Italianate Victorian, three stories, with a round tower on one corner: a bit like the *Psycho* house from the movie, or enough like it to make it a little spooky on dark nights.

I made my way up to the front door and used the light from my phone to fit the key in the lock. The door didn't squeak. Rafe keeps it oiled. I flicked on the porch light and the front foyer light, and went inside and locked the door behind me.

I admit it, I'd been a little worried that Denise Seaver had somehow figured out where we lived and was waiting for me, gun poised, when I walked through the door. I have no idea how she might have done that—I hadn't lived here back in November, when I'd been dealing with her over Sheila's murder, and the house was in Rafe's grandmother's name, Tondalia Jenkins, which doesn't sound anything at all like Rafael Collier, let alone Savannah Martin—but I worried. It's happened before, not once but several times, that I've come home to find that someone has been in my house.

This time I didn't. I walked through the whole house from top to bottom, including the dusty ballroom on the third floor, and there was no one inside but me. Once I was sure of that, I washed my face, brushed my teeth, took off my clothes, and fell into bed and oblivion.

Fifteen

I woke up to the sound of banging on the front door. "Savannah! Savannah!"

Uh-oh.

I rolled out of bed and staggered toward the stairs. Downstairs the banging continued. "Savannah! Open the door!"

"I'm coming." I navigated the stairs as quickly as I could. It's getting trickier every day. The more front-heavy I become, the more worried I am that I'll pitch forward and kill both myself and the baby. "I'm coming!"

I don't think she heard me. Not surprising, over the noise she was making. When I pulled open the door, she practically fell across the threshold.

"Sorry," I said. "I forgot to set the alarm."

It was Tamara Grimaldi, and unlike last night, when all I'd been able to think about was getting into bed, now I remembered that I was supposed to have met her at the office at nine.

It was well past that now, and her eyes were worried. "Are you all right?"

"Fine," I said and yawned. "Just tired. It was a long night."

Grimaldi straightened and followed me down the hall toward the kitchen. I needed to put something in my stomach pronto, and orange juice sounded like just the thing. "Can I get you anything?" I asked over my shoulder.

She shook her head. "I've had breakfast. Several hours ago."

"Sorry." I busied myself with filling a glass with juice. "After we left you, we got word that they'd found Carmen. So we drove back out to Eaton's Creek. After that, Rafe volunteered to break the news to her family, so we drove back down to Antioch. And after that Rafe and the boys got together at the Short Stop to plan how they were going to proceed. They've been out there all night. I went home and to bed, and I was so tired, I forgot to set the alarm."

"But you're all right?"

I nodded and lifted the glass to my lips. When I had taken a couple of swallows, I wiped the back of my hand over my mouth. Very unladylike, but Mother wasn't here. "I don't think Denise Seaver has any idea where we live. I wasn't living here back in November. Neither was Rafe. He was in Atlanta then, and I was living in the apartment on Main Street. And his name isn't on the courthouse records. Nor is mine. There's no reason Denise Seaver would associate Tondalia Jenkins with Rafe. Until last year, nobody knew they were related." I lifted the glass again.

"You want me to go through the house anyway?"

I shook my head. "I did it myself. Last night before I collapsed. It's empty."

Grimaldi nodded and let her hand drop from her gun.

"I'm sorry I overslept," I added. "I really did mean to meet you. I just forgot to set the alarm."

"I'm just glad you're all right. When you didn't show up..."

I nodded. After a year of this, we've all gotten used to expecting the worst. Usually, when the worst happens, it's Rafe in the crosshairs and not me, but I understood why she'd been concerned. "Everything's fine here. Just an oversight on my part."

"At least you got plenty of sleep," Grimaldi said and pulled out one of the kitchen chairs. "Want to tell me what happened last night? With some more details?"

I did, between sips of orange juice: from the initial phone call about Carmen to dropping Rafe off in front of the Short Stop. "They let you know that she'd been found, didn't they?"

Grimaldi nodded. "Jaime called me." Jaime being Detective Mendoza's first name. "I didn't go out there, though. I'm busy with my own case, and I know he can handle it."

"Any news on the baby this morning?"

"Nothing I've heard," Grimaldi said. "The APB went out to everyone, and it hasn't been retracted, so I'd say we're still looking."

I would say the same thing. "I should give Sheriff Satterfield in Sweetwater another call."

"You think she's on her way down there?"

"I have no idea," I said. "I can't think of anywhere else she might go. Her partner in crime—the other doctor at St. Jerome's, the one who helped her with the adoption ring, Rushing—he's dead. And she knows that, because she killed him. Carmen's family hasn't seen her. The townhouse where Carmen used to live has been sold. And the apartment I used to live in has been rented to someone else."

"Have you checked with the new tenant?"

I shook my head. "Do you think it would be worthwhile to do that? She knows I've married Rafe since then."

"But if she doesn't know you've moved, she might think the two of you are still living in the apartment," Grimaldi said. "We can at least ask if anyone's seen her."

I supposed it wouldn't hurt. "Just give me a couple of minutes to get dressed."

"Take your time," Grimaldi said. "I'm going to call Jaime and see if there's any news. After we stop by your old place, we'll go to your office and take fingerprints."

I stopped in the kitchen door. "Did you check the paint scraper?"

She looked up, in the process of manipulating her phone. "Yes. Devon Knight's prints were all over it. The footprint you found matches a pair of tennis shoes found in his car. Along with a pair of jeans and a white T-shirt."

I nodded, and headed up the stairs to get dressed.

Before I moved into Mrs. Jenkins's house with Rafe, I lived in a small one-bedroom apartment on the corner of Fifth and East Main. It was on the way to the office, and the last few times I'd driven by, I'd seen a potted plant and a bike on the balcony. When Grimaldi pulled up to the curb, the plant was still there, but the bike was gone.

"Looks like whoever lives there might be out," I said. "There's usually a bicycle on the balcony. Now there isn't."

"We'll go knock anyway." She opened her door. "If no one answers, we'll see who else we can find."

"You're the boss," I said, and followed her across the street.

The building is set around a central courtyard, which was empty when we walked in. Most of the people who live at Fifth and East Main are young professionals, with a few older people mixed in for good measure. Almost everyone is single, and gainfully employed. The building tends to be pretty empty during the day. Whoever lived in my apartment now, might have taken his or her bike to work. It'd be a quick, easy ride into downtown, just a mile or so down the road, on the other side of the Cumberland River. We could see Grimaldi's office from where we were standing; or could have, if we'd been on the street instead of in the courtyard. The western part of the building blocked our view at the moment.

My old apartment was on the second floor. We went inside, past the mailboxes, and headed up the stairs. The hallway was still carpeted in the same utilitarian gray as six months ago.

Grimaldi knew just where my door was. She'd been here plenty, after all. She knocked, and we waited. No one answered.

She knocked again, and we waited some more.

"Probably gone to work," I said.

Grimaldi nodded, and looked around. "What do you think the chances are that Denise Seaver is inside with the baby?"

I didn't have to think long. "I'd say slim to none. I lived here back in November, when Sheila was murdered, but Denise Seaver had no reason to know that."

"She was your gynecologist, right?"

"My obstetrician, more accurately. I was pregnant last winter, remember? But she was my gynecologist while I lived in Sweetwater, too. While I was a teenager."

"When you went back to see her for the pregnancy, did you have to fill out new paperwork? Did you give her this address, or your mother's house in Sweetwater?"

Good question. "I'm not sure," I said. "After I divorced Bradley and lost his health insurance, there were a couple of years I didn't go to the gynecologist at all. I wasn't sleeping with anyone, and I didn't have any female problems, so I didn't want to spend the money. But then Rafe came along and I got pregnant. I can't remember whether I put this address on my medical forms or not. I might have."

"So she could have gotten it that way."

She could have. I wouldn't say it was impossible.

"Do you hear anything?" Grimaldi asked.

"From inside?" I put my ear to the door. "No. Do you?"

She knocked again, and raised her voice. "This is the police. If you're inside, please open the door."

No one did. Grimaldi fumbled for her keys.

My eyes widened. "You can't just open the door. Can you?"

"I can if I suspect someone inside is in danger," Grimaldi said.

"But there's no sound from inside!"

"The baby could be sleeping. And Denise Seaver wouldn't respond. We're here. We might as well look."

She started fitting what I guessed was a universal key into the lock.

"I'm pretty sure this is illegal," I said, moving from foot to foot.

She glanced at me. "I'm the police. And if that baby's in there, you'll thank me."

I would. Although I didn't think the baby was inside. Not without making a sound.

"Maybe not," Grimaldi said, twisting the key in the lock, "but you know what they say. Better safe than sorry. I'd rather step over the line now, and have them not be there, than not go the extra mile—or step—and miss them."

When she put it like that...

"I'll stand guard," I said.

Grimaldi arched both brows at me. "I'm the police, Ms.... Savannah. Not your disreputable husband. You don't have to make sure no one sees me."

"Good." Because someone had just opened the door downstairs and was moving across the floor.

"Stay here," Grimaldi said and pushed the door open with one hand, while the other went to the butt of her gun. She raised her voice. "Anyone home?"

She disappeared inside. Part of me wanted to know what the place looked like now, when someone else was living in it, but I recognized my own curiosity as being out of place and stayed where I was. Bad enough that Grimaldi was invading this person's privacy; I had no right to do so.

The footsteps started up the stairs. I stayed where I was, wondering whether there was any chance at all that it was Denise Seaver who was on her way up the stairs.

But no, as he kept climbing, I recognized Mr. Sullivan from down the hall. Back from his morning constitutional, it seemed. A trip to the gym—as evidenced by the shorts and sweaty T-shirt, and the gray hair sticking straight up—followed by one to

Brew-ha-ha, the coffee house up the street, for the cardboard cup that was currently in his hand. I inhaled the life-giving scent of coffee—which I couldn't drink because of the baby—and smiled. "Hi, Mr. Sullivan."

Mr. Sullivan squinted at me. "Oh," he said after a moment. "Back, are you?"

"Not really. My friend and I are just looking for someone."

"This the same friend who came looking for you yesterday?"

My spider-senses tingled. "Someone came looking for me yesterday?"

"A nurse with a baby," Mr. Sullivan said.

"Nurse?"

"Looked like she was dressed in scrubs."

Shit! I mean... shoot. I had already noticed how much the prison uniform looked like medical scrubs, and had told Rafe that that fact probably made Denise Seaver happy.

"When was this?" I asked Mr. Sullivan, as Detective Grimaldi came back out of my old apartment and closed the door behind her. "Yesterday, you said?"

Mr. Sullivan nodded. "Late. After seven. Late enough that I thought it was strange she was carrying a baby around."

After seven. We'd been eating dinner less than a mile up the road. If we'd driven past, we might even have seen her.

Rafe and I hadn't, though. We'd gone a different way toward home, and had turned off before we got there.

"How did the baby seem?" Grimaldi wanted to know.

Mr. Sullivan tilted his head to look at her, and she showed him her badge.

He waved it away. "I know who you are, young lady. I've seen you around here before."

It might have been the first time in her life someone had called Grimaldi 'young lady.' Her mouth dropped open, before she closed it again with a snap.

"You want to tell me what's going on?" Mr. Sullivan asked,

sharing a look between us.

I glanced at Grimaldi. She shrugged. I guess maybe she was still speechless. I turned back to Mr. Sullivan.

"Those weren't nurse's scrubs. They were a prison uniform. She escaped from the Tennessee Women's Prison yesterday, along with another inmate. The other woman was pregnant and in labor, and they were on their way to the hospital. Now the guard who was driving them is dead, and the pregnant woman is dead, and the woman you saw took the baby and she's on the run."

A masterpiece of succinctness, if I do say so myself.

"Why was she looking for you?" Mr. Sullivan asked.

"I'm not entirely sure. But I don't think it's because she wants to give me the baby."

Grimaldi snorted, and covered it with a polite, "Can you tell us anything else about the woman? Or baby? Did it seem healthy?"

"Seemed asleep," Mr. Sullivan said. "Wrapped in a small blanket or towel or something like that. I just saw the top of the head. Lots of black hair."

No surprise there. Carmen was—had been—Hispanic, with long, black hair.

And of course Rafe was half black, also with dark skin and hair that was almost black.

"Do you have any idea where they went from here?"

Mr. Sullivan shook his head. "Wasn't watching. Saw them right here in the hallway. She asked for Savannah." He glanced at me. "I told her Savannah didn't live here no more. She asked where you live now. And I told her I don't know."

I nodded. He knew I was still in the neighborhood, because we'd seen each other since I moved, but I'd never had a reason to give him my exact address. Now I was very happy about that. "Then what happened?"

"She left," Mr. Sullivan said. "Walked down the stairs and

out. I don't know where they ended up." He shook his head. "I would have called you, but I don't have your number. If I hadn't seen you now, I would have called your office and asked them to put me through."

"I appreciate that," I said, and dug a business card out of my wallet. "Here. If she comes back, or you see her again somewhere, you can call me."

Mr. Sullivan pocketed it, along with the card Grimaldi gave him. "Anything else you can think of?"

Mr. Sullivan shook his head. Grimaldi thanked him on behalf of the police department, and we took our leave. Back down the stairs and across the street to the car. Where Grimaldi stopped with her hand on the door handle. "What's that?"

"What?" I looked in the same direction she was.

"The yellow building with all the people outside."

"A Catholic church," I said. "They do good works. Feed the homeless and give them somewhere to sleep on cold nights. Those guys are probably waiting for lunch. Or a morning biscuit and coffee."

Grimaldi locked the car again. "Let's go."

"Over there? Why?" But I scurried after her down the sidewalk. She—in pants and low heels—ate up the distance a lot faster than I did. By the time I skidded to a stop next to her, she already had her badge out and was showing it to the older woman in charge. Several of the homeless—mostly men, quite pungent in the warm August sunshine—sidled away, trying to look nonchalant.

"Yes, Detective." The woman behind the biscuit tray kept working. She didn't look at us, her hands kept moving, kept gathering up biscuits and cups of coffee and passing them across the tray into waiting hands, but she spoke to Grimaldi. "What can I do for you?"

"We're looking for this woman." Grimaldi held up her phone. I leaned forward and peered at it.

It was Denise Seaver's mugshot, and believe me, the most awful passport photo in the world couldn't have been worse.

Granted, it had probably been taken just a few hours after I dosed her with pepper spray, so her eyes were swollen and she looked blotchy and horrible, not to mention angry. But still, it's one of the worst pictures I have ever seen.

Normally, she's a plump, friendly-looking woman of the earth-motherly type. All long gray hair and a benevolent—if totally fake—smile. In this picture, the hair was scraped back from her face, and her lips were pinched into a tight line. A much more accurate representation of what she was really like, on the inside.

It made me wonder what Rafe's mugshot looked like, from when he was first arrested at eighteen. Maybe I could ask him to dig it up for me? Or Grimaldi?

The biscuit-and-coffee woman nodded, and dragged me back to the present. "Saw her yesterday. Came in carrying a baby around dinnertime last night. Said her daughter had run off and left it with her, and she needed money. We don't hand out money, but I gave her a blanket and a package of diapers and some formula. We do keep those on hand."

While she spoke, her hands kept moving among the biscuits and coffee cups.

"It didn't occur to you to wonder why she was wearing prison blues?"

The biscuit lady gave Grimaldi a look. "They looked like scrubs. She said she worked there. As a nurse, in the clinic."

And she hadn't even been lying, really.

"What happened after that?" Grimaldi asked.

"She took the stuff and the baby and left. Said she was going to go across the street and look for her daughter."

So now I was her daughter. Great.

"And you didn't see her again?"

The woman shook her head. "We have some regulars here—

" she nodded to a toothless old man as she handed him his breakfast, "take care of yourself out there, Curtis—but she didn't come back."

"If you see her again, can you call me?" Grimaldi withdrew another card.

The woman stopped handing out biscuits long enough to take it, glance at it, and drop it in her pocket. "Homicide?"

"She killed a couple of people last year," Grimaldi said, "and a prison guard yesterday."

"The church should have gotten a bulletin from the police yesterday," I added. Grimaldi looked at me. "Detective Mendoza said he'd put all the churches and shelters on alert, in case she decided to get rid of the baby."

The woman shook her head. "Haven't seen anything like that. It might have come in after she was here."

Maybe. Or maybe someone had dropped the ball. At any rate, there was nothing we could do about it now. Denise Seaver had been here, had moved on to my old apartment, where Mr. Sullivan had seen her, and had gone on from there. Where she was now was anyone's guess.

"Thank you for your time," Grimaldi said politely as the woman continued to hand out biscuits and coffee. The tray was half empty by now. "If you see her again, give me a call."

"Do you think she will?" I asked when we were half a block away, out of hearing range of anyone who's been even remotely close to the biscuit-and-coffee handout.

Grimaldi glanced over her shoulder. "Hard to say. Some of these religious types like to think they can rehabilitate the world with good deeds. She might be one of them."

"Denise Seaver probably won't go back there again anyway." She wasn't stupid, and once someone had seen her, chances were she'd stay away from that person again, just in case someone had gotten to them in the meantime.

"Probably not." We reached the car and Grimaldi unlocked

the doors. "Let's go to your office and get those fingerprints."

I nodded. While Denise Seaver and Carmen's baby might be topmost of mind, Grimaldi had a murder case to solve, and I had promised Tim to find out where Magnolia Houston's money went. And who knew, maybe it would do me good to think about something else for a while.

Sixteen

"Thank God you're here!" Tim said when we walked through the door. For once, he wasn't looking at me, but at Grimaldi.

She arched her brows. "Why?"

Tim was standing over Heidi, who was sitting at the front desk. "We had a break-in!"

A break-in?

I looked around. Nothing seemed out of place. I was looking right at the back of Brittany's computer monitor, and there was the usual low hum of electronics in the air. The company checkbook was open on the desk, with plenty of checks left in it. "How do you know?"

"The petty cash is gone," Tim said.

The petty cash box was sitting on the desk beside the checkbook, lid closed.

There hadn't been much in it when Rafe and I had checked it two nights ago. "Are you sure someone didn't just borrow the money yesterday? For manila envelopes or whatever?"

"Positive," Tim said. "The window in the powder room is broken."

Grimaldi had her notebook out. "Is anything missing?"

"Nothing beside the petty cash," Tim said. And changed it to, "Or nothing we've found so far."

"How much was in the petty cash?"

Tim looked at Heidi. Heidi shrugged. "Sixty-four dollars and change," I said.

All of them turned to me.

"I counted it on Tuesday night. After we caught Devon in here."

Grimaldi scribbled in her notebook. "What are the chances that this has something to do with the missing money?"

Tim winced. I did, too. Heidi blinked. "What missing money?"

Tim opened his mouth. And closed it again.

"There was a problem with the funding for Magnolia Houston's closing on Friday," I said. "The money didn't get to the seller."

"Where did it go?" Heidi asked, and I will say for her that she sounded completely sincere, and sincerely baffled.

"That's what we're trying to figure out. Something happened with the wire transfer." And that reminded me. I turned to Tim. "Rafe has a friend who knows a lot about computers. He said, if he can see the original email, he might be able to tell us where it originated. Would you like to call Lane DeWitt, or should I?"

Tim grimaced, but rose to the occasion. "I'll do it."

"Just ask when someone can come by to take a look at that email if they still have it. Hopefully they do."

Tim nodded.

Grimaldi was still waiting, pencil poised, for an answer to her question, and I turned back to her. "I can't think of any reason why someone who made off with half a million dollars would break in here to raid our petty cash."

Tim shook his head.

"Unless they came back for something else," Grimaldi said, "and took the petty cash to make it look like that's why they broke in."

I looked at Tim. Tim looked at Heidi. "What could they be coming back for?" Heidi asked, right on cue.

"That's what I need to figure out," Grimaldi said. "Have any other emails gone out for other transactions, changing the wiring instructions? Overnight, perhaps?"

Tim turned pale. "I don't know."

"Can you find out?"

"I'd have to call every closing attorney involved in every transaction the company's doing." He flapped his hand in front of his face, as if having the vapors. "Heidi!"

Heidi reached for the petty cash box, I assume to put it away.

"Leave that," Grimaldi ordered. "I want to print it."

Heidi blinked.

"Fingerprints," I said. "If nothing else, we know the intruder touched the box. If we're lucky, maybe he left fingerprints."

Heidi nodded, worrying her bottom lip.

"Come on," Tim said, setting off down the hallway. "If I have to call everyone, I need help." He snapped his fingers at her. She lumbered after him down the hall.

Grimaldi pulled out her fingerprint kit. "I might as well start here. While I'm doing this, why don't you call your husband and tell him that Denise Seaver stopped by your old apartment last night. She has probably left the area now, but if he's trying to put together a timeline of where she's been, you can give him the church and the apartment."

I nodded. I could do that. It would keep me out of my own office, that still had to be fingerprinted—although if nothing else, we knew it wasn't Devon who had broken in last night. And it probably wasn't Brittany either, since she had a key. The same, of course, could be said for anyone else in the office. So if the break-in was related to Magnolia's money in any way—or to Devon's murder—everyone who worked for LB&A were exempt from suspicion.

"Unless they tried to make it look like a break-in when it really wasn't," Grimaldi said, setting up her supplies on the sofa by the wall, where the fabric was too rough to take fingerprints.

"It's never a good idea to jump to conclusions. Go make your phone call, Ms.... Savannah."

"Any objection to me taking a look at the bathroom?"

"Not as long as you don't touch the windowsill," Grimaldi said. "I'll have to print that, too."

Naturally. I took my phone and headed down the hall while I dialed.

Rafe hadn't called me today. I figured that meant A) he had dropped off due to exhaustion and was asleep somewhere, and B) there was nothing to report. If they had found Denise Seaver and/or the baby, I'm sure he would have called. If he'd been awake, I'm sure he would have called, too. I hated to wake him, but Grimaldi had told me to call, and besides, I needed him to know that Denise Seaver seemed to be looking for us.

The phone rang a couple of times on the other end, and then I heard his voice. "Morning, darlin'." It was husky and a bit rough. Gravelly. And quite sexy. That was the first thing I had noticed a year ago, when he'd called the office to report that Brenda Puckett had stood him up for their appointment. His voice, and how it sounded like he had just rolled out of bed. Or was still in it, like now.

"Good morning," I said appreciatively. "I'm sorry to wake you."

"How d'you know I was asleep?" I heard rustling, like he was sitting up.

"I figured you would have called me if you weren't."

"Maybe I was just being considerate, seeing as my wife's pregnant and needs her rest."

Maybe so. "Were you?"

"No." There was amusement in his voice. "I was asleep."

"Good," I said. "You probably needed it."

He didn't say anything, and I added, "Long night?"

"Long enough."

"I guess you didn't find anything?"

"Not the baby, if that's what you're asking. I guess she's still carrying it around."

"She was carrying it around last night." I explained how Grimaldi had come to pick me up when I'd overslept this morning, and we had stopped by my old apartment and the Catholic church up the street on our way to the office. "We have no idea where she went from there. Mr. Sullivan doesn't know where I live now, so he wasn't able to tell her, so I don't think we have to worry about her knowing where to find us."

"Would be nice if she did," Rafe said. I arched my brows, and although he couldn't see me, he added, "At least we'd know where they were at. If I've got her in front of me, I can get that baby away from her. It's a lot harder just having her walking around God knows where."

Indeed. "I'll keep an eye out. If she was in the neighborhood last night, maybe she's still in East Nashville this morning." And if I got lucky, maybe I'd see her walking down the street.

It was quite annoying to reflect that if we'd driven down Main Street last night, on our way home from dinner with Grimaldi at the FinBar, we might have seen her walking down the street then.

"Can I borrow José for thirty minutes later?" I added. "Tim has agreed to contact DeWitts about the original email changing the wiring instructions for Magnolia Houston's money. If they still have it, maybe José can look at it and tell us where it came from."

"I'll let him know," Rafe said. "We're all crashing on his floor. He lives down here."

I assumed 'down here' was the Tusculum/Antioch area, where the Short Stop was located. I also assumed, but didn't mention it, that they'd all been a little bit impaired last night, and hadn't wanted to go far after they left the sports bar. Hopefully José's fiancée had been OK with having three extra TBI-agents—two in training—crashing on her living room floor. There was a whole lot of testosterone in the air when the four of them were together.

"I appreciate it," I said. "I know finding Denise Seaver and the baby has to take precedence, but I could really use him. Five hundred thousand is a lot of money. And if Devon was involved and now he's dead..."

"You don't have to justify it," Rafe said. "If you want him, he's yours."

"Thank you."

"Just don't go thinking about keeping him."

"Why would I want to keep him? I've got you."

"Damn straight," Rafe said, and hung up.

I continued on into the bathroom to inspect the damage.

The powder room is pretty small. Just a commode and a sink, with a window overlooking a small, overgrown gap between our building and the one next door. We've never bothered to cover the window with anything. A small, ruffled, green valance—to match the flower printed wall paper—hung at the top of the window, but there's no way to actually cover the window for privacy. Then again, for as long as I've worked at LB&A, I've never seen a soul in the gap between the buildings.

If you were going to break into the realty office, it was a good place to do it. There are plenty of trees and bushes in the gap, no through-traffic, and the other building doesn't even have any windows on that side. The LB&A building sits on a corner, fronting the street on two sides, with a parking lot at the back, and of course those three sides are all visible from the street. But the gap between buildings is very private.

It's also pretty narrow. Three feet wide, maybe; no more. These days, you wouldn't be able to build two buildings that close together. There's at least a five foot setback on each side, so the buildings would be ten feet apart, minimum. But the LB&A building is a hundred years old, and they didn't have such concerns back then. Also, both buildings are brick, and I guess they weren't worried about fire.

At any rate, someone had slipped sideways into the gap between our building and the next, and had slithered through the trees and bushes over to this window, where he or she had slammed a rock through the glass. The rock was on the floor, a big, gray chunk. Grimaldi would have to have a go at it, although I suspected it was too rough to take prints.

Along with the rock, there was glass all over the floor. No question about this being an outside job. The rock and glass were both on the inside, so whoever had broken the window had done it from outside. That didn't mean it couldn't have been someone from LB&A trying to make it look like a random break-in, of course, but at least whoever had done it, had gone through the trouble of pushing through the overgrown trees and brush outside to get here.

I wandered back to the foyer and gave Grimaldi my take on the situation. She was busy picking up fingerprints on little pieces of tape—a bit broader than Scotch tape, but otherwise it looked like the same thing—and transferring them onto small index cards. On every card, she noted down where the print came from. After the cash box was done, she went on to the edge of the desk, and the knobs and drawer pulls. With that done, she moved the whole operation into my office, and started again. The front office prints were put away in a folder, and a new folder was started for my desk.

About halfway through this process, Tim wandered back in. "Nothing's missing from my office. I don't think anyone's been in there."

Grimaldi nodded. "Good."

"Heidi's been calling the closing companies to double check the wiring instructions for all our closings. So far, everything's A-OK. Nothing's wrong with any other transaction."

"Good."

Tim turned to me. "I talked to Lane DeWitt. He says they still have the email. It was deleted from the inbox after they printed it out, but it was still in the trash. He moved it back."

"Good." That way, there was something for José to look at. I didn't think the printout would have helped him at all.

"He says you can stop by anytime you want."

"I'll send Rafe a text and tell him we're ready whenever José is." I dug for the phone I had dropped into the pocket of my maternity dress.

"Be sure to tell him I send my love," Tim said with a lascivious wink, and sashayed off again.

"That doesn't bother you?"

Grimaldi didn't look up from her gathering of fingerprints. There seemed to be a lot of them on the edge of my desk.

"Not much anymore." I sent off the text to Rafe, and dropped the phone back in my pocket. "It used to. A year ago, when I first met Rafe again. Tim was always drooling over him, and remarking on how hot he is. It was embarrassing, especially when he did it in front of Rafe. But then I realized that Rafe didn't mind, so I guess I got used to it."

Grimaldi nodded. "I have your fingerprints on file. And I took Brittany's yesterday. But I'll need them from everyone here. This could take a while."

"I don't have a car," I said. "We took yours, remember? I'll just stick around until you're ready to go."

"Let me guess. You're planning to tag along with me for the rest of the day?"

"Not if you don't want me to. Although it would be nice if you'd keep me in the loop. We're sort of working on the same case, after all."

Grimaldi refrained from telling me I wasn't working on a case at all. *She* was working on a case; *I* was doing a favor for a friend.

"I thought you'd probably want to come along when I take José to DeWitts," I added. "Unless you don't care about the email."

She moved on to my drawer pulls. "I care about the email. The missing money probably has something to do with Devon Knight's murder. And since it's my job to find Devon Knight's murderer, I definitely care about the email."

"Then I'll just stick around until we figure out what to do." My phone whistled, and I pulled it back out of my pocket. "Rafe says José can be here in forty-five minutes."

"Tell him to meet us outside DeWitts," Grimaldi said, still intent on her fingerprint-gathering. "I'll be finished here by then."

I walked away, down toward Tim's office to ask for the exact address for DeWitts Title and Escrow, so I could text it to Rafe and he could pass it on to José.

By the time I got out of Tim's office, Grimaldi had moved on to the powder room. As I had suspected, the rock was too rough to take fingerprints, but Grimaldi stuffed it into an evidence bag anyway, and busied herself gathering fingerprints from the windowsill.

She spent the next thirty minutes in the bathroom, and when that was done, she went on to get fingerprints from Tim and Heidi and the handful of other agents who were unlucky enough to be present in the office on a Thursday morning. Once it was all done, and properly annotated and filed, we carried it all out to the car and went to meet José at DeWitts.

Tim had declined to accompany us—still upset with Lane DeWitt's accusation about the missing money, I guess—so it was just the two of us headed the few blocks south to DeWitts.

They're located in one of the big turn-of-the-(last)-century four-squares that dot the landscape in East Nashville. When the house was built a hundred plus years ago, the area was a summer playground for the wealthy who lived on the other side of the river. This was when a ten mile trip by horse and carriage from Belmont and Belle Meade would take all day, instead of twenty minutes by car, like now. Although a good many of the old buildings burned to the ground in the great fire of 1916, there are still a lot of lovely, old houses left, many of them on the National Register of Historic Places.

This one was built of pale gray stone with a cedar shingled second story that had been painted a pale aqua. It might not sound like much, but it looked gorgeous. A short, wrought-iron fence encircled the front yard, matching the wrought-iron sign that proclaimed this as the home of DeWitts Title and Escrow (Est. 2006).

José's truck with the Virgin Mary on the window was parked at the curb. José was inside it, and so was Rafe. I guess, since I'd dropped him off last night and he'd had to get a ride with someone, he'd chosen to come with José to see us. And perhaps also to see if he could find any other sightings of Denise Seaver in the last twenty-four hours.

As always, it was lovely to see him. We do the sideways greeting now, since the stomach gets in the way front to front. I leaned in and he slipped his arm around my back and gave me a kiss. It lingered. Or maybe I did. As usual, I got flutterings in my stomach. Not the baby this time.

Grimaldi and José exchanged more proper greetings. They'd met before, during that period between my scheduled wedding and my actual wedding in June, when Rafe was missing. Grimaldi, Wendell, and all the rookies had worked tirelessly to find him.

When all the formalities were concluded, Grimaldi turned to the building. "Ready?"

We followed in her wake through the wrought-iron gate, up the steps, and through the door.

Inside, a plump young woman in a black dress sat behind the front desk. She looked up. "Can I help...?"

The question ended in a gulp when she got a load of the four of us. I'm nothing particularly unusual, other than being pregnant. Grimaldi is all cop, in her usual dark suit and no-nonsense demeanor. Rafe is... well, he's Rafe. Gorgeous, with the kind of sex appeal that can hit a woman between the eyes and knock her backward. Even in yesterday's clothes and with stress and sleeplessness carved in the lines of his face, he was equal parts compelling and terrifying.

And then there was José. He's short for a guy, no bigger than me, with the usual Hispanic glossy black hair, warm skin, and liquid dark eyes. And he works out a lot, so the sleeves of the polo-shirts he favors—this one a dark turquoise—are rolled up almost to his shoulders. Not to show off his biceps, but because the sleeves probably cut off his circulation when he pulls them down.

Rafe is rather nicely muscled, too, but I think José's biceps might have his beat. Or if not, José looks more impressive, simply because he's almost a head shorter.

Anyway, there we were. The three of them and me. The young receptionist stared from one to the other of us, mouth open, blue eyes wide, and I wasn't surprised to see a flicker of fear cross her face. Rafe and Grimaldi separately look scary. Together, they're damn near terrifying.

Grimaldi badged her. "We're here to see Lane DeWitt. He's expecting us."

The receptionist hiked her jaw up. "Yes, ma'am. Detective. Right away."

She lunged for the phone. The corner of Rafe's mouth quirked and Grimaldi wrinkled her brows at him. Only José remained imperturbable.

"Mr. DeWitt?" The receptionist's voice practically quivered. "A police detective is here to see you. Along with two agents from the TBI. And... um..." She glanced at me, obviously unsure where I fit in.

"The representative from Lamont, Briggs, and Associates," Grimaldi said.

The receptionist repeated it, then hung up the phone. "Mr. DeWitt will be right out."

Grimaldi nodded and turned to José. "Savannah tells me you think you can figure out where this email originated."

"If I can get a look at the original and trace it back," José said. "It isn't hard to spoof an email address. All it takes is a server and a little bit of know-how. The trail should go right back to the IP address it originated from."

"A location?"

"That'll take a little longer. But once I have the IP address, you can find out who it belongs to and where the unit is located."

"Excellent," Grimaldi said.

The receptionist was still looking from one of us to the next, her expression halfway between fascinated and wary. She probably knew about the missing money, and she might not have been sure whether we were going to be a blessing or a curse. We certainly had showed up in force, anyway.

Steps on the stairs brought all our heads around in that direction. A pair of elegant, gray slacks were making their way down, followed by an eggplant-purple shirt. The ensemble was topped by a handsome face surrounded by dark hair, artfully sterling at the temples.

He floated off the staircase and toward us. And since his quick assessment dismissed me and Grimaldi, in that order, and lingered on Rafe and José, it was easy to see why Tim and Lane DeWitt had always gotten on well. Birds of a feather, and all that.

"Gentlemen." He smiled winningly before adding, a smidge too late, "And ladies. What can I do for you?"

Grimaldi pulled out her badge again. So did Rafe and José. Lane blinked at finding himself faced with so much hardware.

"We've come to take a look at that email," Grimaldi told him when the formalities were over. "Timothy Briggs called you earlier and let you know we were coming?"

The inflection made it sound like a question, but her tone said clearly that he'd better not pretend not to know anything about it.

"Of course." Lane smiled suavely. "Such a big group."

"It was a big crime," Grimaldi said. "Five hundred thousand dollars is a lot of money. And of course, now that the case includes a murder..."

She let that hang there for a moment, while Lane turned pale and while the receptionist squeaked and covered her mouth with her hand. Her nails were long and pink, and her eyes above them looked ready to pop out of their sockets.

"Murder?" Lane repeated, and his voice had lost most of its oily slickness in the surprise. "Who's dead?"

"I'm afraid I'm not at liberty to tell you that." Grimaldi gave him a tight-lipped smiled. "Suffice it to say, it's someone with a background in information technology, and someone who's attached to one of the companies involved. Or was attached, I should say, since he's now attached to a toe tag in the morgue. Permanently."

"Urk," Lane said, or at least it sounded that way.

Grimaldi nodded. "As you can imagine, we're taking this seriously. If you don't mind, the TBI part of the task force can take a look at the email while I ask you some questions. Will that be all right?"

Grimaldi can be quite scary when she's all cop. She'd certainly scared the crap out of me when I first met her. Lane looked like he was ready to pee his pants.

"Yes," he managed. "Of course. If you'll... um... why don't you come up to my office. Molly—" This was addressed to the receptionist, "why don't you switch the phones off and go to lunch."

Molly blinked. "But... it's only ten o'clock!"

"Long lunch," Lane said, with a look that sent her scurrying for her bag. "This way, Detective."

He steered Grimaldi back toward the stairs. She gave me a sort of significant look over her shoulder. It took me a second to figure out what she wanted, but when she abandoned subtlety and nodded at Molly, I nodded back.

Rafe and José waited for Molly to make her way out from behind the desk before they moved in. José arranged himself in the chair and Rafe leaned over his shoulder with one hand planted on the desk. It was a very nice position to show off the muscles in his very nice arm, and Molly made a sort of little sigh.

"I'll walk you out," I said.

She gave me a startled look. "Oh, but..."

I gave her a friendly smile. "I'm just here to represent LB&A. I don't really have anything to do. And I want to ask you a question."

Molly nodded, but not without a worried look over her shoulder at the staircase to the second floor, where Lane DeWitt and Grimaldi had disappeared.

"It isn't anything to worry about," I assured her, as I closed the outside door behind us. "I just wanted to know if you knew anything about this email. Did it come in to your mailbox, or Lane's, or someone else's? Was there someone already assigned to the Houston/Harper closing, and the email went to them?"

Molly shook her head. The rest of her was shaking, too. Her voice was so soft I could barely hear it. "It came in to the general mailbox. No one had been assigned to the closing yet. On closing day, it just depends on whoever is here and available. We can't really plan things like that in advance. Closings run over, you know: go long, and then people sit and wait..." She trailed off.

"Was there anything unusual about the email? Did you notice anything about it?"

"Nothing," Molly said, quivering like an aspen. "I saw it. It looked like it came from Tim. I forwarded it to Lane. And that's all I know about it."

"When did you realize what had happened?"

"Not until Monday," Molly said. "Tim called and asked to be put through to Lane. Then Lane came running down the stairs and wanted to see the Houston file. And everything went crazy from there."

She glanced lovingly at the sidewalk. Probably wanted to get away from me and my questions.

"Did you submit the claim to the insurance company? You're insured for things like this, aren't you?"

Molly nodded and lowered her voice another degree. I could barely hear her. "They won't pay. They say Lane should have double-checked the email before he wired the money."

I nodded. I thought he should have, too; not that I was about to say so. "I'm sorry to kick you out of your office. This probably won't take long, and then you can go back to work."

"It's all right," Molly answered. "Lane said to take a long lunch. So I will."

She hopped down the front steps without so much as a goodbye, and scurried down the walkway to the street. I took a seat on the porch swing and waited for the others to join me.

Seventeen

Rafe and José came out first, just a few minutes after Molly had gotten into her small hybrid and driven away.

Rafe came over and sat next to me. The swing rocked. "All right, darlin'?"

"Fine," I said. "I figured the two of you were busy inside, and Grimaldi will be out when she's ready. The weather's nice. It's finally getting a little cooler."

It was. Not always the case in late August, which can be just as hot as the middle of summer, but this year—or at least this day of this year—there was a nice breeze and a snap in the air that hinted of fall. Not that that couldn't go away by tomorrow, of course.

"What did you find?" I added.

"José tracked the email to the IP address and the final ISP. Now we have to figure out who it belongs to."

It was like he was speaking Greek. "Could you translate that into English?"

"The email came from a webmail account," José said. "I know the IP address—sort of a code number—for the computer it was sent from, but someone has to check with the internet service provider to see whose account it is."

"You didn't do that?"

"We thought that'd be better coming from the detective,"

José said diplomatically, and he had a point. "It's her case and her body. We're just doing a favor for a friend."

"So what do you plan to do for the rest of the day?" I looked from one to the other of them.

José looked at Rafe. Rafe grimaced. "We still gotta find Denise Seaver and that baby. They gotta be holed up somewhere."

"I can call Sheriff Satterfield again," I offered. "Although I'm sure he'd have let us know if they'd seen her."

Rafe nodded. "She's gonna need clothes. Can't keep walking around in that prison uniform forever. Sooner or later somebody's gonna realize she ain't a nurse."

"She got the diapers and formula free. And she asked at the church for money. That probably means she doesn't have any."

"Just whatever was in the guard's wallet," Rafe said. "And it prob'ly wasn't much. Most people don't carry a lot of cash these days. It's mostly all cards. And Mendoza put a warning on those."

"Maybe we'll get lucky and she'll try to use one."

"Not if she didn't use it to buy diapers," Rafe said. "She ain't stupid. I'm sure she knows we can track the cards."

"So that means she needs to get clothes for free. Mendoza said he notified the churches and shelters and places like that. Where else are there free clothes?"

"People leave them outside thrift stores," José said. "And there are donation bins here and there."

"There's a thrift store up on Main Street," I told them both, "about two blocks north of the library. I think there's a dumpster out back that people toss donations into. And there are donation bins of some sort outside the grocery store, too. For the veterans or abused women or something like that."

Rafe and José exchanged a look. "Worth looking into," Rafe said. José nodded.

"What are Clayton and Jamal doing this morning?"

"Still in Antioch," Rafe said. "Clayton's sitting outside Mrs. Arroyo's house, and Jamal outside Bianca's. I know Carmen won't show up, but just in case Denise Seaver decides to do someone a good turn for once in her life, and hand over that baby."

I shook my head. "I don't see that happening. She took it for a reason, and I don't think it was to give it away."

Rafe nodded, his face dark.

"Nothing from the TBI lab yet, I assume?"

He shook his head. "Maybe tonight. Or tomorrow." He slanted me a look. "Does it matter?"

José looked uncomfortable, focusing on something beyond the porch, as if, if he wasn't looking at us, he wasn't really there.

"No," I said, and I'm pleased to say that my voice was firm. "It doesn't matter at all when it comes to finding the baby. It matters to what happens later, but right now, the only thing that matters is finding it before Denise Seaver does something to ensure we never will."

The door behind José opened, and he looked acutely relieved when he turned to greet Grimaldi. "Detective."

She walked over to join him. Or us. "Were you able to find anything?"

"The IP address of the user. It's a webmail account. You'll have to contact them to find out who owns the computer. Hopefully it's an individual and not a library computer that anyone can use." He handed her a sticky note.

She dropped it in her jacket pocket. "Good work, Agent Garcia." José's eyes widened—maybe it was the first time someone had called him that—and then he grinned and looked at Rafe. Grimaldi added, "I'll arrange for a subpoena."

"How long will that take?" I asked.

She glanced at me, and her brow furrowed a little. Maybe she could sense the tension in the air. "Depends on the judge. Since it's a murder case, and since there's some circumstantial evidence that the money is connected, maybe a few hours."

Sheesh. The wheels of justice grind slowly, don't they? "Molly left," I said. "It seems Lane is upset with her for not noticing that the email was fake, even though he didn't notice it, either."

Grimaldi nodded. "What are you two up to?" She looked from José to Rafe and back.

"Still trying to find Doc Seaver and that baby." Rafe got to his feet and set the porch swing in motion. "At this point, I don't know what the hell to do other than just drive around looking for her. We can prob'ly figure out where she's been, but that ain't gonna help us figure out where she's going next."

His voice had a fairly vicious undertone. It was quite obvious that he was beyond frustrated at having nothing constructive to do.

"You worked the adoption case," I said to Grimaldi. "Was anybody else involved in that? There was the other doctor at St. Jerome's, of course, but he's dead. Was there anyone else? A nurse, maybe? Or a lawyer, to handle the adoption paperwork?"

Rafe looked up.

Grimaldi shook her head. "It was all done through the hospital. There was no adoption paperwork. They just took babies and sold them. And filed birth certificates in the adoptive parents' names. There's no record of the adoptions at all."

"Someone must have put them in touch with the people who wanted babies, though. I mean, it's a question of supply and demand, just like everything else, isn't it?" I avoided looking at Rafe. "You have something to sell—in this case a baby. How do you find someone who'll pay for what you have?"

"I imagine Doctor Rushing had something to do with that," Grimaldi said. "He dealt with difficult pregnancies. Some of those pregnancies probably ended with women finding out that they couldn't ever have a baby of their own."

Possibly so. "That's too bad." Since he was dead. "I was hoping we could find someone else she might go to. Some kind of middle man she's worked with before, that we could hunt up. Just in case she goes to him—or her—to try to trade the baby for money."

"It was a good thought," Grimaldi said. "And I wish I could think of someone. But the nurses just took care of the babies and didn't know what was going on with the adoptions. And none of the other doctors suspected. The other practitioners in Doctor Seaver's practice in Columbia were appalled, and couldn't have been more cooperative when we spoke to them."

I nodded. "I guess all we can do is drive around the neighborhood and see if she's still around, then. Talk to people and see if anyone's seen her."

Rafe looked at José. José nodded, and they headed down the steps toward the truck. Rafe didn't look at, or talk to me.

I turned to Grimaldi. "I guess it's you and me."

She glanced my way. "What's wrong with your husband?"

"He's upset," I said.

Grimaldi scowled after him.

"It's OK. Just as much my fault as his. I said something I probably shouldn't have, and he took it the wrong way." And while I was a bit hurt by that, I understood the pressure he was under, and the fear he probably felt. It was personal for him, even more than it was personal for me. Last night he'd seen Carmen dead, a woman he had smiled at and laughed with and kissed and touched. He might not have been in love with her, but it must still have been upsetting. And now her baby was out there. His baby. He probably thought of it as his baby, whether it would turn out to be or not. He probably had to think of it as his baby, because if something happened to it, and he hadn't done everything he could, he wouldn't be able to live with himself.

Grimaldi nodded when I said so. "You need to cut him a break," she told me. "I'm sure the guilt is eating him alive."

Guilt? "What guilt? He didn't do anything wrong. It isn't his fault that Denise Seaver saw Carmen as a way to get out of prison. And it isn't his fault she left Carmen to die. I'm sure he feels bad about it, but it isn't his fault. None of us expected it to happen this way."

Grimaldi nodded. "Of course. But that's not what I'm talking about."

"What are you talking about?"

She gestured toward the car, and we started off down the steps toward the street. "You've already had to deal with David Flannery. Your husband's son by someone else. And now you learn he's knocked up Carmen. Another baby with a woman who isn't you."

I nodded. "So?"

"He loves you. Can you imagine the guilt he feels about putting you through this? Again?"

I hadn't thought about it, to be honest. I guess I had been a little too busy wallowing in my own hurt feelings. "But it isn't his fault. He didn't plan any of it." He'd been seventeen and drunk when David was conceived, and Elspeth had taken advantage of that, and of him. Perhaps he should have been more careful, but it was a long time ago, and not worth the trouble of holding a grudge. And he had taken precautions with Carmen. It wasn't his fault if they had failed.

"I don't think he'd see it that way," Grimaldi said. "He screwed up. He's probably worried you're going to leave him."

"That's crazy." I wouldn't. Ever. No matter how many illegitimate children showed up.

"Not from his point of view," Grimaldi said. "He doesn't feel like he ever deserved you in the first place, and now he's done something else to screw up your life and make himself look bad to your family. And on top of that he has to spend all his time looking for the baby before something happens to it. He's probably worried it looks to you like he's putting the baby—and Carmen—above you."

That thought had crossed the shameful recesses of my mind

last night, as I drove home from the Short Stop by myself. Like he didn't need me or want me, and I should just go away and leave him alone.

"That baby isn't safe out there with Denise Seaver," I said. "She made a career out of selling babies. She's probably planning to sell this one. And if she can't, it's not worth anything to her. If she can't make money from it, it's just slowing her down. And God knows what she'll do with it then. Someone has to find it before that happens. No matter whose baby it is."

Grimaldi nodded. "Leave it to them. I've got a job for you."

"Really?" I'd thought she'd suggest taking me home now, that we'd done what we'd needed to do at the office. And the last thing I wanted to do, was sit around at home twiddling my thumbs.

"I need those fingerprints checked. And I don't want to have to stop to do it. If I wait, it'll be five o'clock before I can get to it. Do me a favor and use the file to see if you can match them. Devon's prints are in there. So are Brittany's. And Tim's and Heidi's. And yours, from before."

"I'd be happy to." I took the file out of her hand and opened it. She put the car in gear and we rolled away from the curb.

"Where are we going?" I asked after a minute. We were on our way down Shelby Avenue at a good clip, and it looked like we were headed for the interstate. "The prints on my desk are mostly mine. But there's a partial here that looks like it could be Devon's. From the drawer, it says."

Grimaldi nodded.

"Looks like maybe, when he stopped by on Tuesday night, he was going through my desk."

"He'd just seen you that afternoon at the house in Goodlettsville," Grimaldi reminded me. "You may not have recognized him, but he wouldn't have known that."

I nodded. "I guess that means he had something to hide. Either that he had something to do with the missing money, or just that he was involved somehow with Magnolia Houston." Angie at the consignments store had called him her boyfriend. So maybe he was two-timing Brittany and was afraid I'd tell on him.

Although I wasn't quite sure how that squared with them getting married tomorrow. Would he really marry Brittany if he was involved with Magnolia?

Unless the involvement was strictly platonic, of course. Platonic and financial. She had paid him to reroute her money, and that was all. No reason why he couldn't marry Brittany then. He might even have told himself—and her—that he'd done it for them.

"I'll get started on the prints from the window sill," I said. "You should call for that subpoena. The sooner the better."

Grimaldi nodded and picked up the phone. We swung onto the entrance ramp for I-24 East as I hunkered over the window sill prints and listened to her call the office and ask someone to look into a subpoena for the webmail provider José had named.

"Where are we going?" I asked again when we had merged with traffic and navigated the I-24/I-40 split and were zooming toward Hermitage and the lake.

Grimaldi glanced at me. "We're going to see one of Devon's friends. Someone he plays music with. I figured I'd give him a couple extra hours to sleep, since I want him awake and aware when I talk to him."

I nodded. "They aren't Devon's fingerprints on the window sill. And I don't know why I even bothered to look, since Devon was dead when someone broke in. Sorry."

"No problem," Grimaldi said.

"They aren't mine, since I know I wasn't there." I moved my own fingerprint card out of the way and picked up Brittany's. They weren't hers, either. By the time we pulled up in front of a small mid-century ranch somewhere in the wilds of Donelson, I had eliminated Tim, Heidi, and everyone else who had been in the office this morning. Not that anyone in the office would have had a reason to bash in the window. Everyone in the office had a key.

I waited for Grimaldi to tell me to stay in the car, but she didn't. "Come on."

"You want me to go inside with you?"

"Just try to look official. You want to hear what he has to say, don't you?"

Of course I did. I just didn't know whether I had the ability to look like a cop. Somehow I doubted it. It's in the eyes, and I just don't have them. Cop eyes, I mean. I can see just fine. I just don't see—or look—like a cop.

But I swung my legs out of the car and scurried after Grimaldi up to the front door. She knocked and we waited. And knocked and waited. And knocked and waited some more.

Eventually we heard the sound of dragging footsteps inside. It sounded like a zombie approaching the door. When the door opened, it looked something like a zombie, too. Minus the blood and other creepiness, but definitely a zombie-look.

The boy was Devon's age, early twenties. He had dirty blond hair in a Devon-haircut: too long, uncombed, hanging in his eyes and over his ears. Not to put too fine a point on it, but his style looked like it had been achieved by rats chewing and sucking on his hair. He was pale, with eyes barely open, peering out furtively through the brush, and the fact that he had opened the door in a pair of unzipped jeans and nothing else, didn't seem to have occurred to him.

"Yeah?"

Grimaldi showed him her badge. He stared at it for a moment, and I could see the wheels turning over, very slowly, inside his head.

"Shit," he said eventually.

We waited, but that was all there was.

"We'd like to talk to you," Grimaldi said. "Inside."

He glanced over his shoulder. The living room looked like a

frat house. The coffee table had at least a dozen beer bottles sitting on it, all of them empty, and there were empty pizza boxes and gaping chip bags everywhere. Also a couple of ashtrays full of cigarette butts.

"I'm not here to bust you for pot," Grimaldi told him. "Or whatever else you've got sitting around." She waited a second before adding, "At least not if you cooperate."

"Whaddaya want?"

"Like I said, we want to talk to you. Inside."

The young man hesitated another second, and then he stepped back. "Sorry about the mess."

No kidding. It looked even worse up close, and didn't smell so good, either. My nose wrinkled.

"On second thought," Grimaldi said, with a look at me, "let's do this outside. Someone could get high just from breathing the air in here."

No kidding. I backed out again, my head swimming.

"There are some chairs on the patio," the young man said. "We can go there."

"Lead the way." Grimaldi waved at me to go around the house, while she followed the young man through. Maybe she was afraid he'd lock the door with us on the outside, if she didn't keep an eye on him.

By the time I had circumvented the house and garage, they were already seated on a pockmarked but shady patio in the rear. Grimaldi had her book out. "Name?" she asked.

The young man owned up to being christened Hanse Neyman. "But everyone calls me Han."

"Star Wars?"

He grinned. "Yeah."

OK, then.

"I imagine you can guess why we're here?"

"If it's not about the pot," Han said—not the brightest bulb in the chandelier, obviously, "I guess it's about Devon?"

Grimaldi nodded. "You've heard the news?"

"Britt called me yesterday. We had rehearsal last night, and she called to let me know he wasn't gonna be there."

"How often do you rehearse?" Grimaldi asked, settling back in her chair with her notebook on her knee.

Han shrugged. Like Devon, he was pretty androgynous, with skinny shoulders and not much of a chest. A tuft of blond hair showed in the unzippered part of his pants, but nothing worse than that. "Every couple of days, I guess."

So if they'd rehearsed two nights ago, why had they rehearsed again last night?

"We didn't," Han said when Grimaldi put the question to him. "Not two nights ago."

"Brittany said Devon had been at rehearsal from seven o'clock until he got home at two-thirty."

Han shook his head. "Not on Tuesday. We rehearsed yesterday."

"Can you tell me where you were Wednesday morning from one to four?"

"Here," Han said, making a sweeping gesture at the house. "Sleeping."

"Alone?"

"There are three of us living here. But I wasn't sleeping with any of them."

"Can you prove that?" Grimaldi said, and we watched the young man's eyes bug out of the sockets.

"Why would I wanna do something to Devon? We were friends, man. I owe him a lot. If it wasn't for him, we wouldn't be on our way now."

"On your way where?" Grimaldi sounded ready to pull out the handcuffs and slap them around his skinny wrists to stop him from going wherever it was.

He shook his head. "Not like that, man. Devon got us a really good gig playing for Magnolia Houston. We're going places."

Grimaldi looked like she wanted to ask about the places, but I got in first. "Devon did? Devon got you a job playing for Magnolia Houston? All of you?"

Han nodded. "The whole band. We're backing her up on her videos, and when she goes somewhere to perform, we go with her. It's awesome. She has a bus and everything."

I'm sure she did. "How did Devon come to know Magnolia Houston?" They didn't exactly travel in the same circles. Or so I assumed.

"Something to do with his day job," Han said vaguely.

"Computers?"

"Something like that. She had a problem with something and hired him to fix it. He works for—" He faltered for a second before he went on, "—worked for one of those troubleshooting places."

"The kind that comes out if your computer acts up?"

Han nodded. "She called and he went out there. And I guess they got along. Wasn't long before he was banging her."

"Excuse me?" I said.

"You know what banging means, right? You musta had a bang yourself to get like that." He pointed to my stomach.

Grimaldi made a face. Hard to say whether it was humor or disgust.

"Yes," I said, "I know what banging means. You're saying that Devon and Magnolia were having sex."

Han nodded, looking pleased.

"I thought he was marrying Brittany."

"He was banging Britt," Han said.

"They were living together. I guess Brittany didn't know that he was... um... banging Magnolia, too."

The word sounded weird coming out of my mouth.

"He didn't tell her," Han said. "But he wasn't marrying her, neither."

"Are you sure? She told me they were flying to Curacao this

weekend."

Grimaldi was furrowing her brow—I guess maybe I wasn't supposed to mention that—but it was too late now.

Han shook his head. "I don't know nothing about that. We're playing a gig on Saturday. That's what we've been rehearsing for. We're rehearsing again tomorrow night. Magnolia's been invited to sing at a fundraiser at the Ryman Auditorium. I don't think Devon would wanna miss that."

I didn't think so either. Not that I would care personally, but for a Nashville musician, the Ryman Auditorium is the Holy Grail. The Mother Church of Country Music, it's where the Grand Ole Opry performed for years. All the country greats have stood on the stage there. If Devon had a chance to perform at the Ryman, I don't think he would have prioritized getting married. Not when he could have postponed the wedding for a week.

I glanced at Grimaldi.

"Do you have any information about this house that Magnolia was buying in Goodlettsville?" she asked.

"Just what Devon told me," Han said. "Old place. She was gonna fix it up nice and live there. And build a big rehearsal space in the barn. It sounded nice."

He sounded wistful. Maybe without Devon, the gig would be over, and Magnolia would kick the rest of the band to the curb. Giving Han no reason at all to want to get rid of Devon. Not unless he hoped to step into Devon's shoes, I guess.

"Thank you for your time, Mr. Neyman." Grimaldi got to her feet and dug a card out of her pocket. "If you think of anything that might be important, please give me a call."

Han said he would, and padded into the house. Grimaldi and I made our way around the corner and down the driveway to the car.

"That's very strange," I told Grimaldi when we were pulling away from the house. "I know what Brittany told me. She'd gone out shopping, and bought a lot of stuff, and she told me they were getting married and flying to Curacao on their honeymoon."

Grimaldi nodded. "There are tickets booked in both their names. And a hotel room on the beach. I checked."

"Maybe Devon was feeling so guilty about sleeping with Magnolia that he was willing to sacrifice the Ryman gig to marry Brittany."

"Hmmm," Grimaldi said, and it didn't sound like she believed it. I didn't either. No musician worth his salt—especially an up-and-coming one, who had just landed himself and his band a good gig—would give up a performance at the Ryman just to get married.

"Why would Brittany say they were getting married if it wasn't true?"

"That's an interesting question, isn't it?" Grimaldi said, but she never answered it, because my phone rang. "Go ahead and get it."

I picked it up. The number was unfamiliar, and there was no name attached to it. That happens a lot to a real estate agent, though. Perfect strangers call and want to know about properties for sale and that sort of thing all the time. I put a smile on my face, since supposedly it shows up on the other end of the line, and said brightly, "This is Savannah. How may I help you?"

"Hello, Savannah," a voice said.

Eighteen

My jaw dropped, and I almost dropped the phone, too. Grimaldi sent me a worried look as I fumbled, and then a narrow-eyed stare when she saw my expression.

I managed to hit the speaker button. "Where are you? What do you want?"

Denise Seaver giggled, and Grimaldi's eyes narrowed further. She pulled over to the side of the road and stopped the car.

"It's not what *I* want," Denise Seaver said gaily—and I knew even as she said it that she was lying; it was all about what she wanted, "it's about what I have that you want."

"And what's that?"

Not that I couldn't guess, but I wanted to hear her say it. Or rather, I wanted to hear what she was going to say. Call it curiosity. Next to me, Grimaldi had pulled out her own phone and initiated the record function to have a record of the conversation.

The smirk in Denise Seaver's voice was audible all the way from the other end of the metaphorical line. "Your husband's brat."

It took effort to make sure my voice was even. "We haven't found any proof that Carmen's baby is Rafe's."

"You will," Denise Seaver said, and sounded confident about

it.

"How would you know that? Did Carmen tell you it was?"

She made a little humming noise that was either assent or pleasure. It could be either, to be honest. She could probably hear that I was upset, and I'm sure it made her happy.

"So what do you want?" I asked again.

"To make a deal."

Grimaldi arched her brows.

"What kind of deal?"

"You give me fifty thousand dollars," Denise Seaver said, "and I tell you where to find the baby."

Fifty thousand dollars? "Have you lost your mind? I don't have fifty thousand dollars. I sell real estate. I haven't made ten thousand dollars yet, let alone fifty thousand. And Rafe's in law enforcement. We don't make fifty thousand dollars between the two of us!"

Grimaldi scowled at me. I made a face. Yes, I realized that this might not have been the best response. But in the surprise, and the heat of the moment, I hadn't thought about that. Now, all I could do was wait and see how she reacted. Hopefully she wouldn't just hang up the phone and peddle the baby somewhere else.

"Your mother has money."

She does. My father was a lawyer, and of course Mother inherited everything when he died. Including the Martin Mansion, that had been in his family for generations. If she didn't have fifty grand sitting in an account somewhere, a loan on the house would net her many times that.

"While that may be true," I said, "my mother is trying to deal with the fact that her husband had a love child with her best friend, and over the thirty-three years she's known Audrey, nobody said a word about it. I don't think now's a good time to ask her for fifty thousand dollars so I can save *my* husband's love child."

Denise Seaver was starting to sound impatient. Grimaldi was starting to look it. "I don't care how you get the money. Ask your brother or sister. Take a loan. But if you want the brat, you'll get it."

"How long do I have?"

"An hour," Denise Seaver said.

"I can't come up with fifty grand in an hour!"

She sighed. Long-suffering wafted along the air waves. "If you want this baby, you can."

"I really don't think so. I mean, it's not just that I have to find someone with that kind of money just sitting around, and then talk them into giving it to me. But there's getting it out of the bank, too. I assume you won't take a check?"

"Cash," Denise Seaver said. "Small, unmarked bills."

Like in the movies. "Let's say I can make this work, and I can get the money. Then what happens? We'll meet somewhere and I give it to you?"

Denise Seaver agreed that this seemed like a fine plan.

"When do I get the baby?"

"When I have my money."

I shook my head. Not that she could see me. "I don't think so. If you have the money, you have no incentive to give me the baby. I want the baby first."

"If you have the baby, you have no incentive to give me the money," Denise Seaver pointed out.

A classic Catch-22.

"Then what do you suggest we do? Meet on the bridge at midnight, you put the baby down, I throw the duffel bag with the cash in your direction, and you take it and run while I pick up the baby?""

"I suggest you get busy asking your family to fund your husband's brat," Denise Seaver said. "I'll call back in an hour."

She hung up before I had the chance to say anything more.

For a moment, both Grimaldi and I sat there in silence. We

were both too shocked to speak, I think. Then I woke up. "I have to find fifty thousand dollars somewhere."

"Extortion," Grimaldi said with grim satisfaction. "Not that she's ever seeing daylight again, once we get her back behind bars. But the charges are racking up. At this point, she's looking at another count of murder, reckless endangerment and negligent homicide, kidnapping, and now extortion."

"That only matters if we can find her. And I don't know how we will." I was dialing while I spoke. "Darcy? It's Savannah. I need to talk to Dix."

"If this is about your mother..."

"It isn't," I said, although now I had gotten curious. "What happened?"

"Your sister went over there this morning—"

Your sister, too, I thought, but didn't say it.

"—and your mother had mixed herself a blender full of mimosas and was making her way through it."

Sheesh. "Well, at least it wasn't brandy."

"Not this morning," Darcy said. "By now, who knows?" She waited a second, I guess to see if I had a response, and then added, "I'll put you through to Dix."

I thanked her, and waited. A second later, I heard my brother's voice. "Morning, Sis."

"Morning," I said. "I need fifty thousand dollars."

"Funny thing," Dix said. "So do I."

"What do you need money for?"

There was a pause. "I thought you were kidding," Dix said. "What's going on?"

"I told you that Denise Seaver escaped from prison yesterday with another inmate, didn't I? The Hispanic woman with the big stomach? She gave birth in a shack up in the hills north of Nashville after they stabbed the guard and walked off. Denise Seaver left her there to bleed out, and took the baby. Now she wants to sell it to me for fifty thousand dollars."

The pause this time was much longer. "I get the feeling there's more to this story," Dix said.

I grimaced. "There's a chance the baby might be Rafe's."

This time, the pause went on for long enough that I started to worry he wasn't going to answer. I glanced at the phone display, and the line was still open. "Dix?"

His voice sounded sort of dangerous. Or as dangerous as my brother's voice ever is. "He cheated on you?"

"It was before we worked things out between us," I said. "Sometime in late November or early December last year."

"You were together then."

"We'd been together. But after the miscarriage, we weren't together for a while. And anyway, he was undercover in Atlanta. And then he came back here and got involved with Carmen."

It took Dix a few seconds to process the information. "This is the inmate who gave birth in the woods? So what you're saying is that your husband—before he was your husband—slept with a suspect?"

"It's a long story," I said. "And we don't know that it's his baby. We're still waiting for the paternity test. But if it is—hell... heck, even if it isn't—I can't just tell Denise Seaver to do her worst. She will, and her worst is pretty bad. If she can't make money from it, that baby will probably end up floating down the Cumberland River with its throat cut by tonight."

And the mental image of that was enough to bring on a wave of nausea. I put my hand to my stomach, and my own baby turning cartwheels inside, and swallowed hard.

"I don't have fifty grand just sitting around, Savannah," Dix said. "I could probably come up with that much, given a couple of days, but it's all tied up in time deposits and IRAs and mutual funds and things like that."

"I don't have a couple of days. She's calling back in an hour. And if I don't have the money—or the promise of the money— God knows what she'll do to that baby."

"Then I can't help you," Dix said. "It's going to be the same thing for Catherine, by the way. We don't keep that kind of money just sitting around. We've got kids. We've got investments and college funds and stuff like that, but not a lot of liquid cash."

There went my second phone call. "I don't suppose Mother..."

"No," Dix said. "And if you call her and take advantage of the fact that she's drunk as a skunk right now..."

"Darcy told me she's been throwing back mimosas."

"Liquid breakfast," Dix said. "At least she's getting some vitamin C with the booze. But if you call and bother her with this, I'll kill you." He hung up.

"OK, then." I hung up, too.

"What?" Grimaldi asked. I told her what Dix had said, and she nodded. "Good call. And anyway, your mother probably won't be sympathetic to a sob story about your husband's love child right now. Not with what she's dealing with herself."

No. And she had just started liking Rafe, too, after almost a year of not liking him at all. I wasn't about to do anything to change that. "So what do I do now? Try to fake her out with a duffel bag full of newspaper?"

Grimaldi grimaced. "I'm not sure that's going to work. Or that it's a good idea, with the life of the baby on the line."

Me, either.

"Do you think maybe it's time to call your husband?"

Shit. I mean... shoot. I'd been hoping to avoid that. Even though I realized it was unreasonable to think I could. "I guess."

"I'll do it." She dialed. After a moment, she asked, "Where are you?"

Rafe said something.

"There's been a development. Can you talk?"

The response must have been yes, because Grimaldi laid out the development in a few words. "Seaver just contacted your wife. She wants fifty thousand dollars in exchange for the baby."

I could hear Rafe's voice get louder. I couldn't hear what he was saying, but I didn't need to. We didn't have fifty thousand dollars, and didn't know anyone who did.

In the midst of Grimaldi talking the situation over with Rafe, my own phone rang again. I glanced at the display—the Martin and McCall law office. My heart skipped a beat; maybe Dix had changed his mind or come up with some sort of solution? Maybe if he and Catherine and Jonathan pooled their resources, and borrowed a little from the firm...?

I opened the door and slipped out of the car. No sense in having both of us sitting side by side carrying on two different conversations. "Dix?"

"No," Darcy said. "It's me."

"Oh. Hi." I leaned my butt against the warm side of Grimaldi's unmarked sedan. "What can I do for you?"

"I heard about what happened," Darcy said.

I grimaced. "Was Dix loud?"

"That, and I was curious, so I asked." She hesitated a moment. "I'll give you the money."

I blinked. "You have fifty thousand dollars?" She was my brother's receptionist, for God's sake. Why work for Dix, if she had that kind of money just sitting around?

"Insurance payout from my parents' accident," Darcy said. "They died at the same time, so I became the beneficiary for both of their life insurance policies."

I shook my head. "I can't let you spend your parents' money on this. You may not get it back. I'm sure Grimaldi will try to figure out a way to use this to arrest Denise Seaver again, but the money may be lost."

"You asked your brother for help," Darcy said. "And you would have asked your sister and your mother if your brother hadn't told you not to."

She was right. I would have.

"I'm your sister, too. And I want to help."

I wanted to thunk the back of my head against the roof of the car. *Way to go, Savannah, making your new sister feel left out.* "I'm sorry. It's still new. And I didn't want to assume you'd be interested in helping."

"And you didn't think I'd have any money." Her voice held a hint of amusement, so at least it didn't seem like she was unforgiving.

"That, too," I admitted. If my lawyer brother didn't, how was I to guess that his receptionist would? "I sure don't. And I don't feel great about taking yours."

"You would have taken Dix's."

"That's..." *Different.*

"I don't see that you have much of a choice," Darcy pointed out. "And I'm happy to do it."

"But your parents' life insurance..."

"You're my sister," Darcy said firmly. "If it hadn't been for you, I'd still be alone. I want to help. Please let me."

Since she put it like that... "I'll do my best to get it back to you. If there's any way to keep it safe and return it, I will."

"Don't worry about it," Darcy said, which is not what I would have said about the potential loss of fifty thousand dollars. "Just go keep that baby safe. And get that bitch back behind bars."

I promised I would. "She's calling back within the hour. After I speak to her again, I'll drive to Sweetwater and pick it up."

"I'll be ready," Darcy said. "The bank is just across the square and the money's sitting in an account. It shouldn't take long. I'll go there now." She hung up before I could say anything more, even thank you.

I took a second to pull myself together and to send a thank-you up above for Darcy before I opened the car door again and slid in. "We have the money."

Grimaldi stopped in the middle of a sentence—presumably still talking to Rafe—to stare at me. "What did you say?"

"We have the money. My sister is giving it to me."

"Remind me to thank Catherine next time I see her," Rafe's voice came tinnily from out of the phone.

I shook my head. "Not Catherine. Darcy."

By now Grimaldi had put him on speaker. "Darcy gave you the money? Where did she get that kind of cash?"

"Life insurance policy from when her parents died," I said. "Her adoptive parents."

Everyone was silent for a moment while we all contemplated Darcy's generosity. Then Grimaldi shook it off. "Hopefully we can get it back to her."

Hopefully. But— "We'll have to risk the money. We can't risk the baby. The baby is most important. Then getting Denise Seaver back in prison. If we can do that, we can probably get the money back, too. But keeping the baby safe is the first priority."

For a second, nobody said anything. Then—

"Darlin'..." Rafe said.

"What?"

"Are you sure you wanna take your sister's money for this? If we lose it all..."

"I warned her that might happen," I said. "She said it was OK. And it's not like we have a choice. You and I certainly don't have that kind of cash."

"But this ain't your family's problem. It's mine."

"Which makes it mine," I said, "since you're my husband. Which makes it theirs, since they love me. And you. They're not just my family, you know. They're yours, as well."

He didn't say anything at first. Then— "Your mama's gonna go back to thinking I'm the scum of the earth, ain't she?"

"At the moment," I said, "she's deep in her own problems and a blender of mimosas. She might never hear about it. And anyway, she has no room to talk."

He didn't respond to that, and I added, "We don't have a choice. Denise Seaver made it very clear that if we didn't come up with the money, we could kiss that baby goodbye. We have to get it back, whether it's yours or someone else's. Darcy is willing to help. Let's just be grateful. If we lose all her money, we can always promise to take care of her in her old age, or something."

Rafe snorted, but didn't answer.

"By now, we probably have forty-five minutes before she calls back and tells me where and when she wants me to meet her. If there's anything we can do to find her and the baby—or just the baby—before we have to hand over the money, we should do it."

"We've been trolling the thrift stores," Rafe said. "Looks like she bought some stuff in one of'em earlier this morning, just after they opened. A skirt, a blouse, a bag, and a pair of sandals. And she talked the clerk down to twenty-five bucks on a baby stroller. Said she only had fifty dollars total."

"She must have found some money somewhere—"

No sooner were the words out of my mouth than I wanted to smack my own forehead. "Never mind. I know where she got it."

"Where?" Grimaldi asked.

I glanced at her. "I wondered where she'd gotten my cell phone number. I bet if we check the fingerprints on the window sill in the office, they'll be hers. Mr. Sullivan knows where I work. It's just a few blocks from where I used to live. What do you want to bet he mentioned it? She probably went there, broke the window, took the petty cash, and found my phone number in Brittany's Rolodex."

Grimaldi nodded. "There were sixty-four dollars there the other day, you said?"

I nodded. Rafe probably did, too, on the other end of the line.

"That would leave her with fourteen dollars after what she spent. What do you suppose she did with that?"

I tried to put myself in her position. Homeless, newly

escaped from prison, carrying a baby. Chances were she would have wanted something to eat. I hadn't thought to ask anyone in the office whether there was food missing from the fridge, but it would be an interesting question at some later point. Chances were, she'd found something in the fridge or freezer last night. Maybe the Lean Cuisine Chicken Pot Pie I had offered Heidi yesterday for lunch. The baby had formula she'd gotten from the Catholic church, so she was good there. But by this morning, she might have been hungry again.

"Say ten dollars for food," Grimaldi said, when I put the suggestion forward. "She's expecting to get paid today, so she has no reason to conserve her money. And she's been locked up for a while, with no access to nice things. She was a doctor, so reasonably well off. Rather than go to a gas station or grocery store to buy something cheap, she might have gone somewhere where she could indulge in a nice breakfast. Not somewhere too nice—she had the baby—but maybe a coffee shop or something like that."

"Brew-ha-ha," I said. "It's a coffee shop on Main Street just a few blocks from the office. Good coffee. Nice pastries."

"I'll check if they've seen her," Rafe said, from the other side of town. "It's right down the street from where we are."

Grimaldi nodded. "We're on our way." She pulled the car away from the curb and flicked on the lights and siren.

"We'll see you soon," I yelled at Rafe. He yelled something back, but I couldn't hear what it was. Hopefully it was nice.

Nineteen

Grimaldi broke not only the sound barrier, but also a lot of laws on our way back to East Nashville. We hit the interstate ramp at seventy miles per hour, and by the time we were on the highway, the speed had gone up. By a lot. We averaged between ninety-five and a hundred all the way to the Shelby Avenue exit, where we screeched down the ramp like something out of an action movie. It couldn't have been more than three minutes after that, that we pulled into the parking lot outside Brew-ha-ha and cut the engine.

Blessed silence descended. I shook my head to stop the ringing in my ears. "How do you stand that?"

"You get used to it," Grimaldi said, throwing her door open and scanning the parking lot. "There they are."

There they were. José's truck was parked at the other end of the lot, and its owner was leaning against the tailgate sipping from a cup with the Brew-ha-ha logo.

I looked around. "Where's Rafe?"

"Let's ask," Grimaldi said and headed across the lot on long legs. I scurried after her, still looking around for my husband.

José was pointing him out before we could ask. "He's over there, talking to the bus driver."

A bus had stopped across the street, and Rafe had engaged the driver in conversation. She was female, naturally; otherwise,

I'm sure the bus would be gone by now.

"What about?" Grimaldi wanted to know.

"The barista said Seaver was here this morning. Came in wearing the scrubs, came out of the bathroom in the skirt and sandals. Ordered a caramel macchiato and a banana muffin. Sat and ate it. Then ran across the street when the bus came, and got on."

"What about the baby?" Grimaldi asked.

"She had it in a stroller. It must have been asleep. The barista said it didn't make noise."

Hopefully asleep was all it was. It was a newborn. It couldn't be good for it to be dragged all over creation like this.

"And she took it on the bus?"

José nodded. "That's what the barista said."

Across the street, the bus pulled away. Once it had, Rafe sauntered back toward us. Naturally there was a gap in traffic right then, so he could just mosey across. If it had been me, I would have had to dodge between the cars the whole way.

"Was that the same bus driver?" Grimaldi asked.

Rafe shook his head. "But she told me who to call. And she said there are security cameras all over the bus depot downtown."

"Are you sure she went to downtown?"

"It seems likely," I put in. And added, as they all turned to me, "I mean, here we are at Main Street and Tenth. Main Street and Fifth is the last block before the interstate and the river. If she was going to Fifth, she'd probably just walk. It's five blocks. But if she's going all the way into downtown, it makes sense to take the bus. Especially if she wants to get off the street."

Grimaldi nodded. "Bus depot it is. Let's go."

We went. She and I piled back into the sedan, Rafe and José climbed into the truck. And we headed toward downtown.

We were almost there when my phone rang. I pulled it out and looked at it. "It's her. What do I do? What do I say?"

Grimaldi pulled off to the side of the road, right in the middle of the bridge, and put on her blue lights so no one would bother us. Rafe and José were already far up ahead, and didn't notice us stopping. Or if they did, they didn't turn around.

Grimaldi's voice was calm. "Take a breath, then answer the phone. Tell her you have the money. Make sure she knows that first. And then ask her what she wants you to do with it. Anything else you can get out of her is a bonus."

I nodded.

"Do it now. Before she gets tired of waiting."

Right. I turned on the phone. "I have the money."

Denise Seaver sounded amused. "I thought you'd be able to figure something out."

"I found someone who'll give it to me. She's gone to the bank." I wished I could stop babbling, but I was too nervous. "As soon as you tell me where to meet you, I'll go to Sweetwater and pick it up."

She didn't answer, and I added, brightly, "It'll take me about three hours to get there and back. I assume you're still in Nashville?"

She didn't answer that, nor had I expected her to. "Once I have the money," I added, "I can meet you somewhere. I give you the money, you give me the baby. And we both go on our merry way."

Denise Seaver allowed as how that would work.

"You want to tell me where to meet you?"

"No," Denise Seaver said. "I'll call you in two hours. By then, you should have the money and be on your way back to Nashville."

I should. Unless there was a delay at the bank, or somewhere else. Roadwork, or a traffic accident. "It could take a little longer than that. I have to go home and get my car first. And pick up a suitcase or something to put the money in."

It wouldn't fit in my handbag, I assumed. I've never actually seen fifty thousand dollars in tens and twenties, but it seemed like it would take up more space than that.

"Two hours," Denise Seaver said. And hung up.

I turned to Grimaldi. "You have to take me home so I can drive to Sweetwater and get the money. And I have to call Darcy back."

I started to dial, but before I had completed the number, the phone rang again. "It's Rafe."

"Answer it," Grimaldi said.

"What the hell happened to you?" the love of my life asked. I guess they'd arrived at the bus depot, just a couple of blocks on the other side of the river, and realized we weren't behind them.

"Sorry. Denise Seaver called back. I have to drive to Sweetwater to pick up the money. Grimaldi's going to drive me home so I can get my car and a suitcase to carry the money in when I get it."

"I'll go with you," Rafe said.

"There's no need to. I'll be perfectly fine on my own."

"It's a lot of money," Rafe said.

"Yes, but nobody will know that I have it. I'll be perfectly safe. As long as I make sure I have plenty of gas in the car, I won't have to stop until I get there, and I won't have to stop on the way home. I'll be fine. And if I have to wait for you, I'll be wasting time. She said she'd call back in two hours. That's pushing it, even if I leave right now. Stay with José and look at the cameras at the bus depot. Maybe you can figure out where she went and we won't have to give her the money."

He didn't answer, and I added, "You're already there. It doesn't make any sense for you to stop what you're doing and leave again. And if you want to leave, José has to leave, since he drove you. Just stay there. I'll be fine on my own."

"Maybe Tammy can go with you," Rafe said.

I rolled my eyes. "I'm sure Grimaldi would be happy to go with me. But I don't need her to. She has a job to do as well. And a murder to solve. And five hundred thousand dollars to track down. Our measly fifty grand is a drop in the bucket in comparison. This isn't her case. It's Mendoza's. Although I can call him and ask if he'd like to go to Sweetwater with me."

"No," Rafe said. "That's all right. If you wanna go on your own, you go on your own."

I grinned. So did Grimaldi.

"I'll give you a call when I get there," I said, "just so you know everything's all right. Meanwhile, just do what you can to figure out where she is, OK? That way, maybe we can save Darcy's money."

Rafe said he would. "Be careful, darlin'."

"Always," I said, and didn't realize until I'd hung up that I had given him the same pat answer he always gave me. I wondered if it annoyed him as much as it usually did me.

"I can go with you if you want," Grimaldi offered as she pulled the car away from the curb and back into traffic crossing the Victory Memorial Bridge. "If you're worried."

I shook my head. "I'm really not. I've made the drive from Nashville to Sweetwater dozens of times since I moved here, and nothing's ever happened to me. There's no reason to think anything will happen this time. I don't need an escort. You have a murder to solve and five hundred thousand dollars to account for, and I'd much rather have Rafe and José here, doing whatever they can to find Denise Seaver before we have to hand over the money. She's here in Nashville, and if they can find her, all the rest of it will be moot."

Grimaldi nodded, and signaled to turn north on Second Avenue, between police headquarters and the Ben West Building. "I'll drive you home and let you pick up your car. Then I'll get back to work on Devon's murder. With any luck, that subpoena will come in soon, and I can figure out who the IP address belongs to. Once we know who sent the email, we'll be a step closer to figuring out who's behind this."

"It's possible to trace a wire transfer, I assume?"

"With a subpoena," Grimaldi said. "No financial institution is just going to hand over depositor information. And if the account is foreign, that makes it all the more difficult."

"Is this one foreign?"

"We'll have to see," Grimaldi said, and signaled to turn right onto the Jefferson Street Bridge, back across the river. We were executing one big square, and would end up a mile or maybe two from where we'd started, at the house on Potsdam Street. "I'm going to start with the IP address and see where that takes me. Chances are that's located somewhere around here. Someone shot Devon Knight, and it wasn't the Russians."

No, it wasn't. "Will you let me know what happens?"

"If anything does," Grimaldi said. "But you've got some pretty heavy stuff on your own plate right now. I'll probably let you deal with that first. I don't think I'll be arresting anyone today. Not unless we get lucky and nab Denise Seaver. But I don't think I'm close enough to arrest anyone for Devon's murder."

"Do you have a suspect?"

She hesitated. "I have a theory. Actually, I have more than one theory. Several theories. I'm willing to bet one of them is right. But right now, it could go a couple of different ways."

I had my mouth open to ask her to share, when she added, "And I'm not going to tell you anything about it. You have enough to deal with."

"It might make for a nice distraction," I said. With an ingratiating smile.

I got a jaundiced look back. "Now's not the time to get distracted. If things work out tonight, I'll tell you all about it tomorrow. By then, maybe I'll even have some proof."

Fine. "Fine," I said. "Be that way."

"You do realize that I don't have to tell you anything, right?

You're a civilian. By rights, you should be a suspect. Your fingerprints are all over that desk."

"Of course they are. I sat there and worked most of the day Monday and half of Tuesday. It's not like I'm going to take messages wearing gloves!"

"I'm just saying," Grimaldi said, "that you're lucky I'm willing to share anything at all with you. I don't have to."

"You don't seriously suspect me?"

"No," Grimaldi said, "but someone who doesn't know you might. You'd better be grateful this is my case and not someone else's. Like Jaime Mendoza's."

"He wouldn't suspect me, either."

"Probably not," Grimaldi admitted, "although it would be fun to see him interrogate you. Especially with your husband watching."

"They talked yesterday," I informed her. "Over Carmen's dead body. Mendoza was quite nice about us horning in on his crime scene."

"He's a nice guy. And a good cop. And someone should probably get in touch with him and tell him what's going on."

I nodded. "Someone should." But it wouldn't be me.

"Do you think your husband will?"

"Maybe not. Although he might. But he's not used to having to keep other people in the loop on what he's doing."

"I'll take care of it," Grimaldi said. "Give me a call after you hear from Seaver about the money drop. I'll let Jaime know, and we'll coordinate an op between the two of us and your husband."

I told her I would, as we started up Potsdam Street toward the house. "It'll be a couple of hours, though. She knows exactly how long it'll take me to drive from Nashville to Sweetwater. I'm sure she's done it plenty herself, back and forth to St. Jerome's, coordinating all the baby sales with Doctor Rushing. She won't call again until she's sure I have the money."

"No worries," Grimaldi said, and flicked on the signal to turn the car into the gravel driveway leading up to Mrs. Jenkins's house. "We've all got plenty to do while we wait. If he finds her, I'm sure your husband will let you know."

I was sure he would, too. "He has my number."

Grimaldi stopped the sedan behind the Volvo, and I opened my door and started the process of shoe-horning myself out. "Thanks for taking me with you this morning."

"I enjoyed the company," Grimaldi said. And ruined the warm fuzzies by added, "Spending time with you is usually entertaining."

"I'm sorry our problems are distracting you from your own case."

"Don't worry about it," Grimaldi said. "The prison escape and kidnapping might not be my case, but I'm a cop. It's still my responsibility to do what I can. And it was my case the last time. I want Denise Seaver back behind bars as much as you do."

"I appreciate the help. I'm sure Rafe does, too, even if he'll probably never say so." By now I was out of the car and leaning down with my hand on the door. "I need to go."

Grimaldi nodded. "Drive carefully. I know it's tempting to try to get there as fast as possible, but saving Carmen's baby and losing your own because you crash wouldn't make anybody happy."

No. Except maybe Denise Seaver. "I'll be careful," I promised.

"I'll wait for you to get going." She indicated the Volvo.

"It's all right. I have to go inside and get the suitcase for the money." And pee. I always have to pee, and it had been quite a while since I'd had the chance.

"Don't you think Darcy has a suitcase?"

"She probably does. But I'm already taking her money. I don't want to take her suitcase, too. It'll only take a minute." I waved her off. "Just go. Do your thing. There's no need for you to sit here and wait for me to come back out. All I'm going to do, is get in the car and drive away."

I headed for the stairs. The gravel crunched under my shoes. Behind me, Grimaldi reversed and began to maneuver past the Volvo and bike. I climbed the stairs and watched until she was on her way down the driveway. Then I waved and turned and fitted the key in the lock.

I wasn't kidding about having to pee. The first thing I did when I got inside—after making sure the door was locked behind me, obviously—was quickstep down the hallway toward the downstairs bath, without even taking my shoes off first. The heels were clicking on the hardwoods. One of these days I really was going to do as I said and start wearing flats.

For now, I lifted my skirt, pulled down my panties, and sank down on the toilet with a sigh of relief.

I'll spare you a detailed description of the next minute and a half. Suffice it to say I had to pee a lot. And the baby felt like it had taken up permanent residence on my bladder. And I had three more months of pregnancy to go. I could only imagine how much worse it was going to get.

After my business was finished, I dropped my skirt, washed my hands, and headed back into the hallway to go find a suitcase I thought would be big enough to hold fifty thousand dollars worth of small bills.

Only to stop—on a dime, as the saying goes—when I came within sight of the front door. "Hello, Savannah," Denise Seaver said, looking at me down the length of a very businesslike pistol.

Twenty

My jaw dropped. "How did you get here? I locked the door!"

She gestured with the pistol. "Through the back."

"You couldn't have! I would have heard you walk by."

"Three hours ago," Denise Seaver said.

I blinked. "You've been here for three hours? You were here when you called me?"

She nodded. And smiled that beneficent smile that never fails to get on my nerves, especially now that I know what she's really like.

"Why?"

"I thought I'd find you here," Denise Seaver said, with a faintly annoyed wrinkle between her brows now, "but by the time I got here, you were gone."

"Detective Grimaldi came and got me. Someone had broken into the office and taken the petty cash. I assume that was you?"

"I was looking for your new address," Denise Seaver said, "since you'd moved from the apartment you used to live in."

Her tone of voice indicated that I'd had no right to inconvenience her.

"The petty cash was just sitting there, I suppose, and you thought you might as well take it?"

"I needed to buy a stroller," Denise Seaver said. "Even newborns get heavy when you carry them around for hours."

"Speaking of newborns..." I looked around. "Where's the baby?"

She gestured up the stairs with the gun.

"May I?"

She inclined her head, and stepped back as I moved forward. I guess maybe she was afraid I'd make a grab for the gun. She didn't have to worry. I've been shot before—by Denise Seaver, as it happens; the one and only time it's happened to me—and I had absolutely zero desire for it to happen again.

Not to mention that these days, it's not just my own welfare I have to worry about, but that of the baby inside me, too.

So I moved forward and she withdrew into the corner until I had gone past her and was on my way up the stairs. Then she came out of the corner and followed, with the gun no doubt trained on my back.

I stopped in the upstairs hallway. "Where?"

It was so quiet up here, that to be honest, I had grave concerns about the welfare of the baby.

For some reason, I thought maybe she'd put it in the nursery-under-construction down the hall from the master bedroom. That's where our baby would be, once it joined us. But with more than three months to go, the nursery wasn't ready. One item of particular importance that was missing was a baby bed.

So Carmen's baby wasn't there. Instead, Denise Seaver jerked the gun toward the lavender bedroom across the hall from the master. It had been Tondalia Jenkins's bedroom while she'd been living here, and Mother had slept in it the night after my botched wedding ceremony.

The baby looked impossibly tiny in the middle of the queen sized bed. I crept over, as quietly as I could, so I wouldn't wake it.

It was minuscule, it was wrinkled, its face looked sort of scrunched up, and between you and me, it wasn't very pretty. Tufts of black hair alternately stood up on the top of its head, or were glued to its skin. It looked something like the human equivalent of a baby bird.

There was no way to guess whether it was a boy or girl. Not unless I unwrapped it. The face gave no clues whatsoever.

As far as other things went, its skin color was middling. Darker than mine. Maybe not as dark as Rafe's. I didn't think our baby would end up being as dark as Rafe, either, since my Caucasian coloring would probably act like a good dollop of cream in his coffee.

Try as I might, I couldn't see anything of Rafe in the little face in front of me. Hair and skin, sure, but a lot of people have golden skin and black—or almost black—hair. Carmen did, too. It didn't necessarily mean that Rafe had contributed to this one's DNA.

On the other hand, it didn't mean he hadn't.

I didn't recognize any of his features in the tiny face. But since I also didn't recognize any of Carmen's, that wasn't necessarily significant. It was just a tiny, wrinkled, newborn baby. It could have been anybody's.

"Cute," I lied.

Denise Seaver gave me a jaundiced look, as if she suspected I was fibbing. "Pick it up."

I took a step back. "Me? Why do I have to?"

"Because I've got the gun," Denise Seaver said.

And OK, that was a powerful incentive. I thought about offering to take it off her hands, but I didn't think she'd go for it. Or think it was funny. "What about the suitcase? I came inside to get a suitcase for the money. So I could take it to Sweetwater and fill it."

"I'll carry the suitcase," Denise Seaver said, gesturing with the gun. "You pick up the baby."

I didn't want to pick up the baby. First, because I figured it would probably wake up and start screaming if I tried to move it. And second, because I just didn't want to touch it. It seemed wrong.

"We can do this the easy way," Denise Seaver told me, "or the hard way."

Me doing what I was told was probably the easy way. "What's the hard way?"

"I shoot the brat," Denise Seaver said, moving the muzzle of the gun in the direction of the tiny scrap of life in the middle of the big bed, "and nobody has to carry it."

"No." I took a quick step forward. "That won't be necessary. I'll take it."

"I thought you would," Denise Seaver said, with that nasty smirk.

The baby felt even smaller in my arms than it had looked in the middle of the big expanse of bed, and it weighed practically nothing. When I first lifted it, it mewled a little bit, and its tiny face scrunched in a grimace. But then it settled back down in my arms. I had to sort of rest it on the ledge of my stomach.

"Where's the suitcase?" Denise Seaver asked.

"Master bedroom closet." I was too busy holding the baby and looking down at it to even consider whether now might be a good time to try to make a grab for the gun. The baby was small and helpless, and looking at it, knowing that it was my responsibility to keep it safe, at least for the next few hours, was like nothing I'd ever felt before. I loved Dix's girls, and would gladly kill anyone who tried to hurt them. I loved David, and would have mauled anyone who tried to hurt him, with my own hands if I had to. But this was different. This tiny creature was dependent on me for everything. It couldn't move anywhere if I didn't carry it. It would starve if I didn't feed it. Without me, it had no chance at all.

As if it had heard me, its little face contorted, and then its eyes opened. Big eyes, dark. Might be Rafe's eyes. Might be Carmen's. Could be someone else's entirely. It didn't matter. In that moment of holding it, and feeling its fragile body and towering need for comfort and help, I knew that if this was Rafe's baby and I ended up raising it, I could love it. I didn't yet. I could give it up if it wasn't his and we had no claim on it. But if it was his, it was mine, and I would love it as much as anyone could.

It gathered its little body. Its face contorted, and it let out a stomach-curdling scream.

"What's wrong?" I asked, panicked. "What does it want?"

"He." Denise Seaver sounded irritable. I felt a moment of understanding and kinship. If she had listened to wails like this for the past day, I could understand her irritability. The screams felt like they were piercing my ear drums and digging into my brain. All I wanted to do was stop it—him—from screaming.

"Well, excuse me. You've got him wrapped up. It's not like I can see his private parts."

Denise Seaver gave me a look. "He's probably wet and hungry. Why don't you get some practice and change him."

I could do that. I had changed Dix's daughters' diapers before. Different gender, but the same process.

Denise Seaver tossed the bag of diapers on the bed as I unwrapped the blankets around the baby. It was so tiny, with such twig-like little arms and legs that were flailing wildly. The diaper was indeed soggy with wetness, and I took it off. Only to have to jump back to avoid being sprayed again. "God!"

"Boys spray," Denise Seaver told me, not without a fair amount of malicious glee in her voice.

No kidding. I snatched a diaper out of the package and shook it open, and wrestled it around the baby. He kept wailing the whole time. It wasn't until the diaper was on and he was wrapped back up in the blankets that the squealing died down to hiccupping sobs. I picked him back up and cradled him.

"He's hungry," Denise Seaver said dispassionately.

I gave her a look. "You have formula, don't you? The lady at the Catholic Church said she gave you both diapers and baby formula."

For a second, her eyes narrowed. I guess she didn't like the fact that we knew everything she'd done since she escaped from prison.

At any rate, there was formula. I filled up a bottle and was about to sit down and feed the baby when Denise Seaver said, "Time to go."

"Now? But what about feeding the baby?"

"In the car," Denise Seaver said, and waved the gun toward the door. "Go."

Perforce, I went. Denise Seaver followed, wheeling the empty suitcase behind her. "Get your purse."

It was hanging on the newel post in the hallway. I guess she didn't want to risk having me drive without a license, just in case we got pulled over. Although if we got pulled over, she'd have bigger problems than that.

I had to thread the arm with the bottle through the strap of the purse and sort of scoot it onto my arm. It dangled there as we walked out.

"Keys." She let go of the suitcase and wiggled her fingers.

"Hands full," I said, extending the arm with the purse. "You'll have to dig them out."

She scowled but did it, and locked the door. For a crazy second, I contemplated hurtling down the stairs and away while she had her back turned. But she'd turn around and shoot me before I could get out of sight, and with holding the baby, I wouldn't be able to get the car door open, both of us inside, and the car locked again before she killed me. And besides, while Volvos are good, safe cars, I don't think they boast bullet-proof windows.

So I waited sedately, holding the baby and the bottle, for her to finish locking the door. If nothing else, our possessions would be safe. Then I headed down the stairs to the car with the gun pointing at my back.

We hadn't gotten around to buying a car seat, of course, so the baby ended up in the suitcase on the back seat. The seatbelt held the suitcase in place, and the luggage strap inside the suitcase kept the baby down. It wasn't as good as a car seat, but better than nothing. Denise Seaver tossed the secondhand stroller into the trunk, and got into the back seat next to the baby. "Drive."

I turned the key in the ignition. "Where are we going?"

She scowled at me in the mirror. "Sweetwater. You said you'd gotten my money."

"It isn't your money," I told her, as we rolled slowly down the driveway. "It's my sister's money. But I'll take you there to pick it up."

"Just drive carefully. If you try anything, this brat won't survive the trip."

She gestured with the muzzle of the gun at the baby, whom she was feeding with her other hand. She wasn't wearing a seatbelt. On the interstate, I could get the car up to speed and then slam on the brakes. She might go tumbling, while the baby might be OK, being strapped in as it was.

Then again, as Denise Seaver went tumbling, her gun could go off and shoot me in the back of the head, and we didn't want that. It would probably be safer just to take her to Sweetwater, give her the money and the car—if she wanted it—and wave her off. Just as long as she didn't want the baby. I wasn't giving her that.

So I drove. Down Potsdam Street, down Dresden, down Dickerson Pike, past the buffalo statues, and onto the interstate. The gas gauge was at less than half, but I didn't say anything about needing to stop and fill up. We had enough to get to Sweetwater, and what happened after that wasn't my problem. If Denise Seaver wanted my car, the gas would be her problem. If she didn't want the car, I could always fill up before I drove back. At that point, time would no longer be of the essence.

And if she shot me, the gas in my tank would be the least of my problems.

We headed south, adhering strictly to the speed limit and rules of the road. I didn't pass anyone, I didn't cut anyone off, I didn't make eye contact with anyone in another car. I stayed in the right lane and kept moving, slowly but steadily.

We were about halfway there, past Franklin and coming up on Spring Hill, when my phone rang. I reached for it, and Denise Seaver growled.

"It might be Rafe," I told her. "If I don't answer, he'll wonder why."

However, it wasn't Rafe. It was the Martin and McCall law office. "It's me," Darcy said. "I have the money."

"I'm on my way. Where do you want to meet?"

"What's wrong with meeting here?" Darcy wanted to know. "I'm carrying fifty thousand dollars in cash around with me."

While I could understand that she'd prefer to stay safe where she was, I didn't think Denise Seaver would want to park on the square in Sweetwater and walk into the Martin and McCall law office carrying a gun and a suitcase with a baby inside.

Nor did I particularly want to expose my brother or sister—either of them—to that.

"It would be better if we met somewhere else. Somewhere private."

There was a second's pause. I wondered whether Darcy was catching on that there was something not right. But no, probably not. She didn't know me well enough for that yet. To be honest, I'm not sure Dix would have caught on, either, and he's known me my whole life.

Both Grimaldi and Rafe would have. They hadn't known me more than a year each. But they were both in law enforcement and were used to thinking in terms of the worst case scenario. Most people wouldn't really consider that I might be in a hostage situation with a woman holding a gun on me as I answered the phone. But I had a feeling Rafe and/or Grimaldi would.

"OK," Darcy said slowly at last. "Where do you want to meet?"

Here was a chance to maybe give her a clue. If she was adept at all at picking up clues. I had no idea if she was. "Remember where we went Sunday night?"

"Doctor Seaver's house?" Darcy said doubtfully.

"Yes. There."

"You want me to meet you there?"

"Please." I glanced at the clock, and at the gun in the rearview mirror. The hole in the barrel looked big and black. In the suitcase, the baby made a soft, whimpering sound before going back to sleep. "We'll be there in thirty minutes."

Denise Seaver's eyes narrowed in the mirror, and that was when I realized I'd used the plural instead of the singular.

Darcy didn't question it, however. Maybe she thought I had Rafe with me. I wished I did. If I'd only taken him up on the offer of going with me, I wouldn't be in this predicament. "I'll see you in thirty minutes, then."

"If you get there before me," I told her, "you can just go in through the back door—it's probably still open—and leave the money inside. You don't have to wait for me."

Darcy hesitated, probably wondering what was wrong with me, for suggesting that she leave fifty thousand dollars in an unlocked, unoccupied house, and walk away. What I wanted to do, was tell her to stay far, far away so she wouldn't get hurt by the escaped prisoner with the gun, but this was the best I could do.

"I really appreciate your help," I added. "I don't know what I would have done without you."

"It's no problem," Darcy said. "I'm happy to help. Is everything OK?"

"Fine." I manufactured a smile. "Or it will be soon. Once this is over."

"I hear you. I'll see you in thirty minutes." She hung up. I went back to concentrating on driving.

"Where did you go Sunday night?" Denise Seaver asked suspiciously.

I met her eyes in the mirror. "Your house."

"My house?"

"We were looking for your medical records for thirty-four years ago, to see if we could find Darcy's birth mother. I and my brother and sister went there to look."

"You broke into my house?"

"The back door was open," I said. "And it's not like we took anything." Other than some medical records.

She breathed heavy for a minute. To be honest, she didn't smell so good. Stomping around in the woods, helping Carmen give birth, and thrift store clothes, not to mention no toothbrush or shampoo, hadn't done her any favors. I wrinkled my nose, and straightened it back out. "She'll meet us there with the money. I assumed you didn't want to walk into the Martin and McCall office to pick it up."

"No," Denise Seaver admitted after a moment.

"And I thought maybe you'd like to pick up some of your own clothes, too. Those look a little tight."

They did. The blouse gaped across her chest, and she looked like the skirt pinched. The sandals were a size or two too small; just enough that her big toes extended beyond the soles.

There was a pause. "You're being very accommodating," Denise Seaver said, her voice hostile.

I met her eyes in the rearview. "We want the same thing. Or more or less the same thing. You want the money, I want the baby kept safe. We both want to walk away from this. If we cooperate, we can both get what we want. You'll have an easier time getting away without the baby, so you may as well give him to me. And I'm willing to give you the money as long as you walk away."

She didn't answer, and I added, "Besides, you have a gun. I don't want you to shoot me. You've done it once already, and it hurt. Making sure you don't do it again is a pretty powerful inducement to making you happy."

Denise Seaver grunted. It wasn't a dissenting grunt, though. And on that note, we continued south on I-65.

Twenty-One

We reached Sweetwater just before two in the afternoon. The road to Denise Seaver's old subdivision lay past the Martin Mansion, and I glanced up at my childhood home as we moved past. The big, old house stood bathed in afternoon sun, looking like something out of *Gone With the Wind*, but other than that there was nothing to see. Mother had no visitors, and if she had been out today, she'd put the car back in the garage. Unless she was out somewhere right now, but I doubted it. By now, she had probably moved on from mimosas to manhattans, and was sitting in the parlor—or lying in bed—drinking herself into oblivion.

The subdivision was another five minutes down the road. We passed Copper Creek, where Dix lives, and then turned into the next fancy community. I made my slow way through the winding roads before pulling into Denise Seaver's driveway.

"I don't suppose you have a garage opener?"

The look she gave me spoke volumes. She'd been in prison for nine months. Why would she be carrying a garage opener?

"I didn't think so," I said. "You probably don't have a key, either. The back door is busted, though. If you want to go in and open the garage door, I can pull the car in."

"And have you drive away with the brat the second my back is turned? No, thank you. You go around and open the garage door. I'll drive the car in."

Fine. While I'd normally be loath to leave my car in her care, I didn't think she'd drive away with it and the baby and leave me here. If that was what she'd wanted, she'd have done it in Nashville. No, as long as she didn't have the money, we were sticking together.

So I left the car running and the door open. When I attempted to take my bag, Denise Seaver growled, "Leave it!"

I left it, and headed around the garage and over to the back door.

Last year, I had followed Marley Cartwright across her lawn and through the band of trees between her property and Denise Seaver's. Marley had knocked out the window in the back door, and when I came on the scene she was out cold on the kitchen floor, courtesy of a frying pan to the head. And just a few days ago, Darcy, Dix and I had been here, digging through the house for medical records. Being here again brought back memories.

I stuck my hand through the broken window and unlocked the door. Then I walked inside and through the laundry room over to the kitchen, and from there to the door leading into the garage. The remote for opening the car door was on the wall. I pushed it and listened to the door rumble up, letting in a widening band of sunshine for the first time in almost a year. The Volvo pulled into the garage. Once it was clear of the door, I pushed the button again, and the door closed, shutting out the light.

Denise Seaver opened the driver's side door. "Has she been here?"

"I haven't looked," I said. "But I didn't see anything on the way in." And Darcy probably wouldn't have walked all the way through the house to leave the money next to the front door. She'd be more likely to drop it somewhere near the back. "We're a little early."

Dammit. I had hoped that Darcy would have come and gone

before we got here. At least she'd be out of harm's way. Not that Denise Seaver had any reason to hurt her, not if Darcy brought the money, but it would have made me feel safer to be the only one in the crosshairs.

"So we wait." She gestured me back up the stairs to the kitchen.

"We should take the baby out of the car," I said.

"We should leave him there," Denise Seaver answered. "When your sister shows up, she won't expect to see a baby."

True. However— "I thought you wanted the suitcase so you could put the money in it."

"This is my house," Denise Seaver said. "If I had realized we were coming here, I wouldn't have bothered with your suitcase. I have suitcases of my own."

Right. I left the baby where it was, asleep on the back seat of the car, tucked into the suitcase, and headed up the stairs to the kitchen.

No sooner had we both navigated the short staircase, than we heard the crunching of footsteps on the patio outside the back door. Darcy must have arrived and parked her car out front while we'd been inside the garage.

The footsteps faltered a little as she saw the open back door. "Savannah?"

Denise Seaver's brows drew together.

"That's my sister," I said, before she could raise the gun and shoot. "I have two sisters now, remember? This is Darcy."

I didn't wait for her to respond, just called out. "Just put the money down and go, Darcy."

"No, no," Denise Seaver said, and moving more quickly than I thought she could, she shoved me out of the way.

I stumbled and had to catch myself on the kitchen counter. For a second, my stomach—and the baby inside—smacked against the hard edge of the granite. Meanwhile, Denise Seaver leapt like a gazelle for the back door. "Come on in, Darcy. Bring the money." She sounded quite genial, and if it hadn't been for the gun in her hand, I might even have believed she was.

Of course, she had every reason to be. Fifty thousand dollars were walking through the door.

Darcy had the money in a brown paper bag, and as it turned out, I had seriously overestimated how much space it would take up. A suitcase wouldn't be necessary. A medium sized medical bag would do the job.

Denise Seaver snatched it out of her hand. Darcy wasn't quick enough to let go, and one of the paper handles ripped. Denise Seaver clucked and gestured with the gun. "Go on. Over there. Next to your sister."

Darcy took a couple of steps toward me.

"Sorry," I said, still out of breath from bumping into the counter.

Darcy's brows furrowed. "You OK?"

"Not sure. I just hit my stomach on the counter."

"Unless you start bleeding," Denise Seaver said unfeelingly, "you're fine."

"You know," I told her, still cradling my stomach with both hands, "your bedside manner could use some improvement."

It didn't feel like I was starting to bleed, though, so hopefully nothing had happened. I was keeping my fingers crossed that the baby was cushioned well enough inside, that a concussion was unlikely.

Denise Seaver gestured with the gun. "Go on."

"Where?"

"Back in the garage," Denise Seaver said.

It didn't occur to me to say no. I figured she was going to give me the baby now that she had her money. So I traipsed over to the door with Darcy behind me, and opened it. And walked down the couple of steps to the concrete floor.

"Thank you," Denise Seaver said. The next thing I knew, I heard a sort of meaty thunk. I swung on my heel just in time to grab Darcy before she crumpled to the floor.

I staggered. "What did you do to her?"

Stupid question, I guess. The gun hadn't gone off—I would have heard that—so she must have hit Darcy on the back of the head with the butt of it.

"The same thing I'll do to you if you don't do as I say," Denise Seaver said.

This wasn't going the way I wanted it to at all. "I am doing what you say, dammit! And so was she. There was no need to hit her."

Denise Seaver didn't answer, and I added, "What is it you want me to do?"

"Drag her to the car and put her in," Denise Seaver said.

"You know, I'm not sure dragging a full grown woman is the best idea for me, in my condition."

She just looked at me, and I huffed. "Fine." I got my hands under Darcy's arms and hauled. She's tall, my sister—taller than me, and I'm five-eight; she has Audrey's height—but she also has Audrey's build. Tall and lithe. It could have been worse. Even so, it must have taken me a good two minutes to get her over to the passenger side door. I dropped her for long enough to get the door open and my purse out of the car, and then I wrestled her up into the seat. I had to move it back to make it easier.

"You didn't have to do this, you know." I told Denise Seaver breathlessly. "She wasn't a threat to you. I'm not, either. We just want the baby. You can take the money and leave."

"Oh," Denise Seaver said pleasantly—while her eyes weren't pleasant at all, "I intend to. After I take care of you."

That didn't sound good. "What are you going to do to me? I did what you said. You're not going to hit me, are you?"

She smiled. That wasn't pleasant, either. "Not if you continue to do as I say."

"I will. Just don't hurt Darcy. Or the baby." Or me, if you can avoid it.

"Get in the car." She waved the gun again. I moved toward the driver's side, and she shook her head. "In the back."

I opened the door behind Darcy, beside the suitcase with the baby, and slipped in. It was a tight squeeze, with Darcy's seat pushed back so far.

"Good," Denise Seaver said when I had gotten myself and the stomach situated. Things seemed to be OK in that regard. I couldn't feel that telltale trickle of blood between my legs she had told me to look out for.

Carmen's baby was still asleep, its tiny mouth pursed. Denise Seaver put the money bag down for a second to stick her hand in her pocket. "Take these."

They turned out to be a pair of handcuffs. Very official looking. She must have taken them off the dead guard in the van yesterday, along with the gun.

"Loop them around the headrest."

The Volvo has headrests in the same leather as the rest of the seat, attached to the top of the seat with two metal sticks. I looped the handcuffs around one of them.

"Put them around your wrists," Denise Seaver said. The business end of the gun was pointed squarely at me, so I didn't think I could demur.

I used one hand to snap the cuffs around the other wrist, and then I used that hand to close the other half. And just like that, I was a prisoner in my own car.

It was a bit uncomfortable, I guess. I had to keep my hands raised, so over time, they'd probably become numb and tingly. And if the baby woke, I couldn't do anything to feed or change him. But I wasn't really worried. I didn't think she had hit Darcy hard enough to do any real damage. Darcy wasn't handcuffed, so once she woke up, she'd get me out of here. Somehow. We just had to wait it out.

Or so I thought, until Denise Seaver walked away from me

and around to the other side of the car. She opened the door next to the baby.

"You said you'd leave him with me!" I said. "You got your money. You don't get to take him."

She gave me a look. "I have the gun. I get to do whatever I want to do. And you can't stop me."

She was right, I couldn't. But still— "You promised!"

"Calm down," Denise Seaver said. "I don't want the brat. He's all yours."

She left the passenger side door open and moved to the driver's side. And reached in and turned the key in the ignition.

The engine roared to life, and Denise Seaver straightened, looking pleased.

It took me a second, I admit it. At first, I wondered whether she was planning to take us somewhere. It wasn't until she scooped up Darcy's handbag and mine from the concrete floor and started walking toward the door into the house that I realized what the plan was.

"Wait a second!"

She stopped on the top step, looking politely inquiring.

"You can't just leave us here. We'll die!"

"Yes," Denise Seaver said. "That's the idea." She gave me one of those earth-motherly smiles. And then she went out through the door and closed it. I'm sure she locked it, too. Just as I'm sure it was fairly airtight. If some family man decided to do himself in by carbon monoxide poisoning in his garage, the home builder wouldn't want to be responsible for the gas seeping into the rest of the house and killing women and children.

"Shit!" I was upset enough not to bother to clean up my bad language, although I admit to feeling a little guilt over it. "Darcy! Darcy, wake up!"

Darcy didn't wake up. I yanked on the handcuffs. They didn't budge. Volvo builds solid cars.

I tried shaking the seat. "Darcy! Darcy!"

Nothing happened. The baby kept sleeping. Darcy kept being unconscious. And the car kept pumping out noxious fumes that would kill us all.

I forced myself to sit back and take stock of the situation. I had no idea how long it normally takes to die from carbon monoxide poisoning, but I figured the whole garage probably had to fill up before we were in trouble. Once that happened, the baby would probably go first. It was so tiny, with such small lungs. It might even have been born a little early. Denise Seaver had told me Carmen had a couple of weeks left before her due date. If so, the baby was born at least a week before term. Its lungs might not be fully developed yet, and that might contribute to an earlier demise.

Darcy was unconscious and breathing shallowly. That would probably help her—she was taking in less air—although it didn't help me. I'd rather have her awake and able to do something than unconscious and breathing shallowly. As it was, it seemed rescue was up to me. And I was handcuffed to my own car. Chances were, the more energy I expended and the more air I took in, the faster I would start breathing poison.

At the same time, sitting still and doing nothing wasn't an option. Today was not my day to die. Not here, and not like this.

I started yanking on the handcuffs again. It rattled the seat. I could see Darcy's head roll back and forth. "Darcy! Wake up! Darcy!"

Inside the house, I heard Denise Seaver's footsteps rattling down the stairs. A second later, the back door slammed.

"Darcy!" I stretched my hands as far as they would go through the cuffs and started swatting my unconscious sister. "She's leaving! We have to get out of here! C'mon, Darcy! Wake up!"

Darcy moaned, but didn't stir.

"Shit." I sat back and took a breath. Was it my imagination, or was it getting harder to breathe?

Probably just my imagination, I told myself. There couldn't possibly be enough carbon monoxide in the garage yet, to kill us.

Outside the garage door, I heard a car engine roar to life. Darcy's little Honda, I assumed. The one she had driven over here in. A second later, it reversed down the driveway. Then the sound faded as it took off up the street.

"Damn."

There went the possibility that Denise Seaver might change her mind about committing three more murders, and come back to let us out. We were stuck here until someone came by and found us, or until we could get ourselves out. At the moment, it didn't look good.

I rattled the seat some more and called Darcy's name. She didn't respond. When I leaned forward as far as I could and peered over the seat at her, I saw a smear of blood on the leather. Denise Seaver had hit her hard enough to break the skin. She probably had a concussion. For me to keep shaking the seat probably wasn't good for her. Yelling at her probably wasn't, either.

Denise Seaver had taken both our handbags. We had no phones, so we couldn't contact anyone. I kicked one shoe off and tried to twist my body enough to get my leg through the gap between the front seats and across the console to where I— maybe—could turn the car off with my toes, but I couldn't reach. The baby was starting to make squeaky noises. Shortly, it might wake up and want more to eat, and I wouldn't be able to feed it. We'd all just sit here and starve, until the carbon monoxide overtook us, and then we'd all be dead.

And my husband didn't even know where I was. By the time he figured it out, we'd all be rotting.

My eyes filled with tears. Not the most useful response, but I couldn't help it. Blame the hormones. That's what I did.

Anyway, it was the tears' fault that I didn't immediately notice the door from the garage to the house opening.

When a figure appeared in the opening, I did notice, although it took a few seconds for me to blink the tears away enough to recognize him. By then he had uttered a bad word—I couldn't hear it, but I saw his mouth shape the single syllable, and recognized it because I had said it several times myself over the past couple of hours—and slapped his hand on the garage door opener.

Nothing happen, and I wasn't surprised. I had seen Denise Seaver slam the butt of the gun against it as a last salute before closing the door and locking us in. Dix grabbed the end of his tie, held it in front of his face, and plunged down the stairs.

"No," I squealed when he reached over the steering wheel to turn the key in the ignition. "Don't turn it off!"

He stopped and peered at me. His eyes widened at the sight of the handcuffs. "Why not?"

"She took Darcy's car and Darcy's money. We have to go after her."

"The garage door won't open," Dix pointed out.

"It's aluminum. Thin. You can probably bust through it."

Dix bit his lip.

"It's my car. If I'm willing to risk it, you should be."

"Fine." He slid behind the wheel.

"Strap Darcy in before you start."

He reached over and dragged the seatbelt over Darcy's unconscious body. "What about you?"

"I'll be fine," I said. "I'm wedged in pretty tight. I'm sure it'll be all right."

"If you say so." He put the car in reverse and his feet on the gas and brake at the same time. The engine screamed in protest.

"Are you sure about this?" Dix asked over the sound.

"Just do it. Before she gets too far away, and before we die of carbon monoxide poisoning."

Dix nodded and took his foot off the brake. The car responded by leaping backward. It hit the garage door with a crunch. For a second, I was thrown against the seat in front of me. Since it was only a matter of a couple of inches, I didn't think there was any damage done. Then the metal door crumpled like so much scrap metal, and we burst out into the sunlight and careened backwards down the short driveway at sixty miles an hour.

We ended up halfway onto the lawn across the street, and made some nasty gouges in the grass when we first arrived and then, a second later, when Dix shifted gears and we accelerated to take off up the street. Grass and dirt flew, and we took out a bed of mums, too, on the way. The mailbox survived, but it was a close call.

"Any idea where she was going?" Dix asked. He was handling the car competently, skidding around the corners like a real pro. Rafe would have been proud. I knew I was. But I could hear the tension in his voice.

"She didn't say. Away from here."

"I figured that," Dix said, taking the next corner on two wheels.

"If I had my hands free, I'd call the sheriff and tell him what's going on, and to get an APB out on Darcy's car. As it is, there isn't much I can do." Other than hold on for dear life.

"Don't worry about it," Dix said. "I already called it in."

"No kidding? How long were you out there before you came to the rescue?"

He glanced at me in the mirror. "I came with Darcy. She was carrying a lot of money, and I didn't want her to go alone. I didn't know we were coming here until we pulled up in front. If I had, I would have realized something was wrong sooner."

I nodded. "I was hoping she'd catch on. I guess it's good that you did."

"When we got here, I let her go in by herself, while I went around the front and looked in the windows. I didn't see what happened when she first arrived, but I saw Denise Seaver march the two of you into the garage at gunpoint." His lips turned down as he directed a worried look at Darcy.

"Once we got down to the garage floor, she hit Darcy with the butt of the gun," I said. "I put Darcy in the car, and then she made me handcuff myself to the seat. I thought it was just so we wouldn't run away or try to stop her. It wasn't until she turned on the car that I realized she was trying to kill us all. And by then there was nothing I could do. She destroyed the garage door opener and locked us in on her way out."

Dix nodded. "I saw her go upstairs, and a couple of minutes later she came back down with two bags. She threw them in Darcy's car along with the paper bag with the money, and took off."

"And you came inside to save us. My hero."

"Bull pucky," my brother said rudely as we squealed through the gates of the intersection onto the Columbia Highway. "Which way?"

I had a split second to make a decision, and no reason to suspect Denise Seaver had been partial to one direction over the other. There was a fifty/fifty chance I was wrong, but what could we do? "North."

North was the way back to Nashville, but also the quickest way to the interstate, whether she planned to go north or south. And south led into downtown Sweetwater, what there is of it. North leads out of town.

Dix went north. A couple of minutes later we flew past the mansion. "How's Mother?" I asked.

Dix gave me an incredulous look over his shoulder. "You seriously want me to make small talk? Now?"

"Sorry."

"I haven't checked on her since the last time we talked. As far as I know she's fine. Now be quiet and let me drive."

I subsided. However, the baby must have decided it was time

for more food. He started making little squeaky noises, and contorting his little face, and pretty soon he opened his mouth and let out a wail.

"Jesus Christ!" Dix said, almost driving off the road. "What's that?"

"That's the baby. I think he's hungry. But I'm a little tied up here, so I can't feed him."

"He's going to have to wait," Dix said grimly, pushing down on the gas pedal. "It won't hurt him. Maybe the screaming will be incentive to drive faster."

I could well imagine it might be. The shrill desperation of those wails felt like they were drilling into my brain. I sat where I was, with my hands slowly going numb, with a screaming baby next to me, an unconscious woman in the front seat, and with my brother muttering curses under his breath as we tore up the Columbia Highway.

"I don't see her," I said a couple of minutes later. "I think maybe we went the wrong way."

"Bite your tongue." Dix gave the car a little more gas. "There she is."

There she was. Or at least there was a car up ahead that looked like Darcy's blue Honda.

"What are we going to do now?"

He looked at me. "I thought you had a plan."

I shook my head. "I just didn't want her to get away. But I have no idea how to stop her. Just keep following, I guess. Far enough back that she doesn't see us."

"I think it's too late for that," Dix said, as the car up ahead picked up speed and increased the distance between us. "I think she just did."

I thought so, too. "Just stick with her, then."

"I would, but I think we're going to run out of gas soon."

Damn. I mean, darn. Not the way I had envisioned this situation. Denise Seaver was the one who was supposed to run out of gas in my car, not we. "Maybe we just need to let her go, then. Tell the sheriff we've spotted her heading north on the Columba Highway just past Beulah's Meat'n Three, and let them take over."

"They're not here," Dix pointed out.

"But they're coming, don't you think? You said you called them, right?"

He glanced at me. "Do you hear sirens?"

I didn't. Although it was hard to hear anything over the baby's squeals. "How much gas do we have left?"

"The gas light is on," Dix said, "so maybe a gallon?"

"That'll give us about fifteen miles, I think. Maybe twenty. Depending."

"We can spare a couple of minutes." He sped up. "There's a gas station just before the interstate, if we haven't caught her by then."

Since we had no idea how to catch her, I wasn't really worried about it. Although if we got close enough, we could ram her and force her off the road, I guess. If it had been Rafe behind the wheel, I wouldn't have questioned the sense of that kind of maneuver. Since it was Dix, I did. He'd probably kill us all.

And anyway, I'm not sure even Rafe would have risked it, with his pregnant wife and Carmen's baby in the car.

"Maybe you should get back on the phone with the sheriff. Tell him where we are and that if he doesn't hurry, he'll lose her."

"Or I could just drive the car," Dix said. "This isn't easy, you know."

I'm sure it wasn't. And aside from the precious cargo, Dix had two motherless children at home. The last thing I wanted, was for anything to happen to him. The fifty grand was just money. I could spend the rest of my life paying Darcy back for it. As long as we survived.

"You're right," I said. "Just follow her at a safe distance.

Don't try to catch her. If she doesn't run out of gas or drive herself off the road by the time we get to the interstate, just let her go."

Dix nodded. "Anything you can do to quiet that baby down?"

"Not without the use of my hands," I said. "Although I guess I could try singing him a lullaby."

"No," Dix said. "That's OK. Thanks anyway."

Sure. "How's that gas gauge looking?"

"The same as a minute ago," Dix said. "I think we can make it to the gas station. If we lose her at that point, it won't be our fault. We can't drive with no gas."

I nodded. "Hear any sirens yet?"

"No," Dix said. "You?"

I shook my head. Up ahead, Darcy's Honda was making good time up the Columbia Highway. It's a main street with a right of way, so pretty much all the streets entering it has stop signs. As a result, she could just keep trucking while everyone else stayed out of her way.

Until she came to the big intersection with the road to Damascus, a small town southwest of Columbia. Elspeth Caulfield, David's biological mother, lived there before her death.

The intersection kept coming closer. There was a red light, but the Honda showed no sign of stopping. Denise Seaver must be lying on the horn. We could hear the tooting over the squalling of the baby. Cars parted to the left and right like the Red Sea before Moses. Not that there were a lot of cars, but more than we'd seen so far. They scrambled to get out of the way as Darcy's little Honda shot into the intersection and around the corner. Denise Seaver went from her own lane into the next lane and back to her own lane again, sending cars skidding out of the way. And just as she was about to straighten up, stomp on the gas pedal, and take off like a shot up the road to the interstate, a vehicle barreled across the lanes of traffic and clipped the rear corner of the Honda.

It was a three-ton pickup with the Virgin Mary on the rear window. I screamed as it slammed into the little Honda and sent it flying, across the road and into the ditch on the other side.

Dix said a word I never thought I'd hear from him, and pulled the Volvo to a stop at the gravel shoulder behind the pickup. The driver's side was already empty. Rafe was on his way across the road toward the Honda. José was making his way down from the passenger side, looking a little shell-shocked. I guess Rafe had talked him into letting him drive, and José had had no idea what he'd agreed to.

Dix jumped out of the quivering Volvo and followed.

"Wait!" I called after him. "What about me?"

But he was already too far away to listen.

Twenty-Two

An hour later, we were at the Maury County Medical Center. And by 'we,' I mean all of us.

Denise Seaver was in the ICU, handcuffed to the bed. She'd survive to finish out her prison sentence, plus whatever other punishment she had earned for herself with this latest escapade. But she was banged up and had a bad concussion, so she would be spending the night in the hospital before being transferred back to prison tomorrow. It was well deserved, as far as I was concerned. Darcy also had a concussion, if a mild one, and it was only fair that Denise Seaver had suffered the same fate.

Darcy would be going home later, though. Dix had invited her to spend the night at his house, so she wouldn't be alone, but given the presence of Dix's two daughters there, Darcy had said she thought she'd probably get more rest by herself. Part of it might be that she was still a little uncomfortable with her new-found family, but part of it was probably also that she had a raging headache, and spending the rest of the evening with Abigail and Hannah wasn't likely to help that. I had suggested she could call Audrey and tell her mother what had happened, but she had demurred. So I had told Dix to do it. I had a feeling he would, too, once we were out of here.

The Honda had been pretty banged up in its encounter with

the truck, but Darcy had her fifty thousand dollars back, so she could afford to buy a new car.

The truck, of course, barely had a scratch on it, and Rafe had assured José that what there was, would be taken care of.

After the accident, I had watched him, José, and Dix descend on Denise Seaver's car. They had hauled her out and dropped her on the ground, none too gently, before Rafe had handcuffed her. That seemed like justice, too. "Keep an eye on her," he told José, handing José the gun Denise had taken from the DOC guard. "If she moves, shoot her."

José gave him a look, but nodded. I didn't think he'd actually do it, though.

Dix was standing with the phone to his ear, presumably updating the sheriff on the situation, and I was still stuck to my car.

"Please tell me you have something that can open these handcuffs," I told Rafe when he opened my door.

He looked at them. "I could shoot'em off."

"You just gave the gun to José. And anyway, I don't think that's a good idea. The bullet might go through the seat and hit Darcy."

Rafe nodded. "She all right?"

"She's been unconscious since Denise Seaver hit her. It must be fifteen or twenty minutes. I'm getting a little worried."

"Your brother's asked for a couple ambulances," Rafe said, sorting through the keys on his ring. "Sit still."

"Do I have a choice?" But I sat still. And when he unhooked the handcuffs, my hands dropped to my lap like they weighted a ton each. Somehow I managed to grasp a half-empty bottle of formula, and turn to the suitcase. Plugging the baby's mouth with the bottle stopped the increasingly hysterical screams very nicely.

Rafe bent down and peered past me. "Small," he said after a moment.

I nodded. "I think he was probably born a week or two too early. I'm just happy he's alive and well."

He straightened. "He's got a good set of lungs on him, anyway."

I nodded. Yes, he did.

"The lab called."

For a second I froze, then I turned to look at him. I thought I knew what the results had been, just from his demeanor, but I wanted to be sure.

"The DNA wasn't a match."

"Not your baby."

He shook his head.

"I'm almost a little disappointed," I admitted. "I know it's only been a couple of hours. But he grew on me really fast. I would have been happy to have him."

"We'll have one of our own." He squatted beside the open car door to put his palm against my stomach. "Everything OK in there?"

"I think so. She pushed me, and I hit my stomach against the edge of the kitchen counter. She said if I didn't start bleeding, I was OK, but I should probably get checked out anyway. Just to make sure."

Rafe nodded.

"And so should he." I indicated the baby, now sucking down formula with a blissful expression on his small and wrinkled face.

Rafe straightened. "If he's made it through all this, I think he's gonna be OK. But he should get looked at."

"I don't even know what you're doing here," I admitted. "We were following Denise Seaver, and you just came flying out of nowhere."

"We went to the bus depot and looked at the video footage. We saw her get on the bus that runs up Potsdam. Then we tracked down the bus driver. He remembered her. And remembered where she got off."

"At the bus stop down the street," I said.

Rafe nodded. "José and I peeled outta there. But by the time we got to the house, you and the car were gone. We found the broken window, though. So we figured you'd gone to get the money, and that Doc Seaver had invited herself along for the ride."

"That's pretty much what happened," I agreed. "They were already in the house when I walked in. She said she'd hurt the baby if I didn't cooperate, so I did. I thought if she got her money, she'd let me take him. I was pretty sure she didn't want him slowing her down, you know? I just had to keep us all alive long enough."

Rafe nodded. "We drove like hell. And we'd made it all the way down here when we saw the Honda coming around the corner. People don't usually drive that crazy less'n they're trying to get away from somebody. And then we saw the Volvo. And figured we'd better stop her."

"You did a great job." I peered across the street, at Dix and José and the prone body on the graveled shoulder. "She's alive, isn't she?"

"If she ain't, it won't be my fault," Rafe said. "I just clipped the back of the car. She prob'ly hit her head, but there's plenty left of her to serve the rest of her sentence."

"That's good." The baby finished the bottle, and I picked him up and laid him against my shoulder to pat his back. My hands were starting to feel normal again. "I didn't want her to be dead. I'd much rather have her alive and suffering."

"You and me both," Rafe said, and moved to the front seat to check on Darcy.

Then the ambulances came, and loaded up Denise Seaver and Darcy, Baby Arroyo and me. Rafe stayed at the accident scene long enough to talk to the sheriff, before he sent José back to Nashville in the truck. He and Dix took the Volvo to the hospital, and here we all were.

"Everything all right?" I asked when he walked into the hospital room where I was having the baby monitored. My baby, not Carmen's. Baby Arroyo was somewhere else. I was in a bed, with a strap around my stomach, and various beeping and blinking instruments all around.

He nodded. "Doc Seaver has a concussion, but she'll survive. Darcy has a concussion, but she can go home later. The baby's in the maternity ward getting checked out and cleaned up. They're saying he looks good for coming a little early and getting dragged around the way he's been."

"That's great."

"I called Bianca and let her know he's here. They wanna keep him for a couple days, but she can come down and visit. And they know to release him to the Arroyos when he's ready to go. The paperwork's all on file at the prison. Carmen signed it all before she died."

So at least Bianca and Mrs. Arroyo would get Carmen's baby, even though they'd lost Carmen. And maybe that was for the best. This way, the little guy could grow up as one of Bianca's children, without the knowledge that his biological mother was incarcerated.

"Everything good here?" He looked at the various beeping and blinking monitors and machines.

"It seems to be. I'm not bleeding. There's no sign of trauma. The baby's heartbeat is strong." In fact, it was fairly echoing between the walls.

"That's good," Rafe said and sat down on the bedside, where he could lean down and put his lips against my stomach. "Hi, baby. It's your daddy."

I put my hand on the back of his head and felt the bristly fuzz there. It felt familiar and comforting.

We were still sitting like that when the sheriff walked in, with my purse dangling from one hand.

"Oh." He stopped just inside the door, looking acutely uncomfortable. I don't think it was Rafe's posture, or his cooing at the baby, that did it. More likely, it was my naked stomach sticking into the air. The sheriff is a Southern gentleman from a previous generation. "I can come back."

"There's no need for that," I said, as Rafe straightened. "They're just monitoring to make sure the baby's all right."

"And is it?" The sheriff kept his eyes firmly on my face as he approached the bed.

"It seems to be. No signs of anything bad so far." I reached for my purse. "Thank you."

"No problem. We found it on the floor in the kitchen of Denise Seaver's house, along with Darcy's. I've already given it to her, and gotten her statement."

"She's awake? Good."

"Awake and with a killer headache," the sheriff confirmed. "How about you tell me what happened?"

"Sure." I went through it all, from when I walked out of my own bathroom at home, to when we'd come around the corner of the Damascus Road in time to see José's truck career across two lanes of traffic and knock Darcy's Honda into the ditch, and Denise Seaver along with it. "She tried to kill all three of us," I added, just to make sure he'd caught that point. "Me, and Darcy, and the baby."

"And your baby," the sheriff said, with a reluctant glance at my stomach. "That's four counts of attempted murder."

"I guess, once she killed the prison guard and left Carmen to bleed out, she didn't think she had anything to lose. And I probably annoyed her. Besides, it was my fault she went to prison in the first place."

The sheriff nodded. "I don't think I need anything more from you. You're free to go home whenever they release you."

"Thank you." I was looking forward to that.

The sheriff turned toward the door, but before he could

leave, there was the sound of footsteps in the hallway. The clicking of heels, a little uneven. A second later, my mother appeared in the doorway.

She looked, without putting too fine a point on it, like hell. Her lipstick was smeared, her hair looked like it hadn't been combed today, and her shoes didn't match her skirt. If you knew my mother, you'd know how significant each of those things was. Taken together, I could only assume she had given up on life. She was pale, and her eyes were unfocused.

"Savannah!"

The sheriff and Rafe both leapt to grab her, and guided her over to the chair the sheriff had vacated. She dropped into it like standing up was too hard. "Darling!"

"Hi, Mother," I said. At least she didn't seem angry with me anymore. Last time I'd seen her, she'd told me to get out of her house.

Her eyes dropped to my stomach, and the band there. She squinted to get it into focus, and it must have taken her a few seconds to put two and two together. "Is everything all right?"

"With me, fine. Darcy has a concussion. So does Denise Seaver. But there are no ill effects from the carbon monoxide poisoning. Not that we've discovered. I guess we weren't locked in the garage for long enough." Carmen's baby was the main concern in that regard, with his tiny, underdeveloped lungs. But so far he seemed to have come through the ordeal without any lasting damage.

Mother's eyes filled with tears. "I'm sorry I kicked you out of the house on Monday."

"It's all right," I said. "It was probably time for me to go anyway. And I understood that you wanted to be alone."

"It's hard," Mother said.

"I know." Believe me, I knew. But if I could get behind raising Carmen's baby—not that I would have to now, but I'd been willing—then Mother could deal with the fact that her husband had fathered a child before she knew him. "It happened a long time ago, Mom. And Dad never knew. You can't blame him."

"I can blame Audrey," Mother said, with a snap of teeth. "She was my best friend all your lives. And she never told me."

In justice to her, it couldn't have been an easy subject to bring up. *By the way, Margaret Anne, before you married Robert, I slept with him and got pregnant and had a daughter. Surprise!*

I didn't think Mother was ready to be reasonable, though. She was still hurt and angry. "Just give it some time," I said. "Audrey loves you. I'm sure she'll be there when you're ready to talk about it. And so will Darcy."

Mother nodded.

"For now, maybe you could just try to drink a little less? It really doesn't help with the problem, and it just creates another one. Besides, I worry about you. You didn't drive here, did you?"

The sheriff looked worried, too. Maybe concerned that he'd have to arrest his ladyfriend for DUI.

Mother shook her head, and kept shaking it a little too long. "I came with Catherine."

"I'll drive you home," the sheriff said. "Come on, Margaret." He gave her a hand up, which amounted to pretty much lifting her out of the chair. "You shouldn't be here. You need to go home and to bed and sleep it off."

"I'm not drunk," Mother protested, but she let herself be led out.

Rafe looked at me. I looked back at him. "Sorry about that."

His lips twitched. "No problem. Never thought I'd see your mama looking like that."

"Once she gets herself back together, you never will again. We should have gotten a picture."

"I can run after them," Rafe offered.

I shook my head. "That's not necessary. I'd rather have you here. With me. Us."

He sat back down on the side of the bed. "Then that's where I'll be."

I took his hand, and closed my eyes, and listened to my baby's steady heartbeat on the monitors, and waited to be released so we could go home.

"Have you heard from Grimaldi?" I asked later, when we were in the Volvo on our way back to Nashville. The sheriff had taken Mother home, Catherine had driven Dix and Darcy, and Denise Seaver and the baby were still in the hospital, the former under guard.

He shot me a look. "I called her. Figured she'd wanna know what was going on even if it isn't her case."

I nodded. "What about Mendoza?"

"She said she'd update him. He's prob'ly on his way down, to make sure Doc Seaver is under lock and key and not likely to get away again."

Probably. And so he could tie up any loose ends and make it all official with the sheriff. "I'm sure he's glad this one's over. And with no other loss of life." Other than the guard and Carmen, whose deaths were more than enough.

Rafe nodded. "It coulda been a lot worse."

"I did the best I could," I said. "I was trying to save the baby. I figured, once she got her money, she wouldn't have a reason to hurt us. She'd gotten what she wanted."

"I guess money wasn't all she wanted."

Guess not. I hadn't realized that my crime of having her arrested for my sister's murder loomed so large in her mind that she wanted me dead for it. Maybe I should have.

"She's gone now," Rafe added, "and she ain't getting back out again. The next time someone has to go to the hospital, it won't be Denise Seaver going with her. She prob'ly won't be working in the clinic no more, either."

Probably not. And I couldn't say I was sorry. "Did Grimaldi

say anything about the other case? Devon's murder and the money?"

"Just that she's getting close to making an arrest," Rafe said. I straightened in the seat—or tried to; it had been a long couple of days, and I was tired—and his lips twitched. "She said if you feel up to spending some time with her tomorrow, she can fill you in."

I slumped back down, pouting. "She's arresting someone right now? Tonight?"

"She didn't say that," Rafe said. "Just that she's getting closer. Oh, yeah, and she got the subpoena for the webmail account."

I straightened again. "Tell me!"

He chuckled. "You don't wanna wait until tomorrow?"

"No! Have you lost your mind?"

"Then I'll tell you," Rafe said, as the car moved north on the interstate. "The email came from Devon Knight's computer."

"So Devon sent the spoofed email changing the wiring instructions. On behalf of Magnolia, do you think? Have her cake—her house—and eat it, too?"

"That's what it looks like," Rafe said.

"So where's the money? Where did he tell DeWitts to send it?"

"She's got the name of the bank," Rafe said. "But it's closed by now. Tammy said she's going over there when they open in the morning to talk to the manager about whose account it is."

"And she wants me to come along?"

He nodded.

"I accept." I resisted the temptation to rub my hands together in anticipation. It would look a bit stupid. But I wanted to be part of finishing this up.

And then I thought of something. "If Devon stole the money, who shot Devon? Magnolia Houston?" To cover up what he'd done, and the fact that she'd made him do it?

"I guess you and Tammy will find out," Rafe said.

Twenty-Three

Tamara Grimaldi knocked on the door bright and early the next morning. So bright and early, in fact, that I was still in bed and Rafe was just getting out of the shower, naked and wet and with a towel hanging low on his hips.

"If you go downstairs like that," I warned him, "you'll probably give her a heart attack."

He grinned. "She's better'n that, don't you think?"

"I'm not sure," I said, "but I don't want to find out." I liked Grimaldi, and if she drooled over my husband, I'd be forced to take measures. "Just get rid of the towel. Please."

He got rid of the towel. My eyes bulged, and my tongue got stuck to the roof of my mouth.

"You know that wasn't what I meant," I managed when I could speak again.

"I know. But it was worth it." He tucked himself away behind the zipper of a pair of faded jeans.

"Commando?"

"It'll give you something to think about today." He winked.

"I'd probably be thinking about it... I mean, you—anyway."

He laughed as he headed out the door, tugging a T-shirt over his head. "You better get up. She's gonna want you ready to go soon."

She would. I sighed and dragged my pregnant self out of bed

and into the shower.

By the time I got downstairs, Rafe had made coffee and was sitting at the kitchen table across from Grimaldi. Updating her on the specific details of yesterday's excitement, it sounded like. When I walked through the door, they both turned to me, and Grimaldi gave me a careful up-and-down inspection. "You look good."

She sounded faintly accusatory.

"I got a good night's sleep," I said innocently, at the same time as Rafe said, "Good sex."

I flushed. He chuckled, and Grimaldi rolled her eyes. "I'm glad you're all right."

"I'm fine. She didn't hurt me. Just shoved me and threatened to shoot me."

"And handcuffed you to the car and tried to poison you with carbon monoxide," Rafe reminded me.

"Right. But that didn't hurt. Darcy was much worse off."

Grimaldi nodded. "I understand she's doing all right."

"I'm sure she is. She was released from the hospital yesterday evening." And then I realized what she'd said. "Have you spoken to Dix?"

"He called to update me," Grimaldi said.

Good. I was glad they were still talking. "He's fine. He wasn't in the garage until he came to let us out. Denise Seaver never even knew he was there."

"That's what he said." She hesitated. "He said your mother showed up at the hospital last night."

"Drunk and maudlin," I nodded. "She apologized for kicking me out of the house on Monday. The sheriff took her home. She isn't ready to deal with Audrey yet, but if nothing else, I think she realizes that none of what happened was Darcy's fault."

Grimaldi nodded.

"Rafe told me we're going to the bank to find out whose account the money went into."

"If you feel up for it. I'm not going to make you go if you don't."

I shook my head. "I feel fine. Really. The hospital checked me out yesterday, and they said I'm fine. No ill effects from the carbon monoxide. And the baby wasn't hurt when Denise Seaver shoved me. I'd like to come, if you don't mind."

Grimaldi pushed back the chair. "Then let's go. We have lots to do today."

"Rafe said we might be arresting someone?"

"*I* might be arresting someone. You'll be watching."

"That's what I meant," I said. "I have to eat something before we go. You remember what happens if I don't?"

She made a face. "Yes. Make it quick, please."

"I can take it in the car." I opened a container of yogurt, dumped some granola in on top, and stirred. Rafe handed me a to-go cup full of orange juice, and I told Grimaldi I was ready.

"Let's go." She strode down the hall toward the front door.

"Take care of my baby," Rafe told me as I followed.

I nodded. "After yesterday, this will be easy." Nobody was likely to shoot at me today. Or do anything else dangerous. And if anything happened, Grimaldi was armed and would take care of the threat. Nothing at all against Darcy—I hadn't expected Denise Seaver to knock her out, either—but Grimaldi wouldn't have fallen for that one.

"Call me if anything happens," Rafe said, following me to the front door.

I said I would. "You're not doing anything dangerous today, are you?"

"Nothing worse than some hand-to-hand with the boys. Unless one of'em gets the drop on me, I shouldn't come home with any new bruises."

"I doubt they're good enough for that yet," I told him, and headed out the door. Rafe closed and locked it behind me, to go get ready for work—hopefully he'd put on a pair of underwear before he headed in—and I went down the stairs to Grimaldi's burgundy sedan. "Where's the bank?"

"Melrose," Grimaldi said, putting the car in gear and rolling off down the driveway.

"Rafe told me the email to DeWitts had been sent from Devon's computer."

She nodded.

"Work computer?"

"Home computer," Grimaldi said. "Devon doesn't have a day job anymore."

Really? "Brittany didn't say anything about that. I asked her about Devon's day job, and she didn't mention that he didn't have one."

"It's a new thing," Grimaldi said. "He quit a month ago. Gave his notice, said he'd gotten a band gig and needed to focus on that. I spoke to his former boss yesterday. They were sad to see him go, because he was good at his job, but they were happy that he had a chance to pursue his dream."

That was all very nice, but— "If Rafe had quit his job a month ago, I think I would have heard about it by now."

Grimaldi shrugged. We were on our way down Potsdam Street, coming up on the corner of Dresden and the Milton House Retirement Home across the street. "Maybe she didn't think it was any of your business."

Maybe not. "It's strange, though. I mean, it's not like it's a secret. Not if he goes on stage every weekend, and performs in Magnolia Houston's music videos. Those have millions of views."

"But chances are no one's looking at the guys in the back," Grimaldi said.

"That's true. But it's still strange. Unless she didn't know about it. But how can you plan to marry someone, yet you haven't told them you're not working at the same place anymore, and haven't for a month?"

"Don't know," Grimaldi said. "Maybe it's because, as Hanse Neyman put it, Devon was banging Magnolia Houston, and he didn't want his girlfriend to know about it."

Maybe. But Han had also said that Devon wasn't marrying Brittany, and she'd been absolutely definite that he was. They even had plane tickets and hotel reservations in Curacao. So clearly Han was wrong about that. Maybe he was wrong about the whole affair. Maybe Magnolia had decided to give Devon a music gig because he'd promised to reroute her money so she wouldn't have to spend anything to buy the house, and they weren't sleeping together at all.

"Anything's possible," Grimaldi said, when I laid it out that way.

"Have you spoken to Magnolia?"

She nodded. "Yesterday, while you were having your adventures in Sweetwater."

"What did she say?"

"She denied having had anything to do with the missing money," Grimaldi said, pulling the car onto the entrance ramp for the interstate. "But she confirmed that she and Devon did indeed have a romantic relationship. When I asked her if she knew he had plans to fly to Curacao with his girlfriend tomorrow—today, now—she said he hadn't mentioned it to her. He was excited about playing at the Ryman on Saturday, she said. She didn't think he would have missed it."

"Weird."

Grimaldi nodded and stepped on the gas.

The bank where the five hundred thousand had ended up was literally just up the street from Brittany's and Devon's building. I could see the top of their roof from the bank's parking lot. Inside, Grimaldi waved her badge and subpoena. "We're interested in a wire transfer that came into your bank a week ago. Last Friday. The proceeds from a real estate transaction. Five hundred thousand dollars."

The branch manager, an older woman a few years younger than my mother, waved her hand in front of her face. It was either a hot flash or nerves. "Is there a problem?"

"The money didn't end up where it was supposed to," Grimaldi said. "The wiring instructions were changed at the last minute, and the money ended up in someone else's account."

"Dear me. It wasn't an accident, I suppose?"

Grimaldi shook her head. "We're talking grand larceny here. What can you tell us about it?"

"Dear me!" The manager's hands fluttered. "You'd better come back to my office. I'll take a look at the account."

She lead the way across the floor and into a glassed-in office by the wall. "Have a seat."

I maneuvered into one of the chairs in front of the desk. Grimaldi took the other, while the manager—her name plate said her name was Glenda Tulis—made herself comfortable behind the desk. "Can you give me the number of the account?"

Grimaldi read it off, while Glenda Tulis typed it into the computer. "Yes, here we are. And you said you have a subpoena?"

Grimaldi produced it. Glenda looked it over and determined it looked all right. "The account belongs to a customer by the name of Devon Knight. He..."

I must have made a movement, because she turned to me. "Something wrong?"

"No," I said. Grimaldi, of course, hadn't moved a muscle. She'd been expecting it, I'm sure. I should have, too.

"Can you give me the details of the transfer?"

"It came in by wire," Glenda Tulis said, peering at the computer, "late Friday afternoon, just before closing. The sender was DeWitts Title and Escrow."

She looked up. I nodded. Grimaldi did, too.

Glenda Tulis went back to the records. "The money spent the

weekend in the account. On Monday morning, it was withdrawn via personal check."

"May we have a copy of the check?" Grimaldi asked politely.

Glenda Tulis hesitated. Her gaze brushed over the subpoena lying on her desk, and she nodded. "I'll print out a copy for you. I'll be right back."

She pushed a button on the computer and walked out of the room.

"Community printer," I said. "We have one at the office, too. If I'm there and need to print something, I send the document there and go pick it up."

Grimaldi nodded.

"Did you know it was going to be Devon's account?"

"I thought it might be," Grimaldi said. "Once I found out where the bank was. And that the email came from his computer."

"So Devon wired the money to himself. Why would he do that, if he was stealing it—or stealing it back—for Magnolia?"

"Maybe he wasn't," Grimaldi said, as Glenda Tulis walked back into the office, her sensible heels clicking on the marble floor.

"Here you are." She handed Grimaldi a piece of copy paper. I leaned closer and stretched my neck as far as it would go to get a look.

Grimaldi obligingly tilted the sheet so I could see.

Yes, indeed. It was a personal check. It had Devon's name and address in the upper left corner, and Sunday's date written on the date line, and it was made out to cash for five hundred thousand dollars.

"Cash?" I said. I'm sure I sounded incredulous. Five hundred thousand dollars is a lot of cash to be hauling around. I'd seen what fifty thousand looked like just yesterday, and five hundred thousand would be a lot more. I'd definitely need a suitcase for that.

Glenda Tulis developed a tiny wrinkle between her brows, sort of like my mother does when something in my behavior bothers her.

"Is this Mr. Knight's signature?" Grimaldi asked, pointing to it.

The wrinkle between Glenda's brows became more pronounced. Maybe I wasn't the only one she disapproved of. "The teller would have made sure of it."

"How was the money taken out?" Grimaldi asked. "Five hundred thousand dollars is a lot of money. And you're a small branch. Did you have that much cash sitting around ready to go? Was it prearranged?"

"It was turned into a cashier's check," Glenda Tulis said stiffly. "And to answer your question: no. We do not keep half a million dollars sitting around ready to go. That would be our entire operating budget for the day. If we give it all away to one customer, we might as well close up the bank for the day. Any kind of cash withdrawal in that amount would have to be prearranged. There would also be a lot of paperwork involved. Including the notice to the Internal Revenue Service and Homeland Security about large cash transactions."

I nodded. I knew about that. So, obviously, did Grimaldi.

"So a cashier's check. Can we see a copy of that, as well?"

Glenda Tulis began to push buttons on her keyboard. While she did, I asked, "Was it Devon himself who brought the check to the bank? Or someone else?"

"You'd have to ask the teller who handled the transaction," Glenda said, leaning back on her chair. It squeaked.

"We'd like to do that," Grimaldi said firmly. "Along with the copy of the cashier's check, if you don't mind."

Glenda was starting to look mutinous. Grimaldi must have noticed the same thing, because she said, "I should mention, Ms. Tulis, that your customer, Mr. Knight, is dead. Gunned down in his parking garage two nights ago. Anything he did in the days leading up to his death could be important. Especially if it involves five hundred thousand dollars."

Glenda Tulis had turned pale. "Dear me," she said weakly. "We heard about the shooting, of course. There was crime scene tape across the garage entrance, and some of our employees noticed as much. But we had no idea it involved one of our customers."

"I'm afraid so," Grimaldi said. "So I'm sure you understand why we're here, asking all these questions."

"Of course." Glenda nodded rapidly many times as she bounded to her feet. "Of course. Anything we can do. I'll go get you the copy of that check, and bring Ellen in to speak to you. It might take a few moments. I can see she's busy with a customer."

"Take your time," Grimaldi said genially. "We aren't going anywhere."

Glenda made a grimace, but didn't have anything to say to that. She just hustled out the door and over to the printer.

"That was a little mean of you," I said.

She shrugged. "Sometimes people need a little incentive."

I guess so. "So Devon sent the email and had DeWitts send the money to his own account. Then, before Tim even knew the money had gone astray, Devon wrote out a check for the whole amount and had it turned into a cashier's check."

"So it appears," Grimaldi said, examining the printout of the check.

I leaned in. "Something wrong? She said the teller would have made sure the signature was his."

"I'm not worried about the signature," Grimaldi said. "I've seen Devon's driver's license, and this is his signature. If someone forged it, they did an outstanding job. But there's no reason to think anyone did."

I nodded. "What are you looking at, then?"

She handed me the sheet. "Does anything strike you about

it?"

I peered at it. Closely. Again, it was a copy of a personal check from Devon's account. It had his name and address on it. No one else's. Grimaldi said the signature was legit. The bank must have determined the same thing, and with half a million dollars on the line, it stood to reason that they would have made sure. The date was right. The amount...

"Does the word 'thousand' look a little cramped to you?" Grimaldi asked.

I looked at it. And tilted my head and looked at it from a different angle. "Maybe. A little. I mean... yes. It does. But no more than what happens sometimes. He has big, sort of loopy handwriting. He might just have gotten going on the 'five hundred' and then realized he was going to run out of space and squeezed the 'thousand' together before he ran out of space."

Grimaldi didn't answer.

"The line across the t is a little long, though. Almost as if the word 'thousand' was an afterthought. As if he wrote 'Five hundred—' and considered himself done."

Grimaldi nodded.

"But that might still just be a mistake."

"Might," Grimaldi said. "Might not."

"So..." I thought about it. "What you're saying is that Devon wrote out a check for five hundred dollars, and someone else added the thousand?"

Grimaldi opened her mouth, but there was no time for her to answer. Glenda came back through the door towing a young woman with mousy hair in a bun. "This is Ellen," she told us. "Ellen, this is the police."

I wasn't the police, of course, but I didn't bother to mention it. If Detective Grimaldi didn't see the need, why would I?

Grimaldi smiled at the young woman. She can look more or less frightening when she smiles, but this was one of the nice smiles. She must have noticed, as had I, that the girl was shaking.

"Hi, Ellen. I'm Detective Grimaldi. We'd like to talk to you about a transaction you were involved in on Monday morning. A cashier's check for five hundred thousand dollars."

Ellen nodded. "Yes, ma'am."

Grimaldi grimaced. She doesn't like to be called ma'am. I already knew that about her. "Do you remember it?"

Ellen nodded. "Yes, ma'am."

"Can you tell us about it?"

Ellen hesitated.

"We're interested in who came in with the check. And in what happened while they were here."

Ellen nodded.

"Did Mr. Knight himself come in and present the check?"

Ellen shook her head.

"Who presented the check?"

"His girlfriend," Ellen said.

His girlfriend? Normally I would have said that would be Brittany, but after what Han Neyman had told us yesterday, it might equally well have been Magnolia Houston.

I had my mouth open to ask when I caught Grimaldi's eye. She shook her head. I closed my mouth again.

"Can you describe her?"

"Early twenties," Ellen said, "blond hair, blue eyes, big earrings. Pretty."

It could still be either Brittany or Magnolia. That description could fit either of them. They wouldn't look very much alike at all, if you put them side by side, but a pretty blonde in her early twenties with blue eyes and big earrings could be either.

"She looked familiar," Ellen added. "Like maybe I'd seen her before."

"Here? Like she has come into the bank before, maybe with Devon? Or somewhere else? Like on TV?"

Ellen blinked. "TV? Oh, I wouldn't think so."

"I'm going to show you some pictures," Grimaldi said,

opening her folder. "I want you to tell me if you recognize any of these women."

She laid them out on the desk in two neat rows. They were upside down from where I was sitting, but I recognized Brittany. I also recognized Magnolia Houston, looking a bit less glamorous than usual. Maybe it was her driver's license photo that Grimaldi had dug up. Nobody looks good in those. There was also a picture of Megan Slater, a young police officer who has pretended to be me a couple of times. Another blue-eyed blonde. The picture must have been taken a few years ago—maybe when she was in the police academy or something like that—because I'm twenty-eight now, and she's probably close to the same. Not in the same age range as Brittany and/or Magnolia.

Ellen chewed on her bottom lip. "She looks familiar." She pointed to Brittany.

Grimaldi nodded encouragingly.

"And she." Magnolia.

Grimaldi nodded.

"She looks like you." Ellen looked from the photograph of Megan Slater to me and back.

"She isn't," Grimaldi said, and removed the photo of Megan from the lineup. Too distracting, I guess. We didn't want Ellen focused on someone who definitely couldn't have been here at the bank, withdrawing the money. "Anyone else?"

Ellen gave the remaining photographs another look, and shook her head. "Just those two."

Grimaldi shuffled up the others, leaving just Brittany and Magnolia side by side. "Did one of them come in on Monday and withdraw the five hundred thousand?"

Ellen gnawed on her lip. At this rate, she'd chew right through it. "I'm not sure. I just know I've seen them before."

Nothing extraordinary in that, unfortunately. If Devon did his banking here, Brittany probably did, too. And Magnolia's face had appeared in a lot of places, so it wasn't surprising that

Ellen thought she recognized it.

"I don't suppose there are security cameras?" Grimaldi asked, with a glance at Glenda Tulis.

"There are. But we tape over the footage every seventy-two hours. The footage from Monday is gone. Sorry."

If you ask me, Glenda Tulis didn't sound as sorry about that as she should have been.

"Maybe we should take a look at the cashier's check," I suggested. "In case there's some clues in that."

Grimaldi gave me a look, but didn't demur, just held out her hand for the printout Glenda had brought in along with Ellen. I leaned closer.

It was a cashier's check, for sure. For the full five hundred thousand. Made out to Margaret Murphy.

"Who's Margaret Murphy?" I said.

Grimaldi gave me a look, but no answer.

"That's who she said to make the check out to," Ellen said.

She? "Was it Margaret Murphy who came into the bank? Did she want the check made out in her own name?"

Ellen shook her head. "That wouldn't make any sense, would it? She already had a check."

"But not in her name." Ellen looked blank, and Grimaldi added, "You looked at her ID?"

"Of course I looked at her ID," Ellen said, with the first show of spirit she'd exhibited so far. "She had a check for half a million dollars from someone else's account that she had to endorse. I looked at her ID. I even made her put her fingerprint on the check, although she was a depositor with us, too."

Grimaldi's brows rose. "She was?"

"I remember," Ellen said. "She came in with the check. She endorsed it in front of me, and wrote down her account number. Usually that's enough to cash a check. I checked the account, and the signature matched. But since it was for so much, I made her put her fingerprint on it, and I also asked for her driver's license, so I could write down the driver's license number."

"So her signature, fingerprint, and driver's license number are on the back of the canceled check?"

Ellen nodded. Grimaldi turned to Glenda Tulis, who said defensively, "You didn't ask for a copy of the back of the check."

No, we hadn't. Not specifically. Because we hadn't known we needed to. And I guess maybe the bank wasn't in the habit of volunteering anything someone hadn't asked for.

"May we see the back of the check, please?" Grimaldi said with what I thought was admirable restraint.

Glenda sighed. "I'll get it for you. Do you need Ellen for anything else?"

Grimaldi shook her head. "I think that's it. Thanks for your time."

Glenda nodded, and Ellen scurried out of the office and back to her station, with the demeanor of someone who had narrowly escaped being fed to the lions. Glenda followed, her steps measured.

I turned to Grimaldi. "Who's Margaret Murphy?"

"Magnolia Houston," Grimaldi said.

"Hah! I was right."

She arched her brows. "What about?"

"I figured her name wasn't Magnolia Houston. It's just too perfect for a country singer."

"Stage name," Grimaldi said. "A lot of performers have them. She was born Margaret Louise Murphy in Pottstown, Pennsylvania."

As I had suspected. Less euphonious. And nothing even remotely country about it.

"How common," I said with a grin. Grimaldi arched her brows, and I added, "There must be dozens of girls named Maggie Murphy all over Ireland. Magnolia Houston is a lot more distinctive."

"Definitely," Grimaldi agreed.

"You checked her alibi for Wednesday morning, I assume?"

"Of course," Grimaldi said. "She was home in bed, alone. Where most people are at two-thirty in the morning. No one can verify it."

"So she could have snuck out and shot Devon."

Grimaldi nodded. "He'd been with her until a quarter to two, when he left for home. Or so she said. She could easily have followed him. Parked her car on the street for three minutes. Run into the parking garage. Shot him and left."

"Does she have a security system?"

"She does, but it wasn't set that night. She said she was in bed when Devon left, and she didn't feel like getting up to reset it after he walked out."

So she could have walked out, too, right behind him. "Does she have a gun?"

"She does," Grimaldi said. "It's at the lab, awaiting ballistics testing. I'm sure they'll get to it this morning."

No doubt.

"This is going to be big news. Magnolia Houston is a thief and a murderer."

"We don't know that yet," Grimaldi warned.

"Who else could it be? It all makes sense, right? Devon stole the money for Magnolia, and she shot him so he couldn't tell anyone."

"But that doesn't make it true. There are other explanations that could make just as much sense."

"Like what?" I asked.

But before Grimaldi could answer, Glenda Tulis walked back in, with yet another printout in her hand. "Here you are." She handed it to Grimaldi.

I leaned in, for the last time.

The back of the check did indeed have a signature, a fingerprint, and an account number written on it. The loopy, girlish handwriting was easy to read, and not just because I'd seen it before.

Brittany Stevens, it said.

<h1 align="center">Twenty-Four</h1>

"This doesn't make any sense," I complained when we were outside in Grimaldi's unmarked sedan again. "It made perfect sense that Magnolia was the guilty party. She did it for the money. And then she killed Devon after he got the money back for her. But what does Brittany have to gain?"

Grimaldi didn't say anything, but she shot me a look, in the process of reversing the car out of the parking space it had been in.

So I went on, down the track of my thoughts. "She isn't getting the money. It's already out of Devon's account and into Magnolia's name, and anyway, she isn't Devon's legal heir, so she wouldn't inherit it anyway. If they were married, that would be a different story, but they're not."

And now they wouldn't be. She was supposed to be flying to Curacao this afternoon on her honeymoon. Right about now, she and Devon would probably have been down at the courthouse, tying the knot, if he hadn't wound up dead. "And besides," I added, "since he stole the money, it's not like she'd have gotten to keep it anyway. Or so I assume."

I glanced at Grimaldi, but she didn't say anything. So I continued. "And Brittany didn't kill Devon. If she'd found out that he was cheating on her with Magnolia, maybe she'd have been tempted to—" I knew I would have been tempted to shoot anyone Rafe was fooling around with, "—but you said she hadn't left the apartment the night he was killed."

"She didn't," Grimaldi said, pulling the car into traffic on Franklin Road.

"Well, then I don't understand it. Brittany wouldn't be cooperating with the woman who was sleeping with her boyfriend. Would she? I mean, that doesn't make any sense."

Grimaldi didn't respond. We pulled to a stop outside Brittany's apartment building, and she cut the engine. "C'mon."

"Are we going to talk to her?" I opened my door.

"She was at the bank on Monday morning," Grimaldi said, getting out of her side of the car. "She had a check for five hundred thousand dollars signed by her boyfriend. She turned it into a cashier's check in her boyfriend's mistress's name. I'd like to hear her explanation."

Come to think of it, so would I.

I hustled across the street after Grimaldi, and waited while she pressed the buzzer outside the front door.

No one answered. Grimaldi developed one of those wrinkles between her eyebrows, too, and pulled out her key chain.

"Is this legal?" I asked when she inserted a universal key into the lock and got us through the front door into the building.

She glanced at me. "You're welcome to stay in the car. As for me, I have concerns for her wellbeing. Her boyfriend was shot two days ago. I think she's despondent and a danger to herself."

She hadn't seemed despondent to me, but who was I to quibble with the long arm of the law? And if Brittany had been involved in moving the missing money, it wasn't likely that she'd want to quibble with the long arm of the law, either.

So I trotted after Grimaldi to the elevator, and waited while we rose three stories. At Brittany's floor, Grimaldi told me to hang back while she went to knock on the door.

"You told me Magnolia's gun was at the police lab," I pointed out. "And if Brittany has one, it's news to me."

"Just do as I say, Ms.... Savannah."

She stood to the side of the door herself when she knocked. "Ms. Stevens. This is the police. Open the door, please."

There was no answer. Grimaldi knocked again. I pulled out my phone and dialed the number for LB&A. Just in case Brittany had woken up with a new lease on life and decided to go to work this morning.

The phone rang once, and then again. Then it was answered. "Thank you for calling LB&A. This is Heidi speaking. How may I help you?"

"Hi, Heidi," I said, while Grimaldi pulled out her trusty key chain and unlocked the door to Brittany's apartment.

"Stay here," she told me, as she pulled her gun from the holster and slipped inside.

I nodded, not that she could see me, since she was already inside the apartment. I'd spent a large part of yesterday at gunpoint; I wasn't eager to risk my life again. "I guess," I told Heidi, "if you're answering the phone, Brittany hasn't come in today?"

"No," Heidi said. "But she wasn't supposed to. She and Devon were getting married this morning, and going to Curacao."

"Yes," I said, "but Devon's dead."

"Brittany can still go," Heidi said. "I'm sure the tickets were expensive."

I'm sure they had been. And perhaps non-refundable, too. But what almost-bride goes on her honeymoon alone after her almost-husband is gunned down two days before?

Grimaldi came back out of the apartment, holstering her gun. "Empty."

"I have to go," I told Heidi. "I appreciate it."

I hung up before she could ask me when I'd be back to relieve her. I had no desire to spend the rest of the day on desk duty. Not when something was afoot. "Did you check her closet?"

"No," Grimaldi said. "Do you have reason to believe she's there?"

"Heidi reminded me that Brittany and Devon were supposed to be flying to Curacao this afternoon, on their honeymoon."

"The honeymoon Hanse Neyman said they weren't taking," Grimaldi said.

"Heidi thinks maybe Brittany went on the trip by herself. To get away from everything that's happened. And because the tickets were expensive. She had the tickets and the hotel booked, and she'd already requested the week off. Heidi might be on to something."

Grimaldi said a bad word.

"What?"

"I haven't put any restrictions on her travel. I knew she couldn't have killed her boyfriend, so I didn't tell her she had to stick around and not leave town."

She headed for the elevator with long strides. I had to jog to keep up with her. "This was before you knew she had something to do with the money, obviously."

"Obviously," Grimaldi said.

The elevator was still on Brittany's floor, and we got in and headed down. Grimaldi was visibly annoyed, tapping her fingers against the outside of her thigh and glowering. When we reached the lobby, she stormed out with me bobbing in her wake like a dinghy trailing an ocean liner.

"Where are we going?" I asked diffidently when we were back in the car and Grimaldi had started the engine with an angry roar and then taken off in a U-turn that broke several laws.

She spared me a glance. "Put your seatbelt on."

"I'm trying." It was harder to do these days. My arm didn't have as easy a time reaching across my body as before I was pregnant.

"We're going to the airport," Grimaldi said. "Can you

remember when the flight was?"

I shook my head. "I have no idea. I just know what Brittany told me. That they were getting married this morning and going to Curacao in the afternoon."

Grimaldi glanced at the clock. It wasn't afternoon yet. "Do you remember the airline?"

"I don't remember anything. I didn't know anything. You're the one who looked into this. You told me that you'd checked, and that the tickets and hotel were booked in both their names. It was while we were talking to Han Neyman."

Grimaldi nodded. "Hang on," she told me, as we hit the entrance ramp to the interstate. "We have a plane to catch."

I grabbed hold of the door handle and closed my eyes as the car leapt forward, lights flashing and sirens blaring.

We got to the airport in record time. Grimaldi drove as if I-40 was the Autobahn and the world was her oyster. I was used to going fast—Rafe is another speed demon—but this took driving to another level. I think, at times, we weren't even actually touching the ground.

Grimaldi parked the car in a no-parking zone and left it there, lights flashing. My guess was, nobody would be going near it. As it was, all the other cars gave it a wide berth. From there, we went directly to the security office, where Grimaldi badged her way up to the head honcho.

"We're looking for a traveler," she told him, with no introduction or anything. I guess she expected the badge to do it for her, and maybe it did. "Her name is Brittany Stevens. She was booked on a flight to Curacao this afternoon with her husband, but he was murdered two days ago. We think there's a chance she may be on her way out of the country."

The security guy—middle-aged and balding, but with a physique that spoke of time spent at the gym—turned to the computer. "You realize," he told Grimaldi as he typed, "that without a subpoena I don't have to help you."

Grimaldi didn't answer. Afraid to jinx anything, I guess, since it appeared he was helping her even after saying he didn't have to.

"Brittany Stevens. Checked in thirty-five minutes ago. Still planning to end up in Curacao tonight, but changed the first leg of the flight—Nashville to Panama City—to an earlier flight."

"Panama City, Florida?"

The security guy shook his head. "Panama City, Panama."

So if she got on the flight, she'd end up outside the country in pretty short order. With Magnolia Houston's half a million dollars.

"Is she traveling alone?"

The security guy consulted the computer again, and shook his head. "She checked in with one Margaret Murphy. That the husband?"

"The husband's dead," Grimaldi said. "His name was Devon Knight. Is he still on the passenger list?"

The security guy checked. "The ticket was canceled. There's a note that the refund is dependent on getting a copy of the death certificate."

"The M.E. issued that yesterday," Grimaldi said. "Mr. Knight is definitely dead. But I'm not sure she cares about the refund any longer."

Probably not. She and Magnolia must be on their way to Curacao to live it up with Magnolia's five hundred grand.

"When does the flight take off?" Grimaldi asked.

The security guy checked the schedule. "The plane came in from Newark forty minutes ago for a stopover. They should begin boarding within the next few minutes."

"Can you point us in the right direction?"

"We'll take a cart." He rose from behind the desk, and turned out to be around Rafe's height, with an impressive military bearing. "This way."

He ushered us out a side door, into a corridor where a row of what looked like little open golf carts were parked.

He chose one, and got behind the wheel. "Get in."

I scrambled into one of the two rear-facing seats in the back, while Grimaldi took the seat beside our new friend.

"Strap in," she told me over her shoulder. "We're in a hurry."

I had gathered that. And no sooner were we out of the corridor and into the terminal than the cart put on a burst of speed. I was still fumbling to get my seatbelt strapped across my waist, and for a second I was afraid I was going to tumble off the back of the cart. As we flew through the terminal at what felt like breakneck speed, I clung to the seat and did my best not to be bothered by the fact that I was going backwards.

We got to the gate with time to spare. Boarding hadn't started yet. No one was lined up at the gateway. There was a uniformed airline employee behind the podium nearby, though, so it looked like something was imminent.

Grimaldi and I scanned the crowd. "Do you see them?"

I shook my head. I had never actually met Magnolia—either Tim had kept her to himself, or she just hadn't felt the need to visit the office at any point when I'd been there—but I did know what she looked like. And of course I'd been looking at Brittany almost every day for more than a year. "No. I don't see either of them."

"They haven't called first boarding yet," the head of security said. "Once that happens, everyone going on this flight will come to the gate."

Grimaldi nodded. "Let's just sit and wait. If they're going on the plane, they'll show up sooner or later."

Hopefully sooner, or they'd miss the flight.

Of course, the way things were going, they were going to miss it anyway.

So we sat and waited. The two of them peering forward, me peering backward. The first announcement of boarding came and went, with no sign of Brittany or Magnolia.

To be honest, I couldn't quite wrap my brain around this new development. Brittany and Magnolia were working together? Why?

The situation had made sense for as long as I thought Magnolia was behind the wire transfer, that she had talked—or seduced—Devon into doing her bidding, and then had killed him after she had her money. That was neat and tidy, but didn't allow for Brittany's involvement.

Why would Brittany work with the woman who had been sleeping with her boyfriend? Or had that been a setup, too? Had Brittany been in on it from the start? She'd met Magnolia somewhere, they had come up with the plan to buy Miss Harper's house, have Devon reroute the money, give the money back to Magnolia, and get the insurance company to pay for the house.

No reason in that scenario for Magnolia and Devon to sleep together, though. If there were sexual favors to be dispensed, Brittany could have dealt with them.

And there was also nothing in it for Brittany—unless she'd wanted Devon dead, and Magnolia had offered to take care of that in exchange for Brittany's help with the money. Brittany might know how to spoof an email; she'd been living with Devon for long enough to probably pick up some tricks from him.

But why would Brittany want Devon dead? Especially if she was still planning to marry him?

Unless the marriage and honeymoon had merely been a story she'd told me. Just a way to excuse the trip out of the country with the money. But that didn't make any sense, either. It had been Magnolia's money in the first place. Now she had her money back, but if she was in Curacao, it wasn't like she'd get to enjoy owning Miss Harper's house, even if the insurance company did end up paying for it. Magnolia was left with the same five hundred thousand dollars she'd always had. She might as well just have kept it.

The airline employee at the gate announcing general boarding woke me from my rabbit warren of thoughts, and I took a quick look around to make sure I hadn't missed anything. There was still no sign of Brittany and/or Magnolia.

"There," Grimaldi said. I could barely hear her over the noises of people walking and talking, announcements over the speaker system, and jet engines roaring outside the window. "Savannah!"

I twisted in my seat. "What?"

"That's them. Isn't it? Coming out of the bar?"

It took me a second to find the bar. And once I did, it was hard to get a good look at the two women. Until they turned and headed toward us.

They were clearly dressed for the beach, in summer dresses with thin shoulder straps, and flip-flops instead of proper sandals. One was skinny as a snake, in a hot pink dress and with hoops the size of my biceps in her ears. The other was a little shorter, a bit chubbier, and had black, curly hair hanging to the shoulders of a bright blue dress that matched her eyes.

"That's not Magnolia Houston," I said brilliantly.

Grimaldi shook her head. "It's Brittany Stevens, though. Isn't it?"

It was. But— "That's not Magnolia Houston."

"No," Grimaldi said.

"That's Molly. Lane DeWitts receptionist."

Grimaldi nodded. "Molly can be a nickname for Margaret, can't it?"

It could. Of course it could.

"You said it yourself," Grimaldi reminded me. "They're two common Irish names. The combination is no doubt common, too."

No doubt.

"So it wasn't Magnolia."

Grimaldi shook her head. "I'll have to get them into interview before I can say for sure, but I think Brittany probably found out that Devon was cheating. Because she worked for your company, she knew that Magnolia was paying five hundred thousand dollars for a house. She told Molly about Magnolia, and between them, they came up with the idea to use Devon's computer—"

Which had been in the apartment Devon shared with Brittany.

"—to divert the five hundred thousand into Devon's account to make it look like Devon was guilty, and then to shoot Devon and make it look like Magnolia did it."

"And Magnolia couldn't prove that she wasn't there because it was the middle of the night and she didn't have an alibi."

Grimaldi nodded.

"So if Brittany was upstairs in bed, Molly must have shot Devon."

"And got paid five hundred thousand dollars to do it," Grimaldi said. "Or whatever split they worked out between them, for the theft and the murder. The check was in Molly's name, but she might turn around and give some of it back to Brittany."

"I guess the honeymoon reservations was just camouflage, then, so we wouldn't guess that Brittany knew about Devon and Magnolia."

"I would say so," Grimaldi said.

"And Devon's check really was written by Devon. But for five hundred dollars. And Brittany wrote the 'thousand' onto the line behind it. That's why it looked so squeezed."

Grimaldi nodded. "She must have asked him for five hundred dollars for something. The cashier's check was never intended for Magnolia, of course. It was for Molly. Who just happened to have the same name."

While this conversation had been going on, Brittany and Molly had been making their way toward us—or toward the gate, rather. I hadn't taken my eyes off them, and I doubted Grimaldi had, either. Now all that staring seemed to penetrate. Brittany looked up first, straight at me. For a second, she looked blank, like she knew me but couldn't place me, and then panic flashed in her eyes.

She turned on her heel and ran. A second later, Molly had followed suit. They thundered down the walkway with skirts flying. Brittany's ponytail swung from side to side, and Molly's beach tote hit her butt with every two steps or so. Grimaldi launched herself off the cart in pursuit. Our driver, meanwhile, waited until she was clear, and then started the cart up and followed. I stayed where I was, hanging on as the cart moved.

Grimaldi reached Molly first, and knocked her over. They landed in a tangle of arms and legs, and took out a couple of other travelers while they were at it.

"Go!" Grimaldi yelled, pointing after Brittany. "Get her! I've got this one."

She yanked her handcuffs off her belt and slapped them around Molly's wrists. The girl was already crying.

The security chief hit the gas on the cart, and we whizzed forward. Brittany was running like a gazelle up ahead. I swear, at one point she vaulted over a kid in a stroller and kept going. I think even Grimaldi might have had a hard time gaining on her. Or if she could, it was only because Grimaldi was wearing sensible boots, and Brittany had on flip-flops.

No, scratch that. The flip-flops had gone flying. I caught a glimpse of one of them next to the window. Brittany must have kicked them off on the go. They aren't the easiest things to run in.

"She's heading for the escalators," the security chief yelled. Not at me; he was on the radio, or a walkie-talkie, with someone else. Members of the security staff, I guess. "Female, five-six or –

seven, blonde and blue, barefoot and in a pink dress with a ponytail."

The radio squawked. It sounded like static to me, but it must have meant something to him. "Copy that."

He dropped the radio into a holder on the dashboard and gripped the wheel with both hands. I braced myself, just in time to avoid flying when he stomped on the gas.

People and stores flew by, amidst screams and sounds of hysterical beeping from the cart. People stared after us with wide eyes and open mouths. I wondered whether they might have thought I was a Very Important Person who was very late for her flight.

Or perhaps a very pregnant woman in labor who had to get to the hospital ASAP.

We squealed to a stop by the escalators, and this time I really did almost roll off the seat. The only thing that saved me was the seatbelt across my lap. By the time I had straightened up and untangled myself and my skirt, I was alone. My driver had leapt from the vehicle onto the escalator and was on his way down. I could just see the top of his head descending to the next level.

I climbed down, as carefully as I could. My knees were a little wobbly from the wild ride, and I kept my hand on the cart as I made my way over to the escalator.

Brittany was trapped halfway down the down-side. There were a couple of burly guys in security uniforms waiting at the bottom, and my driver was on his way down from the top. Brittany's only option for getting away was to climb to the next escalator, and just as the head of security was about to reach out and nab her, she did. Vaulted over to the escalator going back up, and started running.

The security guards down at the bottom started up after her, their boots pounding on the treads. The security chief turned and started back up the down-escalator, but for every step he took, Brittany outpaced him by two, and the guards weren't gaining fast enough. Brittany was already almost at the top of the escalator.

I stepped to the side. It wasn't cowardice. I just couldn't think of only myself anymore. If she ran into me, and maybe hurt me, she could hurt the baby, too. And I hadn't been carrying it around with me for more than six months just to lose it now.

So I stepped to the side. And when Brittany took the last step off the escalator onto the floor, I stuck out my foot and tripped her. And although I felt just a little bit bad when she fell forward and smacked her head against the fender of the cart we'd been riding in, and lay still, I didn't feel too terribly bad about it.

"And that's what happened," I told Tim several hours later.

He looked quite overwhelmed. And not surprising, since I had just dumped the whole sordid story on him. "I can't believe it. Brittany and Molly stole Magnolia's money? And Molly shot Devon while Brittany was upstairs in bed pretending to sleep?"

I nodded. "And they tried to frame Magnolia Houston for all of it."

I had been allowed outside the interview room while Grimaldi talked to first Molly and then Brittany, and they had confessed to everything we'd surmised. Including the fact that Brittany had made up the story about the honeymoon to make it seem like she and Devon were still together and everything was great. On Tuesday, when she'd told me that, she'd already known he'd be dying the next night.

"You can give this check to Magnolia," I added, and put it on Tim's desk. "Detective Grimaldi said to give it to you to give to her."

Tim peered at it. He must have known Magnolia's real name all along, because he didn't say a word about the way it was made out. And of course he would have known: unless she'd changed it legally, Magnolia/Margaret would have had to sign the paperwork to buy the house with her legal name and legal signature. "So Molly's real name is Margaret Murphy, too?"

I nodded. "She never pretended it wasn't. Molly is just a nickname. She's been Margaret Murphy her whole life. She didn't know it was Magnolia Houston's name, too, until the paperwork for the closing came in to DeWitts a couple of months ago."

"And that's when she and Brittany planned this?"

"After Brittany found out that Devon was sleeping with Magnolia," I nodded. "Up until then, it was just a funny coincidence. But when Brittany discovered that Devon was having an affair, she thought up this way of framing Devon for the theft, and framing Magnolia for his murder, as well as getting to keep the money. All she had to do was talk Molly into shooting Devon. Brittany did everything else."

Tim nodded, looking overwhelmed.

"Did you know they were sleeping together?"

Tim shook his head. "No, and if I had, I would have told her to knock it off. She's Magnolia freaking Houston. What would she want with some two-bit loser like Devon?"

It hadn't occurred to me to ask. Maybe he was really good in bed. Or maybe they connected on some deeper level. None of my business. "Maybe she just liked that he belonged to someone else. Some women are like that."

Tim shrugged and put the check in his desk drawer. "I'll make sure she gets it. And then we'll start the process of closing on the house all over again."

"Better you than me," I said. "It's a nice old house. I hope she does right by it."

"After the check goes through," Tim said callously, "she can do whatever she wants with the house."

I guess technically she could. I would hate to see it painted bubblegum pink with unicorn shaped topiary bushes in the pasture, but if that happened, there was nothing any of us could do about it.

"I appreciate all your work on this, Savannah," Tim said.

"It was no problem. I was happy to help." And it had been fairly interesting. I probably would have enjoyed it more if the whole situation with Denise Seaver and the baby hadn't cropped up in the middle of it and taken a lot of my attention.

"Do you know what they say about the reward for a job well done?"

"No," I said. "What do they say about the reward for a job well done?"

Tim grinned. "Another job. How would you like to be our fulltime receptionist?"

I thought about it. For about two seconds. It would mean a steady salary and a paycheck every other week. It would also mean being stuck here in the office from nine to five every day.

"Not on your life," I said, and walked out.

# # #

About the Author

New York Times and *USA Today* bestselling author Jenna Bennett (Jennie Bentley) writes the Do It Yourself home renovation mysteries for Berkley Prime Crime and the Savannah Martin real estate mysteries for her own gratification. She also writes a variety of romance for a change of pace. Originally from Norway, she has spent more than twenty five years in the US, and still hasn't been able to kick her native accent.

For more information, please visit Jenna's website:
www.JennaBennett.com

www.ingramcontent.com/pod-product-compliance
Lightning Source LLC
Chambersburg PA
CBHW032106180726
48284CB00002B/478